EMERGENCE

ELLIE BEALS

Emergence
Copyright © 2021 by Ellie Beals

tellwell 🖋

Tellwell Talent
www.tellwell.ca

ISBN
978-0-2288-4865-3 (Hardcover)
978-0-2288-4309-2 (Paperback)
978-0-2288-4311-5 (eBook)

Table Of Contents

Year Three Of The Story

Emergence is dedicated to:

- Charlene Rothkopf and Paula Mancuso Rea, who urged me to do this since we were children,
- David, who is Noah, and whose love and calm have anchored me against every deluge we've experienced in our many years together, and
- Fracas, who was Chuff, and gave me fourteen years of joy. I wanted him to live forever, and this was the best I could do.

FIRST YEAR OF THE STORY

1

XAVIER

I had always liked the little bitch best, even before we met, while I was still Just Watching. The others were big, handsome dogs. She had a deep red, curly coat and was scrawny and scrappy, but she had a kind of beautiful crazy movement as if she was dancing through the woods. The others lived for the woman. The little one lived for herself.

I watched them for a long time before we met. The woman never knew, but the dogs did. I learned their names as I watched. The older male, Chuff, got all big, stiff and bristly, low growls, head and tail high, ears swivelling. The younger male, Zeke was scared slinky, tail low and twitching, as he tried on some bullshit big boy growls. But the little bitch, Trinka, was different. She'd know I was there before the others did, and she'd slip away to find me, wriggling with joy when she did, no matter how good my hiding place. It was a great game we played for months. Of course, it wasn't like that the first time, when she was wary. But she quickly came to recognize me, as though she had always known me. She didn't stay long that first time, but long enough to lead to the first of the many Come hollers I observed after that.

The woman generally seemed to keep track of all three dogs, twisting and turning as she walked to know who was where. She called often and gave them treats when they came to make sure they didn't stray too far from her. Every now and then, she'd put this aside for a minute and just get lost in time. It happened most often when there was light and dark spearing through the trees and lots of birdsong. She'd go still and close her eyes, and her face would get soft; she'd look younger.

After this little spell, I'd see her kind of shake herself back into regular time with a start I knew meant, "Where are they?" Her boys were always quickly located. But when she realized she'd lost track of the little bitch, she'd slump her shoulders and give a big sigh. Then she'd straighten up, throw her head back, and yell, "Trinka, come!" Wow, could that little woman holler. I imagined her shout rolling through the forest, knocking over weak trees as the sound rushed through the woods and the fields, and across the lake. The first time, Trinka returned to her fast. Later, of course, as she got more into playing hide and seek with me, that slowed way down.

I saw this all through the binoculars I'd liberated from a group of drunken hunters as they snoozed way too close to their poorly-made campfire. Liberation—that's what Stefan called it. He'd taught me how to hunt and when and how to save stuff stupid hunters didn't take good care of.

2

CASS

You can't allow slippage, not even a little bit, or you'll regret it. Cassandra Harwood knew that; it had been pounded into her ever since she started seriously studying with her obedience mentor. And it was a concept she practiced religiously in training for the ring. But alas, she'd been lax in her real-life activities, which was quite evident right now. She was standing at a cross-road in the woods, trying to repress her irritation after calling Katrinka three well-spaced times, without hearing even the vaguest tinkle of a distant bear-bell, which each of her dogs wore in the woods.

The irritation she felt was as much with herself as with Katrinka. She would never have accepted the minor recall lapses that preceded this when training. She would have clearly "explained" her expectations at the first sign of insouciance, and Trinka would have responded appropriately. But because such interventions intruded on her own Zen in the woods, Cass had not corrected her when Katrinka first started taking her own sweet time to respond to recalls on their walks. And so, the minor lapses matured into the present, when after about two minutes and three shouts, Katrinka finally catapulted out of the woods and onto the trail, wriggling with delight,. No body language demonstration of regret or of giving Cass the figurative finger. *My fault,* thought Cass. "That took too long," she told Katrinka, her voice stern. Trinka averted her gaze. Chuff and Zeke, who had been waiting patiently, now started to dance in glee, clearly recognizing Trinka's return and weak admonishment as the precursor to resuming the hike.

Which is precisely what they did. With cookies dispensed to all three canines, Cass swung into the easy lope that characterized her woods walks. She moved too quickly to undertake the kind of visual observations her sister-in-law Therese specialized in while meandering through the woods. Instead, Cass reveled in other sensations—the wind, the din of birdsong often punctuated by the high-pitched scree of hawks or raucous calls of crows and wild turkeys, the glory of dark woods pierced by bright shafts of sunlight. Except in May and June, these delights more than compensated for the countermanding irritation of insect assaults in the summer and bitter wind and cold during the winter. It took considerable discipline to not react during bug season. However, Cass took that as part of her devotion to the woods walks, even when the throngs of black flies and mosquitos were dense.

They weren't bad on this day; it was too early in May. The sun was warm, and the wind was mild. All three dogs streaked through the fields like fleet golden shadows, and Cass soon regained that blessed state of mindlessness she had finally acquired when she and Noah bought the cabin.

They agreed now, twenty years after the purchase, that it had been a no-brainer—the best decision they ever made. At the time, though it was a no-brainer for Noah, Cass had anguished. This was not a surprise; it had always been her way—a heavy freight of anxiety-laden what-ifs and sleepless nights preceded every major decision or event. However, these were countered by alternative blissful what-if scenarios. It was part of the pendulum of being Cass, which was evident in every aspect of her life. As a consultant specializing in social justice issues and training development for federal offenders, she was a chronic over-preparer for major presentations, who then shucked all her packaged shtick to brilliantly improvise to considerable acclaim. As a dog trainer, the same fastidiousness went into highly technical precision training, which was shucked once she hit the competition ring, for what, at its best, was a polished presentation of shared joyfulness by both dog and human.

So there had been angst as they debated whether to buy the cabin. Cass's main concern was her familiarity with a pattern she'd observed and heard about from many of her friends. They'd buy a place and spend all their time taking care of it—doing repairs, chopping and stacking wood, landscaping, etc.—but they didn't complain. Instead, they seemed to like it. But Cass had no interest and indeed an active aversion to thinking that might be her future. She was neither lazy nor unfit. She was a committed gym rat who'd been lifting weights since she was thirty, but she loathed doing any constructive physical work. It didn't matter whether it was sanding a chair, planting a garden, or chopping wood. She had tried to enjoy these activities but found that not only did she detest them, she also detested the sullen creature she became when engaged in such efforts.

Noah did too. Who could blame him? So he gladly accepted Cass's terms. She would help with the physical stuff if, and only if, she felt like it. Noah would under no circumstances guilt her about it. Their deal was made, as was their decision to buy. Because by then, both were already firmly committed to being there, at Petit Lac Rouge in Western Quebec, where Noah's family had been embedded since the 1930s, and where they had already spent weekends throughout three summers, ensconced in a little camper on Andrew's beach. Andrew was Noah's brother, who had inherited the first family cabin their grandfather had built. Andrew and his wife Therese had invited them to partake of the lake and the family that way and had managed to never make them feel like trespassers throughout those three summers. Being near but not on top of Andrew and Therese was one of the many appeals of the cabin.

Noah was a great storyteller, and in the early days of their courtship, had wooed Cass with tales of growing up at "the cottage." However, it was only one of a panoply of stories he told, and it didn't get the pride of place it deserved until a few months into their relationship when he first took her on the two-hour trip from Ottawa, Ontario to Lac Rouge. And then, everything changed. Cass didn't fall in love or agree to marry Noah because of Lac Rouge, but once she experienced the family enclave, the mountain air, the clear, cold water, the endless variety, and the impact of sun and shadow on a land that was largely unchanged over hundreds of years, she knew it influenced everything after that. She reverberated differently and better at Lac Rouge.

The cabin was perfectly situated, close enough to the family enclave to allow visits but preclude intrusion. It nestled into the steep hillside on ten wooded acres that tumbled down into a small rocky bay with no other buildings in sight. The family enclave was ten to twenty minutes away, whether you walked, kayaked, or skied. It yielded the best of both worlds—privacy and accessibility—in every season.

When you stepped out of the cabin, and away from the lake, there were endless routes through the woods and fields. Cass, an experienced camper and hiker but a poor navigator at the time, started her treks with Noah. Having grown up as a directionally-challenged big city girl, she surprised both of them with her quick mastery of the network of logging, snowmobiling, hiking, and deer trails that threaded through the hundreds of acres of crown land in which Lac Rouge nestled. Cass called this vast expanse of crown lands that started just west of the main road the back bush. Acutely aware of her native lack of navigation skills, Cass carried a radio, a compass that her backwoods girlfriends had taught her to use in her early days hiking in Canada, a pad on which she noted each decision point when she explored, and a roll of colored tape. Cautious but determined, she tied the tape around trees to mark every decision point so that when she got confused—and it happened a fair bit—she could, like Hansel and Gretel, follow the cookie crumb tape trail back to familiar terrain.

And, of course, there were the dogs. They could flawlessly retrace the route they'd taken so that if she ever experienced momentary confusion, unable to see her markings, she could—and did—just follow the dogs.

It wasn't long before Cass, a more dedicated hiker than Noah, often undertook her adventures without him. Noah, not completely comfortable with this, suggested that she see whether Therese, who walked daily, might be a good hiking partner. Cass tried, but it didn't work. Her sister-in-law Therese, a deeply spiritual human who knew a tremendous amount about the Lac Rouge flora and fauna, took slow strolls designed to facilitate her observations   very Zen. Therese's approach was not compatible with three rambunctious canines who required a fair bit of lung power to control, nor with Cass's drive for a high-quality cardio workout. Given her admirable fitness, that meant Cass had to walk hard and fast. So she walked alone. But she never felt that way since the dogs were always with her.

They were so much a part of it all. The first time the full Harwood household of humans and dogs took a real hike at Lac Rouge, striding through fields of long grass with the dogs racing ahead of them, falling behind, rolling, checking back, and giving physical form to pure joy, there was an almost audible "click" of recognition. Cass felt that an ancient human memory, a deeply buried evolutionary button, had been pushed. The sense of rightness in moving through long grass surrounded by dogs was the most profound she had ever experienced. It never left her after that.

Over the years, she and Noah reshaped their lives around the cabin. Because they were both self-employed, Cass as a consultant, and Noah as a software designer, they could both schedule their work to allow a full month at Lac Rouge mid-December to mid-January, and the whole of the summer. Because they could both work from the cabin when needed, they also spent extended weekends there when Cass and Noah weren't competing. In the early years, that meant most weekends. But as Cass and Chuff, and Noah and Katrinka became increasingly powerful competitive teams, there were more competitions to secure the National Top Ten ranking that Cass craved and that both teams earned regularly. They attained a bit of celebrity status in their subculture—they were the first husband/wife team to achieve consistent national rankings. The weekend visits became more sporadic and thus were treasured even more.

Most of the time, cabin life was reclusive, given that their city lives with high-pressure professions, dog training and competition, obligations to aging parents, and an active circle of friends, was hectic. And coaching added to those pressures. When they started coaching together, they took on only a few select fellow-competitors. But as it became apparent that they were indeed very good coaches, their practice grew. Cass found it extremely rewarding but very "noisy," not just because of the intense interactions but also because of the pride of place coaching challenges started to assert in her introspections.

Thus, getting away was attractive to both Noah and Cass. At Lac Rouge, the silence was welcome, though liberally punctuated by music. They both read prodigiously. Outdoor exercise, good food, lots of weed, and frequent and prolonged sex rounded out their typical cottage agenda when they were on their own, and it wasn't all that different when they had guests.

3

CASS GUESTS

Cass, childless by choice, having abandoned her urban Jewish roots and the cloying web of family obligations that ensnared her throughout her less-than-happy childhood knew that she was inherently selfish. Choosing the very private, professorial, athletic, and undeniably Gentile Noah was consistent with this perspective. Thinking about his gentility always made her smile, remembering her mother's classic Freudian slip as she inevitably called Goys "reptiles" instead of "gentiles." Noah's family appeared devoid of such bias. They were pleasant, welcoming, and non-judgmental, accepting that Noah and Cass preferred family ties that were flexible and non-binding, with no sacrifice required. More like a spider-silk safety-line than a conventional web—or noose? It was a good fit.

Cass felt that the only real splash of generosity she harbored resided in the passion she felt for her many friends. She loved giving them some of what she treasured most—the cabin experience. So there were frequent visits, which were always initiated by Cass since Noah was emotionally self-sufficient and socially self-contained. He needed Cass, the dogs, the cabin, mind-twisting intellectual challenge, whether it was computer coding, reading physics, or simply engaging in crosswords to keep his frenetic synapses firing, music, and sex—lots and varied. He had two friends: his brother Andrew, and Yates, their closest friend throughout the thirty years the Harwoods had been together.

Over the years, Cass invited many of her friends to the cabin. After each visit, there was an assessment of the degree to which the uber-private Noah felt comfortable with the chosen visitor. While Cass found this irksome, she understood it. The cabin was tiny, with a single just-the-necessities bathroom. The master bedroom—all 8' x 10' of it, was in the upstairs loft, and the hybrid storage/guest room was much smaller and situated next to the bathroom. Sound traveled well in these confined spaces, so privacy—a highly-prized commodity for both Noah and Cass—was necessarily compromised while visitors were on site.

Of the array of guests who were auditioned over the years, just a select few got Noah's nod of approval for anything other than very short visits. Yates was one of these. He was a frequent cabin visitor, fitting flawlessly into the Harwood lifestyle rhythms in the bush.

The other most welcome guest was far more surprising to anyone who knew all parties involved.

Lori was Cass's first cousin, who still lived in Baltimore, where she, Cass, and the whole extended Freeman clan grew up. Though Cass was the middle of three sisters, she was much closer to Lori when she was growing up than she was to either sibling or to anyone else in her constantly hovering, controlling family.

Even when they were children, the closeness between the two surprised, indeed, flummoxed the rest of the extended family. The academically-gifted and highly articulate Cass and her cousin Lori were perceived as opposites in all aspects but one—their shared dislike of the omnivorous and critical attention of their tightly-knit extended family. Cass and Lori were rightly perceived as the family rebels.

Lori was two years older than Cass. For the whole of her life, she had the Barbie doll looks that caused a hushed silence to fall over high school study halls when she sashayed in always late and with not the slightest hint of concern. Cass was often told by Lori's admirers just how much Lori resembled Jane Fonda or Marilyn Monroe. Cass thought the latter comparison more appropriate since what made Lori so compelling transcended her beauty and voluptuousness; there was a quality of vulnerability she projected.

Which was real. Lori's father was, in the parlance of the time, "strict." Today, he would likely be deemed to be, at the very least, emotionally abusive. Early on, Lori learned to use the assets she had to attempt—generally unsuccessfully—to assuage his contempt and—considerably more successfully—to garner interest, admiration, and sympathy from others. Cass studied how Lori did this, which gave her the grounding she needed in adolescence and later to charm her way into or out of a range of dilemmas.

Lori was reputed to be flighty and not-too-bright. Her marks in school were merely okay. This put her at a remove from the other Freeman cousins, all of whom excelled academically, as they were expected to.

Cass recognized from the start that Lori was not who others considered her to be. Her beauty was the first thing anyone and everyone noticed about her. And that beauty, for reasons little Cass didn't understand, but adult feminist Cass came to, was perceived to be antithetical to being smart. Cass knew that Lori was indeed very smart, and funny, generous, sexy, and exhibitionistic. She shared all of that with Cass.

When Cass was eight and Lori was ten, they had a tandem sleepover at Bubby Freeman's. Their grandmother's bedroom had two beds—one for Bubby and the other for whichever grandchildren happened to spend the night. One night, while Bubby was still working in the kitchen, but Lori and Cass were in bed, Lori brightly asked, "Hey, wanna see something?" When Cass immediately agreed, Lori proudly pulled up her nightshirt to reveal budding breasts and pubic hair. Cass was first gobsmacked. "Wow! Are those real? Can I touch them?" Then she was delighted to hear that she was going to experience similar developments soon.

Not long after that, Lori showed Cass her first menstrual blood. And at intervals along the way, she shared quick verbal snapshots of the sex acts she witnessed based on her occasional unexpected forays into her parents' bedroom. "They were both naked, and he was lying on top of her and kind of moaning like it hurt." Lori was Cass's angel of sex, and they shared an avid interest in it.

As they grew up together, Cass concluded that Lori's beauty was a two-edged sword, making some things easier for her, but making the process of gaining respect infinitely more difficult. This set Cass up for a lifetime of sympathy for the chronically good-looking. Her friends included many in this category, whose looks always caused most people to perceive their shyness as snobbery or their high-spirits for vapidity. Throughout her promiscuous young womanhood, her girlfriends wondered at how often the charismatic but not gorgeous Cass landed beautiful young men. Cass would refer them to her well-known abilities as an accomplished flirt. True, she had had a brilliant role model. But the real "secret" was that she was sympathetic to and not intimidated by the truly beautiful.

Lori was the only one of the Freeman cousins who did not go to university and graduate school and move from there to a high-powered professional career. However, she was a successful administrator who was always able to take care of herself and insisted on doing so, despite endless sugar-daddy-driven offers. Questioned about this by a pre-teen Cass, Lori explained that if she did accept the gifts, the sugar-daddy would believe that in some way, he owned her. "Nobody owns me but me," she said.

Cass went through a long period of consciously distancing herself from most of her family, which was facilitated by her move to Canada at the age of nineteen after a university girlfriend introduced her to hiking in Ontario. Cass immediately fell in love with the country and the distance it provided, but that distance never included Lori. Indeed, Lori was the only family member who encouraged Cass to make the move during the long and agonizing months that Cass debated with herself over making such a life-altering decision. Lori said that she believed that as long as Cass failed to create a substantial physical distance between herself and the rest of the Freeman clan, she would continue to find herself enmeshed in the uncomfortable combination of love, anger, and guilt that made her so unhappy during her stormy adolescence. She accurately observed that Cass hated being angry but was almost always near rage about the family efforts to direct and control her. "You need to lose some of that anger if you want to be happy," was Lori's wise counsel. Cass heard her and made her decision.

Lori often visited, both before and after Noah entered Cass's life. The real surprise was how Lori clicked with Noah's remote sensibilities. A close relationship between the reserved and professorial Noah and the exhibitionistic show-girl lookalike Lori did seem unlikely. But Lori's entry into the insular world Cass and Noah created together at the cabin started with the dogs and reinforced Cass's belief that in one critical characteristic, Noah was as doglike as a human could be. Just like dogs, Noah appeared to be impervious to how any human looked. It was not that he was unaware; it just didn't matter to him. This was sometimes troubling for vain Cass, who wanted reassurance that she was always a visually desirable commodity. But more often than not, it was a source of great comfort. Noah loved her, full stop, and no conditions imposed.

With regards to the dogs, Trink and Zeke's responses to Lori were not unexpected. Katrinka was always a social slut—groveling, wriggling, rolling on her back, shoving her face far too close and often into her target human's sphere. Zeke was a flirt—spinning, inviting play, zooming in to touch, grinning in a bow with his butt in the air, vibrating with fun, bouncing away to tease. Both produced the expected grab-bag of behaviors, notable when they met Lori only in that their attentions were more prolonged and intense than usual, and didn't lose that intensity once the novelty wore off. Their actions clearly said: this human is fun!

But Chuff, Cass's senior boy and benign household alpha, had a truly notable response to Lori. Chuff was a cordial guy, always amiable when meeting new people but seldom fully engaged with anyone except Cass. He reminded Cass of a maître d'hotel, inviting and allowing someone into his domain and then stepping back. Unlike Trinka, Zeke, and most other Golden Retrievers, Chuff was a one-person dog, and his person was Cass. He never strayed from her side. The light in his eyes and the dance in his step when he was in her presence was constant. His ceaseless delight in being with his beloved was evident to everyone who watched Cass and Chuff in the ring together. Their mutual adoration lay at the heart of their competitive success. And Chuff responded to Lori with an immediate devotion very like the way he related to Cass.

Cass believed that one can't lie to dogs, that their bullshit detectors are infallible. And Cass knew that the quality that elicited the kind of response she experienced, not just with her dogs but with all her students' dogs, was a genuine interest and delight in the soul of the dog before her. The way that a person's interest and delight was expressed was immaterial, whether it was Cass's extravagant verbal and physical displays or Noah's quiet calm.

So Cass was never sure if Noah took unconscious direction from the dogs in the way he responded to Lori or whether he, like them, detected her openness, receptivity, and capacity for joy. Whatever the case, Noah liked Lori immediately and never faltered in that feeling, despite everything that would happen.

4

XAVIER – FIRST OBSERVATIONS

As far as I recall, I've always lived in the bush. Stefan tells me that we spent the first year of my life in an apartment in Notre-Dame-de-Grace, where he and my French-speaking mom were barely able to make ends meet. But by the time I was a toddler, they moved into the wilds of Quebec to Lac Rouge, which is the only world I've known.

Stefan says he loved it from the start. He had a head-start, coming from a hunting and trapping family in Northern Ontario. He learned more about living and working in the bush by reading about it. His family was not impressed. Stefan's heavy reading made his family think he was . . . strange. He didn't stay in touch with them after he moved to Quebec to work as a logger. But my French-speaking, small-town mom fell for him, and even though her English was bad and his French not much better, somehow they came together. I have one picture of them, and it was taken back then. They were both beautiful. That was before he got hurt. He had an accident and injured his back at a logging camp. He couldn't work after that. He was on disability, meaning he got money because he'd been hurt while working. You usually couldn't tell; mostly, he moved okay, but sometimes it got so bad that the way he moved changed. And he got mean then, too. I was always very careful when he looked like his back hurt.

Stefan says that one of the things that kept him and my mom together at first was their shared "disdain for the waste, commercialism, and superficiality of the mainstream culture." He really didn't like any of the kind of standard practices of "mainstream culture". Once, long ago, I asked him why I called him by his given name instead of "Dad" or "Papa," as I by-then understood was how mainstream kids referred to their biological fathers. He responded that it was because he "didn't want to affirm the power tropes of patriarchy." Stefan told me he was a "political and ideological survivalist." Over the years, I came to understand this to mean that he fed us as much as possible from stuff we killed ourselves, that he trusted only himself and his ability to take care of me, and that he wanted nothing to do with the government, schools or any of the other stuff he called "societal bullshit." He said this all meant that he was an anarchist, and he was proud of that. He belonged to an anarchist organization and wrote for their journal. He spent a lot of time writing about that kind of stuff.

The thing I remember most about my mom is that she used to hug me a lot, but only when Stefan wasn't around. When he was around, she reminded me of a stray dog—hopeful you will be nice to it but worried you won't be. If my mom was a dog, her tail would have been between her legs any time Stefan was around. The other thing I remember well was what seemed like endless loud arguments in French and English, high voice and low, wrapping around each other, confronting each other, and constantly rising, like two warring hummingbirds during mating season. My mom left when I was about eight. She didn't say goodbye and never told me she was going or why she was leaving. Stefan said that the isolation of the tiny cabin in the dark woods didn't work for her. Though I often asked in the first years after she left, Stefan always said he didn't know where she was and was not interested in finding out. When I asked, he'd put his super-calm face on, which often came before scary outbursts. I knew enough to leave it alone when he said, "I am your father, and that's all you need." Under pressure, he seemed more accepting of the power tropes of patriarchy. Then he added, "Women are just cheap distractions."

I looked up "distraction" just to be sure. We have tons of books, including many reference books, in the cabin. Stefan uses them for my home-schooling, and any time I have a question, he makes me look it up. That kind of pisses me off, because he is very smart and knows almost everything. But I do like knowing how to find out stuff myself. Here's the dictionary definition of distraction: "a thing that prevents someone from giving full attention to something else." So maybe I did first become interested in the woman because she was a cheap distraction.

I was very busy when I first saw her. I was in one of our many hunting stands. This one was high in the trees that ringed a large open meadow, so I could see what was going on in both the woods and the field. I had all my Just Watching supplies with me, some (the binoculars and hi-tech water bottle) liberated, and some (notebook, pen, colored pencils, field guides) stuff that Stefan had bought for me and taught me to use to "see the world truly" starting when I was littlelittle. I was observing a porcupine, who had surprised me by showing a fair bit of speed as he made his way high into a tree not far from me. I couldn't figure it out at first.

Then I heard the bells, which got louder as I heard crashing through the bush getting closer. I knew about bear bells and figured it was dogs—ones that knew nothing about stealth. As they burst into the field, I saw how right I was. I've always been very interested in dogs. We had a book about dog breeds, so I knew them all, even ones like the Leonberger, which I'd never seen in person. I've studied how the dogs around Lac Rouge act, and I've watched every movie I could about dogs. These three dogs were Golden Retrievers, a popular breed with the summer people. One was a small bitch, who went crazy with her rolling, whirling, and spinning as she hit the field. There was a young male, sleek and well-muscled, who just wanted to run, and did it like he was driven by the wind. And there was the big, older male. He held his head and tail high, showing that he was afraid of nothing. But he also danced, racing ahead but then twirling to look back at whatever it was that made him jitter his feet like he was dancing in place. He was watching the woman.

And although the dogs were beautiful to watch, I could see why he watched her like that, and why all of them seemed to orbit her, the way planets circle the sun. She walked fast but relaxed, looking toward the horizon like she was speeding toward whatever she saw there. *What? Why?* I thought and scanned the distance for whatever she was chasing. I didn't see anything. I learned over time, that was just the way she always moved when she was with the dogs, as though she was going somewhere interesting, and wanted to get there. It was unlike the way of walking I had seen in the many other summer visitors and hunters I'd observed. Usually, they weren't alone—there were at least two of them. They were slow, maybe because they were so busy talking, and it didn't matter if it was English or French; nothing I overheard sounded like anything that needed to be said. And they walked without purpose. I used the thesaurus. They meandered, they strolled, they ambled.

But not the woman. She strode. She was small but looked strong. She walked like she owned the earth under her feet. But not mean, right? Not like the earth was dirt under her feet, but like it filled her with the same joy the dogs felt. She had long hair that flowed free that first day. Because of her hair and how she moved, I figured at first she was young. But once I zoomed in on her face, I saw that she wasn't. Not old, not young. I guess she was around Stefan's age, who I figured was about fifty. He wouldn't tell me, so I figured it out as best I could.

So, yes, I was immediately distracted. Observing these four was a lot more interesting than watching Porky, who chittered in distress as the dogs raced past his tree. "Observing" is the proper word for what I call "Just Watching." It's what naturalists do when they study animals and what spies and detectives do when they "tail" someone. But we all have our own favorite, private expressions. In my mind, I've always called this kind of study "Just Watching" because it means that's all you're doing; you're not going to interfere with or harm your subject. And your subject doesn't know you are there, so he acts naturally.

Happily, on the day of that first sighting, the wind was blowing toward me, so I wasn't concerned about the dogs smelling me. And the amount of noise they made and the fact that they hadn't heard Porky's warning made me suspect that with my ability to move quietly, they wouldn't hear me, and they didn't.

So I was able to track them throughout that first Just Watching, as they climbed up and down steeply wooded hillsides and eventually traveled down a trail with several summer places around it. One that hadn't been opened for the summer yet had a big, flat lawn around a large workshop. The quartet stopped there, and the woman pulled a huge blue bag from under the raised porch. As she rooted through it, both males became wildly excited. "Not today," she told them as she completed her inspection of the contents of the bag and pushed it back under the porch.

Well, when? I wondered. *What?* I was already pretty into Just Watching these guys. Their journey ended that day at a log cabin well-hidden on a steep wooded hillside. There was no sign of kids, but so many different types of collars, leashes, and what I assumed were dog toys hung on pegs on their porch! How could anyone need so much dog stuff, even for three dogs? There was also a good stash of weight-training equipment. I didn't have any but recognized it from movies I'd seen where people worked out in gyms.

There was a bearded guy stacking wood as they arrived. He didn't look like a weightlifter. He was tall and lean but in a wiry kind of way. However, he had big forearms, given how skinny the rest of him was. He called out to the woman, "Hey, Cass!"

and they exchanged a brief kiss as he put his hand on her ass and squeezed it. As it turns out, I guessed correctly that this was her husband and this was where they lived. It is important to know where the critter you are interested in is nesting. By the end of that first day of my distraction, I had learned that her name was Cass, the little bitch was Trinka, the young male was Zeke, and the big older male was Chuff. I didn't know the husband's name yet.

For quite a while after that, I Just Watched them, tracking and trailing them on their almost daily treks. They had several different routes, visiting most of the ponds, marshes, and little lakes scattered along the big network of trails they used. I was impressed; Cass kind of sewed together snowmobile and logging trails with much smaller deer trails, much the way Stefan had taught me to do. Hunters did that, but cottagers usually didn't.

I enjoyed shadowing Cass and the dogs. It was a good test of my skills. There was no problem with Cass, but the dogs sometimes reacted to my presence. But their growls, or the times they froze, heads high, trying to figure out whether my smell or the sound of my almost-silent movement through the woods posed a threat, didn't seem to alarm her. She was used to them acting that way, given the hundreds of critters constantly moving through the bush. The only ones she cared about were bears, which she never saw, and skunks and porcupines, which she sometimes did. When that happened, and the dogs leaped into the chase, holy shit did Cass let loose a holler. It was so big that all the dogs, even Zeke, who was really into it, actually left off their chase to return to her for some very big cookie rewards.

Though I enjoyed tracking them in the bush, my favorite Just Watchings were the times Cass carried a big backpack, and they went to the workshop, where she trained the dogs, but only the boys. It turned out that Trinka was her husband's dog, so she'd just tell her to settle and wait, and then she'd work with one or both boys.

It was beautiful to watch. They all had so much fun. Sometimes Cass threw a dumbbell that the dog had to bring back, sometimes even over a jump. Sometimes she did this silent thing where the dog would walk next to her—I learned that's called "heeling"—and then she'd stop with the dog and signal him to stay while she moved far away. Then she'd turn to face the dog and give him hand signals to first lie down, then sit up, then come to her—that is called a "front." Then she'd signal him to go to her left side again—that is called a "finish." I learned what everything was called because sometimes her husband would be with her, and when she asked him to "call a routine," he told her what tasks he wanted her to do.

Trinka liked it when Noah—that's what Cass called her husband—was there. Then she'd get to do the same exercises with him that Cass did with the boys. But usually, Noah wasn't there, and Cass would get so focused on what she was doing that she'd kind of forget Trinka, which is how I got to know her. While Cass worked with the boys, Trinka explored.

I'd made several good disguised hunting stands I could use to Just Watch the training. On the first day that I met Trinka, I was late getting aloft, so she found me just as I was getting ready to climb. I very quietly called her, and she did this funny little forward-backward thing, as though she wanted to greet me but also wanted to run away. Eventually, forward won, and she did this excited little dance and let me pet her. Then she left. But after that, I knew she was looking for me, and we became very good friends. I started to bring cookies for her. Sometimes, I tried to get her to do some of the stuff I saw Cass doing with the boys. She did them well! I tried to remember to send her back when it looked like Cass was winding down her training. But every now and then, I'd forget, and those were the times I could see that Cass was getting upset at how long it took Trinka to come back. But I usually remembered to send her back in time.

But I screwed up one time during the summer when Boobs was there. I just called her that until I discovered that her name was Lori. But before that, I called her Boobs because when she was around, that was all I could see. She kind of looked like Cass, but if Cass was a movie star with these great big, high, bouncy boobs. She was helping Cass move jumps, and she called routines too. I watched through the binoculars and didn't even leave the loft when Trinka came to visit. And then, I got careless when I climbed down and fell the last few feet and hit my head. I was kind of stunned and stupid after that, and I think—but I am not sure—that Cass might have seen me for an instant.

5

CASS – CASS'S TRAINING, LORI'S UNEASE

One of the reasons for Cass's early ambivalence about buying the cabin was that she recognized the challenges this would pose for her ability to train. In the city, where their large finished basement was kept empty but for dog training equipment, she could grab a dog and scoot downstairs to work on whatever she chose whenever she chose to. And this was just "extra," since before their coaching clients arrived, she had one and a half hours, three days a week at their training facility, for the kind of dynamic work she most loved. Despite her dissolute hippie past, Cass seldom acquired a high better than the way she felt when she was moving quickly and smoothly, with a dog at her left side, looking up at her, high-stepping and laughing with delight at the heeling dance they were doing together. She always smiled at how many of her Facebook friends misspelled "heeling" as "healing." She knew it was unintended on their part, but to her, it was so much truer.

Their cabin, set into a steep hillside, offered no space where she could do dynamic training. Early in their tenure at the cabin, she scouted alternate locations. Her first choice was a field of Jean-Luc's. Jean-Luc was an only occasional Lac Rouge denizen. She and Noah met him shortly after he moved into the dilapidated and previously long-vacant, vine-covered cabin that appeared to be sprouting, dark and mushroom-like, out of the loamy woods in which it was set. His English was about as good as their French, so on the rare occasions they met, they all spoke Franglais—a Western Quebec specialty in which English and French phrases are intermingled. The large, rough-hewn Jean-Luc was always cordial. Going through his property, west of the cottage road in the terrain Cass called the back bush, would allow them speedier access to the crown lands they hiked, and he immediately invited them to cross his property if they wanted to. He professed to be okay with the dogs that always accompanied them. His only condition was that they did not smoke. Since neither of them smoked and they both welcomed this evidence of common sense on his part, the Harwoods were pleased to accept his offer. They tended to avoid using this access on the rare occasion they saw his truck in the yard. But if they saw him on their travels, neighborly waves and brief, pleasant chat characterized their meetings.

They knew little about Jean-Luc, other than that unlike most other Lac Rouge seasonal people who came from Ottawa or Montreal, he traveled many hours to the lake from his home in Val-d'Or, considerably further northwest of Lac Rouge in Quebec. They were baffled as to why he would travel the four hours to Lac Rouge for the hunting that seemed to be his primary interest when he lived where hunting opportunities abounded. But they didn't spend too much time wondering. Laissez-faire was the Lac Rouge way. It also governed their response to how Jean-Luc maintained his property. He had several fields surrounding the small patch of bush in which his cabin nestled, which he kept flat and empty.

Though she found this configuration peculiar, Cass felt it would augur well for training: a large flat field within a fast fifteen-minute walk from their place, isolated enough that she would not feel like she was infringing on anyone's privacy. So she was optimistic when they approached Jean-Luc to offer to rent one of his fields for a generous amount. Amiably but firmly, he declined their offer, saying that except during hunting season, he kept those fields stocked with feed attractive to deer so that they would become habituated to the area and thus facilitate the fall hunt. Jean-Luc said that the frequent and prolonged presence of dogs and people would make this less likely. Already acclimated to the pride of place hunting held in the local culture, Noah and Cass got it, said they did, thanked Jean-Luc for his courtesy, and looked elsewhere for training space.

Happily, after hearing of their quest, Andrew offered the large flat plot that housed his utility shed—the workshop for a wild array of chemical and engineering "experiments" when his kids were young, and for the construction supplies and motors of all ilk with which the Harwood males of all ages loved to tinker. Always concerned about intruding on the family, Cass and Noah would never have asked but were delighted to accept Andrew's offer. But there were still the many "atmospheric" variables to deal with: rain, heat, and more than anything, bugs. Though a significant part of her task was to train a dog through a host of distractions, she found that schooling herself to remain relaxed, focused, and happy despite these conditions was difficult. The difficulty appeared to be more hers than the dogs. Each spring, when Cass hauled the huge training bag that housed all her portable jumps and other training equipment out from under the shed, her boys grew hysterical with excitement. Katrinka, who was Noah's partner, not so much. Indeed, Trink would often disappear.

Though she was usually truly patient with her dogs, Trinka's disappearances troubled Cass. Though it was almost inevitable when she stopped by the training place, it happened at other times during their treks. In the early days, such absences were occasional and short-lived. One good, high-volume call to Trinka would quickly result in her hearing Trinka's bell moving toward her. But later, the recalls became increasingly delayed and frustrating. Cass felt helpless and inept, which made her angry—an emotion she firmly believed was inappropriate in dealing with canines.

It was also embarrassing when it was witnessed by others. She could almost feel the covert grins of Harwood kin who might be around and clearly enjoyed the signs of "normalcy" in the legendary obedience dogs in their midst. Happily, that was not the case when Lori, who enjoyed watching the training, was with her. Once, after repeated and increasingly frustrated calls, Lori grabbed Cass by the shoulders, faced her, and asked, "Serenity now?" Perhaps Katrinka heard Cass's laugh in response because she appeared seconds later. For all their dogs, laughter was intoxicating. For Chuff and Zeke, the very best reward they could get in the ring was to elicit a laugh from Cass.

It was after this session, as they walked home with an exuberant Trinka and the two other nicely fatigued dogs, that Cass saw Xavier for the first time. It was just a fleeting glimpse of a long-haired, slender lad of about twelve, crossing the trail quickly and then fading into the woods. Though the other dogs appeared to have missed the sighting, Trinka immediately started toward the boy. However, newly chastened and near, she responded immediately to Cass's, "No. With me, Trink."

"Did you see that?" Cass asked Lori.

"See what?" responded Lori.

This was a noteworthy exchange in that it reversed what was more typically a situation in which Lori asked the question, and Cass responded in the negative to what she perceived as Lori's paranoia.

Like Cass, Lori grew up as a city girl. And like Cass, she resonated with the woods and the wild as soon as she was exposed to them. But her exposures came through her visits with the Harwoods, and thus were later in life and sporadic. She had never had the extensive and protracted camping and hiking trips that Cass had experienced with her girlfriends during her early years in Canada. During those years, she gained a deep sense of comfort in the bush. This kind of comfort seemed to be developing during Lori's early trips to the cabin. But later, a darkling fear started to intrude. "What is that?" she would gasp at something Cass failed to see or hear or find out of the ordinary. When Cass would shrug her shoulders, Lori would object, "It feels creepy, as though we're being watched. Look," she'd command, displaying her tanned forearms, where indeed, the hair was standing on end.

Cass tried to reassure Lori that there was all manner of critters in the bush, more often insinuated through sound and the swaying trail of their motion through tall ferns than through direct observation. She thought it understandable that this was disconcerting to Lori, who spent so little time in the bush. She sometimes gently chided Lori, saying, "You've always thought people were watching you."

"Because they always were," Lori responded. Cass knew this to be emphatically true on city streets full of hormonal men but believed the odds on the wildlife being interested in Lori's good looks were pretty damned remote. Happily, it never stopped Lori from looking forward to and undertaking long hikes through the bush. It just injected a certain . . . frisson . . . into the mix. Knowing Lori's history of falling for bad boys, Cass thought Lori just might crave a hint of danger in her life. Both certainly had when they were growing up together.

This in-the-woods-paranoia of Lori's became evident during Lori's summer visit that preceded her winter visit with Mike. That's when it escalated.

SECOND YEAR OF THE STORY

6

CASS – LORI AND MIKE'S JANUARY VISIT

Over the years, the Harwoods and Lori developed a kind of rota for visits. Autumn was Lori's favorite season, and in the early days, she had agitated to visit then. But Cass and Noah had nixed that since they avoided Lac Rouge during hunting season. Trekking lost its luster then since they had to stay out of the woods and were relegated to feeling tame and suburban as they walked the dogs, which were used to running free in the bush, only on the main road. Both humans and dogs were clad in orange vests since the Harwoods were well-acquainted with stories of tragic mistakes made by careless hunters. Beautiful though it was, for the Harwoods, autumn was a time for Ottawa and dog shows, not for Lori and Lac Rouge.

Though it was never set in stone, it evolved that consistently, Lori would arrive for a week-long cabin visit during the month that Cass and Noah were there from mid-December to mid-January to take advantage of cross-country skiing and snowshoeing. Another week or two was typical during the summer: lots of hiking, kayaking, and drinking and toking in the gazebo while watching the hummingbirds. And occasionally, there were other, shorter visits, typically when Lori wanted to disentangle from her man of the moment.

There was always someone. To Cass, it seemed like this aspect of Lori's life was preserved in amber. It was a pattern established when they were kids, and it never seemed to change. The man of the moment was inevitably a high-flyer, typically a successful sales executive, who was expensively coiffed and Rolex-bedecked. These were men who enjoyed Las Vegas, car-races, expensive meals, hard-liquor, and displaying a curvaceous blonde like Lori. These were the kind of men you'd see on the Real Housewives shows. They were the antithesis of the outdoorsy, intellectual hippies that Cass had always favored, and Lori professed a longing for. But of course, it would never have occurred to men like Noah, Andrew, or Yates to approach her. First, such men did not frequent the clubs and bars where Lori was likely to be on the prowl. And even if paths crossed, the hippie and showgirl personas just didn't seem to synch up all that well, in theory. In practice, Lori was smart, earthy, and practical, and Noah, Andrew, and Yates all recognized that and enjoyed spending time with her.

Until Mike, there was no connection between the cabin and Lori's love life, other than her tendency to dump a guy and then retreat to the cabin to avoid the endless imprecations, flowers, and desperate pleas that typically followed the dumping. But Mike stayed in favor with her longer than any of his predecessors. Lori talked about him with unusual enthusiasm during her summer visit and, eventually, asked if she could bring him with her when she came for her next winter stay. Impressed that she that was confident of another six months with a man of the moment, the Harwoods replied, "Of course." But in the time that preceded the visit, Cass felt a little dash of anxiety, hoping the chemistry would work, worried that it might not.

Lori and Mike arrived in time to celebrate New Year's Eve at the cabin. There was already a lot of snow, and Mike's Caddy didn't have four-wheel drive, so they invoked the winter protocols the Harwoods had developed over the years. Lori phoned as they turned off the highway and onto the narrow twisting road that ran through the mountains to the cabin's dirt service road. Because this road was so treacherous without four-wheel drive, it had been widened at spots to allow people to park and then be picked up and transported to their destination in vehicles able to handle the steep, icy service road. This was most difficult around the Harwood place, in which jagged rock outcroppings lined the road, which both narrowed and twisted right across from their cabin. Neither Cass nor Noah ever took this little drive for granted, but they were used to it. By the time Lori and Mike arrived, Cass and Noah were waiting for them up-road in a warm, idling van. They transferred the luggage to the van and were at the cabin within five minutes.

This arrival method meant that the dogs got to meet Mike before Cass and Noah had a chance to do anything other than say a quick hello. Lori had briefed Mike on the canine crew, and he professed to be comfortable with dogs. Not so much, the other way around. Trinka groveled as she approached Mike, head low and tail tucked, a small line of subservient pee trailing behind her. Zeke retreated, barking with his hackles slightly up. He then skipped delightedly around Lori before again backing away from Mike. And Chuff—good cordial Chuff—greeted Lori delightedly and acted as if Mike wasn't even there. It was the same behavior Cass had seen him display countless times when encountering an aggressive male dog. "I don't see you. I don't hear you. I don't have any time for or interest in you." She was gobsmacked at seeing this display for the first time with a human.

Cass tried hard to not allow her dogs' opinions to color her own response to Mike. He was a large, florid, well-muscled man, slightly larded over with the kind of weight typical of former athletes who were heavy drinkers. Rolex—check. Coiffure—check. Attired in spanking new rustic garb: expensive and immaculate insulated boots, pristine down vest, flannel shirt, and cords that still retained their packing creases. As soon as he entered the cabin, he turned his attention to Cass, folding her into a full-body hug, then holding her by the shoulders as he inspected her. He ignored Chuff's rumble, as he said, "Well, I can see that sexiness runs in the family." Turning to Noah, he shook his hand and said, "Lucky man. Beautiful cabin, beautiful wife, beautiful dogs."

A late dinner, bottle of wine, and some very good joints dispelled that first-meeting discomfort. Mike regaled them with tales of stock market exploits, his fitness regime, and not-so-long-ago adventures with minor-league starlets with whom he'd shared winter vacations past. The Harwoods were heartened to hear that he was an experienced and highly-skilled Alpine and Nordic skier. They had both covertly inspected the equipment he brought, glad to see that his skis were indeed the touring skis they'd recommended. They were quite like Lori's, though she said there had been rather heated discussions about buying them and leaving behind the skinny skis he'd used in the big resorts he'd talked about. "Hey, it wasn't the money that was the issue," Mike quickly interjected. "It's just that I always feel the need for speed."

"I suspect skiing in the bush may change that a tad," was Cass's arch response.

That first evening, as they said their goodnights, Mike again folded Cass into a hug, running both hands down her back and then resting them on her hips. She stiffened, and perhaps it was that or Chuff's grumble that caused him to disengage more promptly than he had before. Grinning, he turned to Noah and winked. "We've got some hot ladies here, 'bro. Hope you have as much fun as I'm going to tonight."

Noah had turned away to silence Chuff. "Have a good night," he said as he and Cass headed for the loft.

The next morning dawned crisp, clear, and cold—a perfect day for skiing in the bush. Cass was proud of the network of trails she had set in the few weeks they'd been there before their guests arrived. Being a more avid skier than Noah, with a higher tolerance for the heavy physical burden of setting trails through deep snow, this had traditionally been one of the tasks she assumed in the Harwood division of labor.

The foursome worked out well, at least for the first hour. Cass led, with Lori, who had on her first winter visits, surprised them with her abilities as both a skier and snowshoer, right behind her. They were both faster than the men, who trailed behind them, sometimes far enough back that the women took a short break while waiting for them to catch up. The dogs ran ahead, ran behind, ran in-between. Mike, who had never skied with dogs before, clearly expressed his irritation when Zeke sometimes stepped on his skis or paused in front of him, causing a delay. At one point, Lori interjected, "Hey, he's just being a dog. What's the issue?"

"I can't get a good rhythm going with them doing this shit," Mike responded.

Noah observed that rhythm was a pretty difficult thing to establish, given the skiing conditions in the bush. "Different aesthetic out here," he said. "It'll come to you."

But it didn't seem to. Deep into the crown land behind Jean-Luc's place, Mike slowed considerably. When he and Noah caught up to the women, his stride was uneven. He explained that an old football injury was acting up, saying it never had intruded on cross-country skiing in the past. "Understandable, buddy," Noah reassured him. "No grooming here. Skiing in the bush is different."

Mike pulled a flask out of the small pack he carried and chugged before offering it to the others. "This will help; fine Canadian Scotch." They demurred, and as Mike took another long draft, Lori suggested that it might not be a good idea, given that they still had a good while to go to get back to the cabin. "Don't you fucking mother me," Mike retorted, before breaking into a grin and adding, "You're too damned gorgeous to pull it off." As she turned around to lead them back home, Cass heard

Mike mutter, "Fucking bitch," *sotto voce*. She didn't know if he was referring to her or to Lori and had no interest in finding out.

But good humor was restored when they encountered Andrew and Therese's oldest son, Paul, on a snowmobile on their return trip. Paul, a self-employed software designer, much like his Uncle Noah, spent most of his time at Lac Rouge. And unlike the rest of the Harwood crew, Paul was both a snowmobile and an ATV enthusiast. Mike was immediately interested, saying, "Now that's the way to explore the bush, and still get some real speed." Paul, who had several snowmobiles, invited Mike to go with him the next day. Mike immediately agreed.

And so, the activity pattern for the visit was established. Sometimes the four of them skied together. Cass chose shorter, less challenging routes not likely to be problematic for Mike. More often, Mike went snowmobiling with Paul, which, based on Mike's condition upon return, appeared to be liberally laced with the use of that flask. When Mike went with Paul, welcoming time alone, Noah would stay at the cabin so that Cass and Lori had time alone together with the dogs.

These were Cass's favorite times. Though she didn't share this with Noah, she generally preferred to make her cabin treks, be it skiing, snowshoeing, hiking, or kayaking, on her own. It played to her selfishness; she didn't need to accommodate anyone else's skill, speed, and routing preferences. The dogs were happy with whatever route and pace she established. Lori was perhaps the only person she was happier to have with her than she would have been solo. They had a rhythm together, a harmony of athletic motion that she achieved with no one else. This surprised Cass when she recognized it in the first of Lori's cabin visits since she thought of Lori as an urban girl. But she also knew that like her, Lori was profoundly sensual and assumed that their shared love of movement was an expression of that. She often wondered if their athletic compatibility was some magic endowed by shared blood.

But there were stressors during Mike's visit that hadn't been there previously. Up until then, Lori's paranoia in the bush had been mild and occasional. Not so, during Mike's visit. Lori became vocally and observably uneasy, particularly when the dogs were out of sight. Once, both Trinka and Zeke were AWOL, and as Cass commenced calling them, Chuff, who was still with them, went stiff-legged and alert, curling his lip and emitting low growls as he directed his attention to the direction in which they'd gone. "Look, look at him," Lori gasped. "Someone is watching us; he knows it."

As they bounced on their skis to keep warm, Cass assured her that she'd seen Chuff react that way in the past when she'd done strident recalls. "He knows that I'm pissed, and he's just responding to that," she assured Lori, far more blithely than she felt. "Watch - he'll lighten up as soon as they get back." Zeke returned first, and Chuff gave him the cold shoulder when Zeke groveled him a lip-licking greeting. Lori's concern mounted as Trinka's absence continued. When she finally returned a good five minutes later, Chuff abandoned his danger stance, and Cass was so relieved and so fucking cold that she didn't even chastise Trinka. Indeed, this was one of the few situations in which she had never been sure of the best course of action. She didn't want to make Trinka less willing to come by being harsh with her once she had indeed returned. Cass knew the best approach would be to intervene while Trinka was ignoring her. But to do that, she had to catch her, and in the thick bush, that was completely impractical. Cass had discussed this with her field-training friends and knew she should be considering using an electric collar to remedy this behavior. But she hadn't done it and knew that she probably never would.

Despite these occasional uneasy episodes, while skiing companionably side-by-side on areas of track widened by snowmobile traffic, Cass and Lori shared the kind of intimate chats they always had. Lori told compelling stories about the plight of the many U.S. veterans associated with the service organization she administered. Impressed by Lori's ability to see beyond the sometimes-disfiguring injuries of many of her clients, Cass was surprised by Lori's revulsion when she had to relieve Zeke of whatever dead thing he had scavenged. Cass told her the story of Moose Crossing—a trail they'd so christened fifteen years ago after she and Noah had found a large dead moose right on the trail. It took two seasons for clear evidence of the great animal to vanish. But at intervals for a good ten years after that, a thighbone reappeared in vastly different locations, on both the east and west sides of the road. That was one busy bone, and Cass was sure it wasn't only her own dogs that were contributing to its travels. She tried to share her enthrallment with the way death in the bush was not necessarily followed by resting in peace, but Lori wasn't buying it. The quotidian talk was more successful, as their childhood practice of sharing sexual revelations continued unabated.

Lori described Mike as a kind of sexual Svengali, which explained why they'd been together so much longer than Lori's generally low boredom threshold allowed. Ominously from Cass's perspective, Lori professed that being with Mike had allowed her to better understand why her mother tolerated her domineering husband. Concerned, Cass probed as to whether Mike displayed the same propensity for emotional abuse that characterized Lori's father, who had been Cass's least favorite uncle. Lori clarified immediately, saying, "No, he's not like that at all. It's just that he's . . . so male. He knows what he wants, and he's not afraid to go after it, whatever it is." When Cass later recounted this episode to Noah, they wordlessly exchanged a grimace and shoulder-shrug at this concept of masculinity. But hey, different strokes . . .

The visit wrapped up without incident, and in assessing it afterward, the Harwoods agreed that on a ten-point scale, it was a seven-point visit. Neither of them had become truly comfortable with Mike, but both were willing to have him visit again, which he suggested at their leave-taking. "I gather Lori comes here in the summer, too. Bet it's great up here then. I'm looking forward to it."

"We are too!" they burbled. When their guests were gone, they agreed that the likelihood of Lori and Mike still being together six months from then was minimal, not enough to worry about.

7

XAVIER - WINTER WATCHING

Just Watching was a lot harder in the winter. The first problem was the cold. Because sound travels farther and scent is easier to follow in the snow, it meant I had to stay farther away and stay motionless longer to prevent my subjects from becoming aware of me. Though Stefan had spent years teaching me how to ignore the cold, I've never been that good at it. It's a little better now that I'm bigger than when I started Just Watching Cass. I was still skinny then, and after a while, I'd start shivering so much I was afraid the dogs would feel it, even from far away. And as bad, sometimes I couldn't even draw to keep myself busy, because my fingers were frozen. For a while, I had these cool mitts I'd liberated, with tops you could flip off and fingerless gloves underneath. But I outgrew them. Too bad.

I also needed to be smarter in the winter than when I watched in other seasons. Though I suspected Stefan might do it, I wouldn't take off my snowshoes to climb a tree, so I couldn't watch from above, which is something I like to do, and that feels safe. I had to hide near to where Cass made her first decision about which route to take. Then I had to figure out which trails she was likely to take from there and pick a different route that would let me stay close to but always downwind from where she was going. I couldn't cross over her trail at any point because even Cass would likely see the snowshoe tracks and be concerned about them coming out of the woods and then going back into them. And there would be no way that Trinka wouldn't follow my tracks or that Chuff wouldn't get kinda chuffy at knowing that I was around.

The cold was also a problem for getting started on winter watches. Cass didn't seem to keep to any kind of a schedule. Sometimes she hit the trails at nine in the morning, other times not till two in the afternoon, and she could start any time in between, which meant I had to just kind of hang around, hiding until she finally showed up. Sometimes I got so cold I just gave up.

It was easier when Boobs and Big Dude were there, because then they started out at about ten each morning. I shouldn't call her Boobs; I know that. She seems to be a nice lady whose name is Lori. It was easier to think of her that way, as Lori, in the winter when I couldn't see those big boobs bouncing around under all her ski clothes. But I knew they were there all right. So did Big Dude. You know how male dogs get when there's a bitch in heat? Heads high, necks arched, muscles tense, noses working like crazy? Well, Big Dude was like that—for a human. And he didn't keep it only for Lori. I saw him doing it around Cass too. Noah and Chuff saw it too. I figure that's why Noah, who could have gone faster, always hung back with Big Dude as if he couldn't keep up with the women. And Chuff just didn't like Big Dude; he kept his distance. He loved Lori though. She surprised me by being able to keep up with Cass who, on skis like when she walked, was fast.

Stefan was the other Just Watching problem I had that winter. He didn't go all super-calm and quiet throughout the season, which was a relief because that always meant trouble. But he wouldn't give me a break on my schoolwork, either. He said it was important that I show how well-educated I was in both French and English, in case the authorities he hated ever wanted to check whether I was getting good homeschooling. He gave me tests every couple of weeks to make sure we were good. He'd go scary-quiet if I didn't test at least two grades higher than I should, based on my age. Sometimes bad scores brought an explosion, in addition to extra assignments. I studied like crazy that winter because I wanted to be Just Watching instead of studying in my room.

I suggested to Stefan that we should move our lessons together to the evenings, so I had more time in the daylight to carry out my observations. Observations are important to him. He taught me about them first when I was littlelittle, telling me about Mr. Charles Darwin and how he changed everything we understand about the world by observing. I call that Just Watching, but I know it's not the correct term because an important part of observing is drawing pictures and making notes about what you're watching. Stefan said that like Mr. Darwin, we are naturalists, and naturalists need good supplies. He always made sure that I had notebooks and colored pencils for my observations. Sometimes, he asked to see my notebooks.

Because of that, I was careful about what I drew when I was so busy Just Watching Cass and her dogs. I drew all of them but put most of them in a second notebook I didn't show Stefan. I put a few in my main notebook, and I was careful to put in other drawings too, so it didn't look like my main job was watching Cass. I'm very good at drawing turkeys and their tracks. I did lots of them that winter, along with foxes, martens, minks, and coyotes.

Stefan asked to see my notebook the night I suggested we change the timing of our lessons. He slowly flipped through what I'd done since he last looked. He asked me who Cass was and asked what I'd learned about her, about her dogs, and their relationships to each other. He went very quiet after I'd answered those questions. *Uh-oh,* I thought. But instead of what I thought might happen, after a quiet minute or two, he said there are special challenges in watching really smart subjects. He told me to wait, disappeared into his room for a minute, and returned with a couple of books. They were all by a lady named Dr. Jane Goodall. He told me she is old now, but she was young when she wrote those books. He said she was a "latter-day naturalist" like us. He told me to read those books. I did. I love Dr. Jane Goodall.

But when he gave me those books, I didn't know how much I would love them, and I didn't think they'd help me with my problem about when we did school. Stefan got up early and usually went to bed at about nine, and he liked to have the evenings free for his own reading or to go to the auberge—an old hunting lodge that been turned into a kind of saloon. So he was not happy about moving school to the evenings. He sent me to our reference books to study what "negotiation" was. Once I thought I understood it, we practiced by negotiating my request. We eventually agreed to move our lessons to six in the evening, two nights a week. That helped.

Despite, or maybe because of the challenges of winter watching, I saw some good stuff and learned a lot about my subjects that winter. On one of the last days of Lori's visit, I found out that Cass was tougher-minded than I thought she might be.

I was watching as she and Lori skied out of the wooded trails where they'd been spending their time into one of the big open fields that surrounded that weird-looking patch of woods with the dark, spooky cabin. I'd asked Stefan about it. He'd picked up a little bit of information about it at the auberge. The guys he drank with there said it was owned by a guy named Jean-Luc, who lived closer to Quebec City. He didn't know anything more about him. I'd seen a guy I assumed was the owner once or twice, making sure he didn't see me. I didn't learn much other than that he's a big guy.

Anyway, only Chuff was with Cass and Lori. I don't know where the others were; they hadn't been with me. Cass did one of her big hollers. I could tell from how long it took to hear the bells that the dogs had been a long way off. Trinka came out of the woods and into the field, running fast. I knew she had cookies on the brain. But Zeke was doing his victory dance and taking his time about it.

In his mind, Zeke was a hunter. When he spotted or scented a critter—whether it was a deer, possum, or turkey—he was on it. So were the others. But unlike Trink and Chuff, who stopped when Cass called them off, sometimes there was no stopping Zeke. He was a pretty good hunter. I saw him grab a low-flying partridge out of the air once.

But hey, he was a Golden Retriever. I'd read about them, of course. They're designed to bring stuff back to humans, not go out and kill it. And Zeke was serious about his job. I can't even count the times that he proudly brought back bits and pieces of something dead he'd found. Each time, he did his victory dance: tossing his head, waving his tail, running in ever-smaller circles until he finally sat in front of Cass, holding whatever his newest treasure was in his mouth, grinning and wagging his tail. "Aren't I a good boy?"

Cass was good about it; she didn't yell at him, but she sometimes made disgusted faces and sounds as she fished whatever he had out of his mouth. It usually looked like small bones or nasty old wings. But then she had a real problem. Because those dogs were retrievers, if she threw away whatever it was, all three of them thought it was a great game and went to fetch it. Because she was short, when she tried to put whatever it was in a tree, the dogs would then refuse to leave, trying to climb the damn tree. It seemed as though she eventually started carrying plastic gloves and bags in her pack, and for the stuff that wasn't too big, she'd put it in the bag and in her pack.

But that wasn't going to help her this time. I realized what Zeke had long before the women did. *This is going to be interesting,* I thought. I could hear what they said to each other because the wind blew their conversation toward me. They thought maybe he'd found a branch he liked, though Cass thought it was weird because he was doing such a big victory dance. He streaked toward her, snow flying and shining like diamonds in the sun as he ran and around her, ever closer, proudproudproud, with the front leg of a very long-dead deer flopping from the knee joint as he ran. As he got closer to Cass, she saw what he had. "Oh Fuck," she said, but instead of getting all freaked out as I kind of expected, she just went into her pack and got out the plastic gloves she had in there. They were big enough to fit over her tight ski gloves.

Zeke was less happy to give up this prize than usual, but after Cass repeatedly said, "Leave it," he did. Lori was not helpful. She kinda turned her back on them and told Cass to let her know when it was okay again. So Cass then had to figure out what to do with the leg. She decided to bury it. The snow was soft and deep, so she got down on her knees with her skis on and shoveled out a half meter deep pit. Then she got Lori to help her cover it, and then they kinda flattened it with their skis. I thought they did a pretty decent job of it, for two city-ladies.

But of course, the minute they started off again, all three dogs ran to the spot and started digging. Cass had to give them a very big, mean-sounding "Leave it!" Then she got out a bunch of cookies. She put both ski poles in one hand and the cookies in the other and gradually kind of lured the dogs away from the spot. Once she figured she was far enough, she then threw cookies ahead of her. But she wasn't far enough away; the dogs grabbed the cookies and then ran back and started digging. "Fuck!" yelled Cass. I started to laugh, which was bad because the dogs heard me. All three of them froze, with their heads up, pointed in my direction. I stopped breathing.

Luckily for me, Cass was too involved in her problem to pay attention to what the dogs were saying. She went through the whole routine again, covering up the leg and then skiing it flat, then luring the dogs away, much farther this time. When she threw the cookies ahead of her this time, it worked. I stayed where I was, watching the five of them slowly disappear into the distance.

This had been a near-miss. If my subjects had been more alert, they might have found me. It was not a super-cold day, so I stayed where I was for a while, sat against a tree, ate a protein bar, did a sketch of Zeke doing his dance with the leg in his mouth, and thought about Dr. Jane Goodall. Eventually, when she realized how hard observing would be if she had to stay hidden, she decided that she needed to let her subjects see her enough to get used to her, so they would act naturally when she was around.

8

CASS – THE BEST WINTER

Cass loved having guests at the cabin. She was a whirlwind of anticipation and activity as she awaited the arrival of Lori and Mike. Menu-planning, shopping in French in the small village grocery store, and making the tiny guest room as habitable as possible was all part of that delicious "waiting" state.

But no matter how good a visit was, the feeling of blessed relief when guests departed was at least as great as the anticipation before they arrived. Now comes the spiral down into complete selfishness! No need to talk; she and Noah could go hours—happily, companionably—without saying a word. No need to present and facilitate options: What would you like? Music and dope? Wine and a movie? Cards, bullshit, and munchies? With the guests gone, no options were required. She and Noah had no need to entertain themselves or each other, except for some lovely catch-up sex, given the privacy constraints guests imposed. Cass believed, of course, that options are good. But they always impose the onus of decision-making. So the fewer options, the fewer decisions that needed to be made, the more life felt like it was unfolding as it should of its own accord, instead of coming out of a Cass Harwood playbook. An inveterate planner, Cass loved not planning.

And in the winter, the selfish freedoms were more profound than at other times of the year since training the dogs and weight-training—activities she factored into the choices she made at different times of year—were not viable in the snow. The only decisions Cass had to make each day were whether to ski or snowshoe, when to do it, and what to wear when she did it.

The winter of Lori's visit with Mike was the best of the many winters they'd experienced at the cabin. There was snow—lots of it—but not so much in any single dump that Cass couldn't refresh her ski trails. There had been a couple of winters when a storm would bring more than three feet of snow in a day or two. Despite Cass's strength and determination, re-setting trails in thigh-deep snow even on skis was simply beyond her ability. When that happened, she had to wait until whenever snowmobilers showed up, and then she'd have to ski in the tracks they made—a considerably less aesthetically pleasing approach than the two narrow tracks she laid down through interconnected deer trails. In this best winter, there was no ice. Ice storms were common in Western Quebec. In 1998, there was one that brought down the power grid across the province for more than a week. The Harwoods were fine because they had plenty of food, a high-tech wood-burning stove, and a generator. But winter sports were severely compromised for the whole of that winter. In the many years after that, ice storms were common, though less severe. Having a whole winter without one, without a thaw, and with just steady cold and lots of snow, was a gift.

Cass made the most of it. She kept expanding her network of trails beyond Jean-Luc's place. And because Jean-Luc posted highly visible *Domain Privé* signs and security cameras all around his property, snowmobiles, with their noise and their smells, were encountered only rarely—in the places where Cass's trails, too narrow and overgrown for the machines, briefly intersected the groomed trails maintained by the snowmobile association. The trails Cass made got hard and packed down as she skied them, and then blissfully softened as new snow fell almost every evening. Throughout that winter, in the wildlands behind Jean-Luc's, she and the dogs danced, flew, and cavorted through diamond dust. When Noah, who didn't enjoy being out as long as Cass and the dogs did, accompanied them, they generally skied elsewhere, closer to home.

Despite the perfect weather and unparalleled skiing, Cass was surprised to find that Lori's paranoia seemed to have infected her. The dogs would suddenly stop, heads up and tilted to the side, ears and noses aquiver. "Wazzat?" And despite her many reassurances to Lori about this being just business in the bush, she now found that in Lori's absence, it was the hair on Cass's arms that was standing on end. It got tedious, as Cass made clear when she addressed herself, "Shit woman, will you stop with the piloerections!"

Dog behavior, in general, was just a tad off that winter. All the dogs knew all the trails, and typically the fore-runners would pause at every decision-point, looking questioningly at Cass as they clearly asked, "Which way do you want to go?" But during this winter, Trinka started to show that she had her own preferences. She would start taking the trail she wanted and would drag her heels when Cass told her, "No, not that way." And she also became harder to keep track of. Cass would bliss out for a few minutes, paying attention to nothing other than the rhythm she'd established, the cool air in her lungs, and the sun tickling her face as it broke through the dark woods. And then suddenly—*zip*—she'd be back. Chuff would be with her, of course. She could hear Zeke's bell, not all that far in the distance. And Katrinka? Where was Katrinka?

This occasioned high-volume recalls. Yell. Wait. Nothing. Bellow. Wait. Nothing. Shriek. Wait. Nothing. And as the minutes of each prolonged recall ticked on, Cass's fear battled her frustration. What if Trinka didn't come back? What if she'd been hurt? What if Cass couldn't find her? By the time Trinka finally showed up, the Zen of the ski had been at least temporarily compromised as Cass experienced an uncomfortable combination of rage and relief.

It was after the most prolonged of these recalls that she met Xavier. Cass had been stalled at the intersection of one of her own ski trails with a heavily traveled snowmobile trail. This was probably the longest recall imbroglio ever, and she was getting panicky, thinking that Trinka could have potentially been hit by a snowmobile. So her relief when Trinka appeared as a tiny dot on the side of the snowmobile trail was profound. But Trinka was not racing toward her, and Trinka was not alone. She was accompanied by a human on snowshoes. Cass skied onto the snowmobile trail to intercept them.

From this great distance, all Cass could tell was that the human was not large and that Trinka was remarkably comfortable with him or her, trotting alongside the way Chuff typically traveled with Cass. It was obvious that Cass did not need to yell, *"Ils sont amicaux,"* which was her traditional salvo when she and the dogs encountered humans while trekking. Clearly, this human already knew that Trinka was friendly. So Cass told Chuff and Zeke, neither of whom displayed their typical "who the hell is that and are they safe?" postures and vocalizations, to sit and stay while she silently advanced. As the duo grew closer, Cass could see that the person on snowshoes was small. Closer yet, a kid, maybe a young teenager, gender not yet identifiable. And closer yet, a boy of perhaps twelve or thirteen, a bit taller than Cass, and rangy, even in traditional rural Quebec hunting wear. He was fast on his snowshoes, and he appeared to be jogging effortlessly. She thought he might be the kid she'd glimpsed once after training. She waited to say anything until he drew close, but the kid seized the initiative when he was perhaps one hundred yards away. *"Est-ce-que c'est ton chien?"* he yelled.

"Oui! C'est mon chien," Cass bellowed in return. Ownership thus asserted, she then called Trinka, who happily bounded toward her, seemingly unaware of her intransigence.

Cass stopped and waited for the kid to approach, which he did with a fair bit of confidence. And there was no reason for timidity. Released from their stay, neither Chuff nor Zeke acted even remotely concerned. Indeed, Zeke greeted the newcomer as if he were a friend. As this happened, the kid again initiated, *"Bonjour. Comment ça va?"*

To which Cass replied, *"Bien."* And then added, *"Parlez-vous anglais? Mon francais n'est pas bon."*

The kid immediately responded, *"Pas de problème,"* and then flipped over into perfect vernacular, unaccented English. Cass was impressed, and in the next few minutes, established that the kid often bushwhacked in the area on snowshoes and had encountered Trinka before. He said he'd always tried to send her back before she'd been away long enough for Cass to get worried. But today, he apologized; he'd made a mistake by sharing a sausage he'd been eating when she showed up, and she then wouldn't leave when Cass called. So he felt he had to bring her back.

The kid said it was hard to hear from so far away. "Are you calling her Trinka?" he asked. When Cass confirmed, he asked what that meant.

"I don't think it means anything," Cass replied. "I just liked the name Katrinka, and the way it turns into a great call name, Trinka."

"What's a call name?" he asked. Cass then explained that purebred dogs like hers have formal names registered with the Canadian Kennel Club, which always start with the name of the breeder's kennel. Her breeder's kennel was called TriGold, so her senior dog's registered name was TriGold's Heavy Breathing. But each pedigreed dog also had a shorter name like a pet would, and that's what you call them. So in real life, TriGold's Heavy Breathing was called Chuff.

Cass was intrigued. He was a cool kid, with great confidence, responsiveness, and curiosity. Those were qualities she always sought in a puppy, and she found them similarly attractive in a young human. She continued to chat with him as she made her way back to her trail. She asked where he lived. But though she caught the general direction he pointed out, she got lost in the welter of other descriptors, taking away only that his place was not directly on the lake and was some distance from hers. When she got back to her trail, she signified that she preferred to go solo by thanking him and saying it had been nice talking to him. As she did so, she realized they hadn't exchanged names. She introduced herself and asked his name. He told her, pronouncing it the French way, "Za-vee-eh," and then spelling it for her in English.

Cass by-passed her astonishment at his acumen about what Anglos do and do not know and instead responded, "Xavier— what a cool name. What does it mean?"

"I don't think it means anything. But my call name is Xavvy," he responded. They were both laughing as they parted company.

She occasionally ran into him after that, often in the deep bush behind Jean Luc's, but once or twice in the terrain she skied with Noah. She was grateful that the kid seemed to understand her drive for solitude. When she encountered him when Noah was with her, he sometimes accompanied them for a few minutes before parting paths. When that happened, Noah's feelings were a bit injured when they had to call Trinka back from following Xavier rather than staying with them. When Cass was out solo, Xavier invariably picked up her cues and did not attempt to attach himself in any way, except when she invited him to. She did that every now and then, primarily because she was so interested in, perhaps even enthralled by how Trinka acted when Xavier was around. She saw the kind of single-minded focus then from Trink that Chuff had always exhibited with her. Regardless of the legal niceties of ownership, Trinka's soul belonged to the kid. Cass didn't know how that happened, but she found it mysterious and beautiful. She was thus impressed but not surprised when, as they parted ways with Xavvy, Trinka always appeared poised to follow him. Each time, Xavvy turned to her and said sternly, "No. Stay." And she did. *Holy shit,* thought Cass.

9

CASS – LATE MARCH

In that glorious best winter, March was unparalleled. It can be a mercurial month for cross- country skiing in the bush, often punctuated by thaws that leave the snow skiable but not terribly rewarding. But the spate of unbroken below-freezing temperatures that had characterized the period of November through February continued into March. Temperatures warmed, but never to the point where the snow grew punky and clumpy.

To take advantage of the superb conditions, Cass and Noah canceled coaching for a week in late March and spent that time at the cabin. On one of the last days of the visit, Cass set out with the dogs to go beyond Jean-Luc's place to take advantage of some new trails she'd developed and push them a bit farther. It was the best ski day of her life. The sun was bright, and there was an unmistakable spring warmth in the air, but it was still cold enough for the few inches of new snow that had fallen overnight to remain in winter-powder condition. For over two hours, she flew smoothly through the diamond dust that the dogs raised all around her as they celebrated the conditions or perhaps simply picked up on Cass's joy. Trinka was the essence of ecstasy. She rolled and tumbled, flirted with Zeke, and even managed to engage Chuff in a brief game of chase. There were no recall battles, which Cass now recognized probably meant that Xavier was nowhere around.

More than two hours in, after setting about fifteen minutes' worth of new trail, Cass paused for some water, raising her face to the warmth of the sun as she drank from her water bottle. Chuff and Zeke clustered around her while Trinka explored the terrain bordering the deer trail where Cass had set new tracks. As she drank, Cass heard a distinct *click* and then a high-pitched yelp. *Shit,* she thought, recognizing the indicators of many minor canine mishaps in the past. The sound had come from Trinka, who appeared to be exploring a large slatted wooden orange-crate sitting inexplicably in the snow just off the trail. Whatever she was exploring was interesting— when Cass called her, Trinka didn't move. And then she did. Her hindquarters demonstrated that she was trying to withdraw her head from the crate without success. And she started making a high-pitched sound, halfway between a scream and a gasp.

The day, previously punctuated by sweet wind sound and birdsong, went silent. Time slowed and skewed into a slow-motion rubbery medium, through which Cass frantically pushed to reach Trinka. She sank to her knees and moved the box. Okay. But that didn't dislodge the animal trap that had been in it and was now closed tightly around Katrinka's neck. Trinka's feet drummed and her gasping scream continued as Cass tried desperately to understand the trap and how to spring it. She did not. She could not. As she focused every fiber of her being on this task, she heard a woman from afar, wailing and gibbering, "Oh God, oh God! Trink, Trinka, oh God!" It was not until much later that she realized that it was she who'd been wailing. It didn't matter. None of it mattered. Profoundly helpless, Cass pulled Trinka, neck still encased in the trap, into her arms and loved her fiercely as her little red girl went quiet and still in her arms.

Silence. Cass looked up through the trees at the bluest sky she'd ever seen. Trinka's last sky. She looked down from the sky into which she had somehow ascended and saw Cass, still on skis, kneeling in a shaft of sunlight with Trinka in her arms. Chuff and Zeke sat unmoving like sentinels where she'd left them. She had not given them a stay command. But there they'd stayed. Cass stayed there for hours. She stayed there for seconds. It didn't matter. None of it mattered until eventually, the soundtrack resumed. Cass climbed shakily to her feet as her hearing returned the sounds of wind and birdsong, punctuated by the low-key whimpers of anxiety coming from Chuff and Zeke, still unaccountably frozen in their self-imposed stays.

She comforted the boys and told them to stay. She used her skis to stomp a sizable clearing around Trinka's body and marked the entire area with the red trail tape she always carried with her. She got out the radio she always carried, knowing that the odds of reaching Noah this far from home were negligible and that she'd need to get out of the shadow of the mountain before she was likely to succeed in contacting him. No luck. No luck. No luck. It didn't matter. None of it mattered.

She had to urge the boys to go with her as she started the trek home. They plodded next to her as she skied the long ninety minutes before she was finally able to reach Noah. Trinka was his partner. When she finally reached him, her report was brief. No tears. There were no tears. "Trinka got caught in a trap. I think she is dead. Meet me at the turn-off to Jean-Luc's place. I'm still about a half-hour away from there."

To reach the turn-off to Jean-Luc's, Cass needed to ski out from the dark woods into the open terrain they called the turn-off. It was a very large meadow, and the late afternoon sunlight was blinding. She could see Noah and the van a good quarter-mile distant, but at first, doubted that it was him. That was because of the color. The blue sky, the white snow, the evergreens, the dark amber of the dog's coats—everything had acquired a circus-like brightness she'd seen in the past only when looking up at large downhill ski hills full of the mad poetry and psychedelically bright clothing of 1980s skiers. That couldn't be Noah! His parka was a dull rust color. The man she viewed in the distance was attired in a blood-red crimson parka. The light, the colors, speared her vision, painfully bright.

But it was Noah. When she reached him, Cass threw herself into his arms. "I am so sorry. I am so sorry. I am so sorry." She couldn't stop saying it. She couldn't stop feeling how wrong it was that she wasn't crying and, in fact, felt flat. She felt nothing except guilt. Trinka was Noah's partner, and she had died on Cass's watch. There was no end to the guilt she felt, especially given that she had already become aware of a seed of relief that it hadn't been one of her boys.

Noah, beautiful Noah, reassured her even before he extracted details of what had happened. He reminded her that they both knew and accepted that there were risks in being in the bush and that he would never hold her responsible. And he then extracted the story, confirming in the process that Cass was in no way responsible.

They agreed that their next step should be to go the auberge, where they could call Paul or find someone else with a snowmobile to enlist in the task of reclaiming Trinka's body. So Cass took off her skis and tossed them into the car while the boys clambered into the back seat. They remained subdued; none of the hijinks that typically accompanied post-ski reunions.

At the auberge, they found the normal smattering of snowmobiles and winter-clad French-Canadian males. As Noah, whose French was better than Cass's, explained why they needed to use the phone, silence fell over the usual din of beer-drinking chatter. Cass felt all eyes on her. And again, she felt nothing. She was a husk of a human, not knowing how to feel or what to do under these circumstances.

And then, suddenly and helpfully, there was a script. Cass had done lots of amateur theatre as a kid, and one of her university majors had been drama. And so she was incredibly grateful when the emotional void she was inhabiting was invaded by a voice-over of an appropriate script: *Wanting to avoid any contact with the curious males assembled, she found an isolated table and placed her hat and gloves there. Feeling both faint and nauseated, she spread her legs wide and lowered her head to between her legs.* Obediently, Cass followed the scripting, keeping her head down until Noah sat down next to her and put his arm around her. He told her that Paul was on his way over and that they'd go retrieve Katrinka. Cass could give him enough information so that they were both confident that he and Paul could find her. A few minutes later, Paul arrived, and he and Noah took off.

With their departure, Cass tumbled back into the void. And once again, the voice-over script obligingly reappeared. *The covert attention focused on Cass once Noah and Paul left was overwhelming. She needed to escape it; she needed to find physical contact and reassurance. So she went out to the car to be with her boys.* Again, Cass obediently followed her script. Chuff and Zeke whimpered and wriggled with anxious empathy as she climbed into the backseat with them, entwining herself with them until she could no longer tell which limbs were hers and which were theirs. About a half-hour later, she realized they might need to relieve themselves and took them out of the car to attend to that. As they all returned to the car, she first heard and then saw Paul's snowmobile approaching, Paul driving, and Noah perched behind him, holding . . . something, which, as they parked and then walked toward her, she knew was Katrinka.

Time stood as still as Cass did. The silent void descended. She was a discarded snake-skin, an empty carapace, watching her husband and nephew approach her vacant husk. The script was slow in coming, and then blessedly appeared when Noah had come close enough for her to see little Katrinka, freed from the trap, resting in his arms with her head lolling as it never had in life. The voice-over continued: *As she saw what was left, what was no longer Katrinka, Cass emitted a long, low, quavering wail.* Which, of course, is what Cass did. The sound, which she heard from afar, seemed to hang in the air forever. And then it stopped. Noah handed what wasn't Katrinka any longer to Paul, who headed to the auberge while Noah went to Cass. "There was nothing you could have done," he said. "The trap was so strong that it took both of us—Paul and me—to get it open. You couldn't have done it, even if you knew how to." Noah gently guided Cass into the car, telling her that he'd go back later to get Katrinka.

He did. Early the next morning, he drove to the auberge. When he returned, Cass numbly watched him remove one of the large ice chests they used to transport food to the cabin from the car and carry it to the shed. She still felt very little, just flatflatflat. She and Noah had decided they'd return to Ottawa to get Katrinka cremated, but only after consulting with a Quebec conservation and wildlife officer. Paul, outraged by what had happened, had suggested and arranged this, looking to find out if the trap that killed Trinka was legal.

At around noon, the officer, on a snowmobile, stopped first by Paul's place so that Paul, on his snowmobile, could guide him to the Harwood cabin. During the brief introductions, he expressed his condolences in English. It was clear that he understood the impact of losing a dog to a trap. His manner was grave and courteous. They then set off, with Noah seated behind the officer and Cass behind Paul. The weather had changed. The sky was low, gray, and sullen.

Once they arrived at their destination, Cass hung back while the three men examined the site. The officer crouched down and carefully inspected the trap, which Noah and Paul had left still chained to the tree against which the wooden crate had initially been placed. He and Paul chatted in French. When they returned to Cass, she immediately asked, "Was that trap legal?" The officer flipped into English as he replied that it was indeed a legal trap. "But I don't understand," said Cass. "I skied over completely virgin snow. I was laying tracks in deep snow. Nobody had been there in ages. Don't trappers have to check their traplines?"

The officer took a deep breath and responded, "I am very sad to have to tell you this. A good trapper will check his lines frequently. But this is not a legal requirement. The trap used was in compliance with regulations and was tagged."

"Yes," interjected Paul, his voice hard. "We know who the son-of-a-bitch who set the trap was. It was Jean-Luc."

Cass and Noah looked at one another in shocked silence. A long pause, before Noah asked, in disbelief, "Jean-Luc?"

"If his last name is Tessier, then yes," responded the officer.

Cass interjected, her voice quivering with rage, "But we know him. He gave us permission to go through his property. He knows we travel far back in the bush. He knows we have dogs. He never said anything about having traplines. Surely that's wrong?"

Again, the officer, clearly upset by the turmoil of emotion around him, paused before replying very quietly, "I agree, *Madame*, that it is wrong. However, it is not illegal. There is no legal action available to you for the loss of your dog. I am very sorry."

The roar of the snowmobiles obviated the possibility of conversation on the way home. And there was nothing to say, anyway.

10

XAVIER – BAD NEWS

Introducing myself to Cass was a good idea. I thought a lot about how to do it ahead of time, and it was a good plan, and I was a good actor. That's the way I thought of it. I had to pretend; I had to act like I didn't know anything about my subjects, and I had to have a good reason for why I was introducing myself. So after Trinka found me in the woods, I did what Cass does when she trains and wants the dog to have a good time. I played chase and kind of play-fought with her, and then sometimes I hid, and she got all excited when she found me. And I wasn't lying about the sausage. I gave her pieces while we played like I'd seen Cass do. Then, when I could tell from her hollers that Cass was getting upset, I told Trinka, "With me," like Cass does, and made my way onto the snowmobile trail. Trinka did stay with me! I could understand why Cass trains. It feels good when a dog just stays by your side like that, looking up at you and looking really happy. If dogs could laugh, Katrinka was laughing that day.

Another good part of the plan was making believe that French is my first language and that I didn't know that Cass is Anglo. Maybe French is my first language; I don't really know. I've spoken both French and English my whole life. We speak mostly English at home, but Stefan says he needs to keep his French fluent, so sometimes we switch, and we'll have a French week. Stefan's French is very good, but he says it gets harder all the time because he writes in English. He's been writing a lot recently because his back has been too bad for him to do more active stuff. And he says the anarchist journal that publishes his stuff likes it and bugs him for more. Even though his French is good, I can tell that he has to work harder when he speaks French. I don't. They're both easy for me.

After that first meeting with Cass, it was much easier to Just Watch in some respects. Cass knew that I was around sometimes, but I succeeded in showing her that I wouldn't get in her way or stop her from being alone like she likes to be. And she got it; she seemed more comfortable. You know what? All animals, including humans, do the same thing when they are on alert or are alarmed—they stop, with their muscles tensed and their heads up. If it's a deer or a dog, they swivel their ears and flare their nostrils, trying to locate a clue in sound or scent. Humans rely on their eyes and ears, so they do a lot of head swiveling. And the interesting thing is that the Alarm Show is catching, between different kinds of critters. When Cass heard something that caused her to do the Alarm Show, the dogs caught it right away and immediately did the dog version of the show. And if the dogs did it first, then Cass picked it up from them. Cass was nothing compared to Lori, who was super-aware, so I was glad that her January visit was short.

After I arranged the first meeting with Cass, she became alarmed less often. I was glad, but I thought it was not smart of her. She shouldn't have assumed that I was the only other critter out there or that there were no other dangers she should be looking out for. But, of course, I couldn't tell her that, because a good naturalist doesn't get involved with his subject.

I knew from Dr. Jane Goodall that you can't do that perfectly. You are a human, and it is only human to start to care about subjects you are observing so often and so long. But I successfully reminded myself to always act with Cass, so she saw a Xavvy I kind of made up, not the real me. And I had no problem with Zeke and Chuff. They just didn't have all that much interest in me once they realized that I wasn't dangerous. But I failed with Katrinka. I just couldn't stop myself from getting more involved with her than I knew a naturalist should. But she loved me so much. No one else in my whole life made me feel the way she did.

I knew I had to manage the situation, and so I did. It was a wonderful winter, a great time to be in the bush. I made sure to do more traditional observations in all sorts of places, so I wouldn't run into Cass too often. It wasn't hard because she and Noah spent more time in the city after their long winter visit and were usually here just for long weekends—like from Friday morning to Monday morning.

But they came up for a whole week toward the end of March. It was a good decision because the weather was beautiful. I prefer snowshoes to skis, but I knew that the snow was great for both, and I was happy for Cass that she was having such a good time skiing. I could tell when I watched her. She was so happy when she skied that week that she looked beautiful. I didn't want to upset her, or my ability to Just Watch her, by having Trinka make her wait too long, too often. So I only went to the bush beyond Jean-Luc's once or twice that week, spending most of my time doing other observations and my schoolwork. Stefan and I had gotten used to having dinner early and then doing our lessons together from about six to eight at night, which left him time to go to the auberge if he wanted to.

One morning, after he'd been to the auberge the night before, he made me breakfast. That was weird because he was usually up earlier than me and made himself a hot breakfast. I also got up early each morning—but after him—and I made my own breakfast, usually toast and cereal. But this morning, he seemed to be waiting for me, and he made me pancakes, which is one of my favorite foods. Then he made me a hot chocolate and sat down with me while I ate and asked me what I'd done observation-wise the last few days. When I told him, he said, "So you weren't in the bush beyond Jean-Luc's?" I didn't like the way he asked that. I could feel myself falling into an Alarm Show. Something was going on.

"No, I wasn't," I said. "Why?"

"I heard that the woman you watch—the Harwood woman— had a little trouble back there a few days ago," he said.

"What kind of trouble? Is she okay?" I asked very quietly, the way I'd talk to him in the woods when we went hunting. He told me that she was okay, but that one of her dogs got caught in a trap and died. He was watching me very carefully, and I knew this was a test, but I didn't know what I had to do to pass it, and I didn't care. When I asked him if he knew which dog it was, he told me, "The little one. The bitch you draw all the time."

I could feel the blood leave my face and rush down into my feet. And I heard the ocean. I have never been to the ocean, but I've seen it and heard it in movies. And Stefan has a big shell, and if you hold it up to your ear, you can hear the ocean in it. And that's what I heard inside my white, bloodless head: the sound of the ocean, like waves breaking inside me. And then they broke through the shell of my body. I cried and cried; it was like the ocean inside me was spilling out of my eyes and running down my face. But I didn't make a sound. I thought that might be part of the test. I couldn't cry like a baby.

We sat there while I cried. Stefan didn't get angry, so I figured I'd passed whatever the test was. Finally, after what seemed like a long time, I asked him, "Who was the trapper?" He told me it was Jean-Luc. "Was it legal? What did he say about it?" I asked. Stefan told me that Tessier probably didn't even know about it; he wasn't around very often. I got mad. "That's not right!" I yelled. "You shouldn't have traps set if you're not going to take care of your lines! And you sure as shit shouldn't have traps set where you know there are people with dogs messing around!"

Stefan looked at me, kinda sad, and shrugged his shoulders. "The Harwoods had a conservation officer check it out, and the trap was legal," he said.

He told me he was sorry that I was sad. Then he tried to make me feel better. "So, your birthday is coming up soon. You will be thirteen. In some religions, that's when you are considered to be a man. So, I want you to think about it today and tonight, and give me a list of three things you want. I will surprise you with one of them on your birthday." Funny—that was the first time I ever felt sorry for Stefan. It was obvious that I had passed whatever stupid test he'd made up and that he wanted to make me feel better. But I knew that losing Trinka was much bigger than a birthday gift. No one might ever love me that way again. But I needed to give Stefan a list that night; I was good at recognizing his tests. So I gave him the list: a crossbow, a camera, a dog.

11

CASS – WINTER RECEDING AND SPRING

Cass, who grew up in Baltimore, where spring was a glorious three months of color and warmth, always said there was only a week or two of real spring in Eastern Ontario and Western Quebec. Instead, winter was followed by Winter Receding, which was typically the months of April and May when the snow grew punky and then disappeared, roads and trails were a patchy quagmire of ice and mud, the skies were gray, the rain was frequent, and sleet and snow were not rare. If you were lucky, there were a couple of weeks of spring-like weather in June before the surprisingly hot and humid summer descended.

Cass and Noah did not return to Lac Rouge until Winter Receding was almost done, about six weeks after Katrinka's death. In Ottawa, there were competitions to attend, and before that, an acclimation process as Noah, now partner-less, undertook the work required to compete with Zeke. Four-year-old Zeke, who had been trained and handled by Cass, was initially confused by this change. But all the Harwood dogs had learned to deal with confusion. Cass felt that this was one of her greatest training victories. She had made the learning process such a positive one that rather than becoming upset when they were confused, both of her boys remained cheerful and expectant, trusting that the human would help them resolve the confusion and that the celebration and rewards when the light bulb went on would be exuberant. Both Cass and Zeke felt a pang at the loss of one another, but this was transient. Chuff remained the centerpiece of Cass's life as a dog trainer, as he had been since they brought him home as an eight-week-old, ten years earlier.

And though it was unspoken, both Cass and Noah recognized that a Lac Rouge hiatus was welcome until the most immediate grief over the loss of Katrinka abated. By the time they returned, it was mid-May, and except for shaded patches in the woods, the snow was gone. It felt like a page had been turned.

Their nephew Paul had continued to spend most of his time at Lac Rouge and dropped in to chat shortly after they arrived. There had been developments. Paul, fluent in French and completely comfortable in the rural Quebec culture of fishing and hunting, had maintained a simmering anger over Trinka's death. He had dropped in on Jean-Luc.

Noah and Cass expressed surprise. As far as they knew, Jean-Luc was seldom around. It was fortunate that Paul had found him in. "Not so much," said Paul. He explained that he kept looking for a truck in the small lot in front of the house, and failing to see one, turned away. Until on his third attempt, he noticed smoke coming from the chimney and tire tracks leading away from the house and around the cleared fields to a large outbuilding where he surmised Jean-Luc parked. It was a long way from the house and very inconvenient, which was Paul's first intimation that Jean-Luc was, "A sincerely hinky guy."

They had seen one another at the auberge, but Jean-Luc didn't recognize him. When Paul knocked on his door and introduced himself, he said he was the nephew of Cass and Noah Harwood. Jean-Luc kept him outside at the door and very coldly asked what he wanted. Paul suggested that they talk inside. They did. Paul said the kitchen was dark and "smelled funky." Jean-Luc neither invited him to sit nor offered him anything to drink—both significant derelictions of the protocols of visits between rural Quebec neighbors. The entire conversation was conducted in French, with both very large men standing. Paul, a gentle giant, said Jean-Luc's body language was troubling. Very aggressive. He wondered if he'd made a mistake, but being large and calm, he stood his ground.

He didn't have to do that for long, because contrary to his expectations, Jean-Luc initiated the conversation. With no preliminary amenities, he launched, "You tell your aunt that she is no longer welcome to go through my property," he said. "I have cameras everywhere, and if I find she has been here, I will call the *Sûreté.*"

"What the fuck, man?" responded Paul, his voice shaking with anger. "You killed her dog. What are you pissed about? What would you complain to the police about?"

It became apparent that it was the inspection by the conservation officer that had enraged Jean-Luc. Evidently, the officer had returned when Jean-Luc was around and discussed the inappropriateness of laying traps where people and dogs might encounter them and having a trapline that was only infrequently inspected. Although no charges were laid, Jean-Luc had evidently felt sufficiently pressured by the officer's warning that he would monitor the situation, to decide that he would no longer trap in the Lac Rouge area. "So your aunt, she took that from me!" he hissed at Paul. Paul tried, very briefly, to reason Jean-Luc through the situation. His aunt's dog had been killed. Most people in those circumstances would want to know if the trap was legal. And it had never occurred to them that Jean-Luc would be the trapper. Otherwise, surely he would have warned them, knowing they had dogs and traveled deep into the bush?

Paul reported that it was quickly apparent that he would gain no traction in this conversation. He expressed regret at the absence of neighborly feeling in Jean-Luc's dealings with the Harwood clan. Jean-Luc expressed hope that Paul would fuck himself up the ass and added that he'd better remember to tell his aunt and uncle that they were now forbidden to access his property.

"*C'est tout, c'est ça,*" Paul concluded.

But it turned out that wasn't all there was. After a long silence, while Cass and Noah digested Paul's story, he added one additional fact: he had already started cutting alternate trails they could use to access the back bush without traversing the Tessier place. And that became a major male predilection for the remainder of that Winter Receding and the brief spring that followed it. Both Noah and Paul loved hard physical work, and the business of cutting down trees and stacking and chopping firewood was dear to them. Trail-cutting fit nicely into their tough-bug-covered-but-loving-it personas.

Cass did not get involved. Nor was she expected to, given her long-standing and well-honored agreement with Noah that waived any expectation of or guilt about her resistance to productive labor. So while the trail-cutting efforts were ongoing, she got her kayak into the lake to survey the coming of spring and continued her treks with Chuff and Zeke, staying away from the area near Jean-Luc's where her fellas labored. She encountered Xavier on one of these jaunts. It was a surprise because until then, their paths had intersected only in the back bush beyond the Tessier place. There, when they encountered one another, Xavier inevitably halted and waited to see if Cass would beckon him to come chat, in which case he'd join her until she subtly intimated that they should part paths. If she just waved, he did the same thing and quickly found another trail to take. But this time, he halted, took a good look at her, turned his head to look in one direction at Chuff and in the other direction at Zeke, and then held both arms out at his sides in a classic questioning gesture.

Cass sighed. She had been dreading this encounter, knowing the kind of bond that had existed between the boy and Trinka. She beckoned him to join her. As soon as he did, he asked where

Katrinka was. So Cass told him what had happened, noting how still he became. He insisted that she provide details about Trinka's last moments, and as he listened, he trembled, and a few large tears trickled down his face. When Cass instinctively reached out to touch him, he drew back and, for a moment, turned his back on her, apparently to collect himself. When he turned back to her, he said, *"Je suis vraiment désolé,"* and then caught himself. It was the first time he had lapsed into French in his dealings with Cass. He then reverted to English, saying, "I am very sorry that happened," he said.

"I know," said Cass. "So am I. I miss her, and I know you will also. She really loved you."

"Oui, je sais," responded Xavier. "She was a very good girl," he added.

Xavier then asked if they'd ever been able to figure out who the trapper was. Cass told him it was Jean-Luc Tessier. "That big guy who owns the little cabin before the back bush?" Xavier asked. Cass confirmed and was surprised that Xavier had no further questions. It appeared that his display of emotion had embarrassed him. He bid her farewell and bushwhacked away from her, pushing his way through the thick undergrowth, evidently unwilling to wait until there was a natural parting place where trails intersected.

Yates visited during that period, and though he was not as woodsy as the other two, he joined them for one of their trail-cutting adventures. But most of the time, he accompanied Cass on her treks. For the thirty years that the Harwoods and Yates had been close, Cass and Yates had a special bond. Noah respected this and had no problem with a feature of every visit: for a couple of hours every day, Cass and Yates would walk together. Both loved walking, and they walked well together since both were fast and found it a relief not to alter their pace for a companion. And they talked.

Yates knew, of course, about Trinka's death and the role Jean-Luc had in it. He had not met Jean-Luc when he labored with

Noah and Paul in the woods adjacent to the Tessier property. But he told her he had seen him from a distance and that what he saw he found "quite creepy." They had worked late that day. They were deep in the woods, which got dark early. Because they were getting ready to depart, there was no noise from either their chainsaws or ATVs.

In the quiet dusk, they saw a panel van enter Jean-Luc's lot and then travel across the open field to the large outbuilding where Paul said he believed Jean-Luc parked. The driver got out of the van and looked around. Yates said there was something furtive about the guy's body language. Evidently, the scene he surveyed passed muster. He knocked on the building's big double doors, which were then opened by a larger man Paul identified as Jean-Luc. He was accompanied by a kid, maybe thirteen or fourteen years old. Both men threw open the back door of the van, into which Jean-Luc vaulted. He quickly re-emerged and signaled the other guy to drive into the outbuilding. The doors to the building were then shut by the kid, with both men and the van still inside. The kid disappeared into the woods, happily not in the direction where the trail crew was hidden.

The four of them talked about it later that evening when Paul had joined them for a toke and a beer. What the hell was going on? When they added this potentially sinister scenario to Jean-Luc's rage at having an officer of the law visit, the remote parking, his unwillingness to have Paul enter his home, and the funky smell in the house . . . "A meth lab?" Cass wondered.

But they all agreed the smell would have been different and more noticeable. And the presence of the kid was troubling. Did Jean-Luc have kids? No one knew. Based on the description, Cass said it sounded like Xavier. But when she'd told the boy about Trinka's fate, he hadn't mentioned knowing Jean-Luc. Which meant nothing, she realized, since Xavier chatted readily to her about things observed in the bush but never volunteered anything about himself personally. And it was obvious that after hearing about Katrinka's death, he wanted and needed to be alone. Given Jean-Luc's part in that story, it seemed unlikely to her that the kid they'd seen was Xavier.

It was a mellow night at the Harwood cabin. Music, beer, and weed brought about the relaxation they all welcomed. No conclusions were reached other than that it was most likely a considerably more innocuous situation, something like Jean-Luc having a son or a nephew with him and taking possession of a second-hand bed or sofa. Boring. The speculation had been fun, but they put it aside. They all agreed they would not allow Jean-Luc Tessier to take up any more space in their lives.

12

CASS – SUMMER

That summer was as glorious as the winter that preceded it. The snows had melted gradually, leaving water levels high and flood risks low. Cass spent less time in the bush to spend more time in her kayak. They had two, but Noah found kayaking to be tedious. That was fine by Cass, who quite typically relished the time alone. The only drawback to kayaking was that she was really alone because she was dog-less in those hours. She had tried to teach the dogs to lie quietly in the kayak, between her knees. However, she had no luck with any of them, and Cass didn't spend all that much time trying. There was a certain selfish freedom in being dog-less for a few hours. She felt guilty at the dejected looks from Chuff and Zeke when they realized from what she was wearing that she was heading to the lake without them. But she'd grown up a Freeman; Cass could handle being guilted.

She often waited to kayak until the afternoon when the wind was high because she loved the hard work and exhilaration of paddling against the wind. She wondered what it said about her, that she so preferred going against the wind rather than running with it. She knew that it was probably just the power of optics, which made it feel like she was moving very fast because of how the waves passed under her prow. But on another level, it felt symbolic that most of the choices in her life had been to run against rather than with the wind. What else would allow a Jewish girl from Baltimore to flourish in Lac Rouge? In the kayak, she hummed one of her favorite songs, *Running Against the Wind*, by Bob Seeger. "*We are older now but still running against the wind.*"

Mornings, which were almost always calm, were also attractive for kayaking, especially if she chose to go out early when fog drifted across the lake. She loved the feeling of eerie mystery as she paddled through the fog. She was atavistic. She was primeval. She was a time-traveler. She was making her way back to the beginning of time. By the time she'd worked her way toward the marsh at the far south-end, the day had resolved into brightness, allowing her to watch the loons encountered on her way. Twice that summer, she saw an eagle. The first time, he was lazily circling the marsh. The second time, she saw him perched on a spar embedded in a great rock outcropping she'd paused under. She looked up at him. He looked down at her, his yellow eyes weighing her; she was too large to consider edible. She was insignificant. His disdain seemed evident as he took off, looking for something more attractive.

From the lake, she could turn off into several very narrow, twisting streams, shallow but navigable until the water level got too low, generally in late August. But because the water had started off so high and there was moderate rain that summer, the streams stayed good the whole season. Red-winged blackbirds dominated some areas, and kingfishers issued their strident calls as they skittered close to the water, looking for prey. And on one memorable day, two blue herons flew lazy intersecting figure eights above her, the entire time she worked her way down-stream.

Lori was with her that day. It was a day both would remember for its gentle perfection. Nothing dramatic. The mist was just clearing as they set off, paddling into a very gentle breeze, the sky impossibly blue. Birds screeched, cawed, whistled, and sang in jungle-like cacophony, but there was not a single human-generated sound: no motorboats, no jet skis, no clamor of distant chain saws. Before heading down the stream of the herons, they paddled the full length of the lake, close enough to one another to chat had they wanted to. But they didn't. They'd done plenty of that the night before. What they did instead was throwback to some of the happiest memories of their childhoods when the extended clan gathered at Bubby Freeman's for Friday night dinner. Inevitably, one of the older cousins would take possession of the little piano, and all the girl cousins would sing together. All were competent, at the very least, able to hold a tune. And Lori was better than competent; her voice was sweet, high, and strong. That day in the kayak, she started them on an Eagles medley. They did indeed have a peaceful easy feeling.

It was even more welcome than usual, given the spiritual baggage Lori had brought with her. As usual, she had been totally committed to her summer visit. Her challenge had been finding a time when her adamance that Mike did not accompany her coincided with a time when it would simply not be possible for him to do so. As far as Lori was concerned, Mike was well and truly over. Lori had been trying to end it with him for months, but he did not accept this gracefully. As Lori described it, he was veering wildly between angry outbursts and woeful apologies accompanied by grandiose bribes. And some of the outbursts had been frightening, leaving livid finger-sized bruises on Lori's upper arms and shoulders. The greater the anger, the more opulent the apology gift. Lori arrived wearing a diamond bracelet she said Mike had refused to take back. Cass, well-aware of Lori's penchant for finery, suspected she hadn't tried as hard as she might have.

Fortunately for Lori and the Harwoods, Mike had been doing a considerable amount of business in Mexico in recent months and was considering relocating there. When a two-week exploratory trip with potential Mexican partners was planned for July, Cass and Noah found that, presto, given their many other commitments, that was the only real window for Lori's visit. In reality, except for Yates, their dance cards were mercifully empty. But Mike was not to know that.

So considerable time had been spent in the evenings the three of them had been together since Lori arrived, talking about the challenge of ending it with Mike. Cass, whose consulting had included a fair bit of work around domestic abuse, was very concerned. Though the relationship had not yet devolved into significant physical abuse, the cycle of possessive monitoring of Lori's movement and emotions, escalating anger when Mike felt she was defying his control, and histrionic regret afterward were all part of a classic picture that too often escalated into serious sexual or physical abuse. The three of them were basically working up a playbook for Lori to follow upon her return, which included new locks, an alarm system, and, if necessary, a restraining order. Lori, the mistress of myriad breakups, was concerned but not to the extent Cass and Noah were. She'd weathered many breakup storms—too many to want to spend the precious hours she had in Canada, angsting about Mike. Lori, who, of course, had heard about Trinka's death, was eager to hike the work-around trail that Noah, Paul, and Yates had by then completed. "If that's okay with you?" she asked Cass. "Are you okay going back there? You're not freaked out because of what happened to Trinka?" In fact, though she felt that "freaked out" was an overstatement, Cass had not been into the back bush since the March day that Trinka died. She hadn't really thought about it; just somehow ended up hiking on the less-wild east side of the road, rather than the west side where the Tessier place and the great unbounded back bush was.

So even as she jovially rejected the idea of being freaked-out to Lori and Noah, Cass acknowledged to herself that she must be. And that acknowledgment immediately gave birth to the goal of confronting and defeating that simmering unease. "For sure, tomorrow," Cass sang out. And uncharacteristically, she strongly encouraged Noah to go with them. And uncharacteristically,

Noah agreed. He'd worked hard cutting the new trail but hadn't hiked it yet.

It turned out to be a good day for a long hike; cloudy, breezy, and a bit cool. It was great weather for both humans and dogs. Chuff and Zeke were hysterical with excitement when it became evident that they were headed for the back bush. They cavorted through the few remnants of wildflowers dotting the meadows that were randomly interspersed throughout the predominant dark woods. And there were quite a few of them that were new to all of them because the access route was different. They'd follow a deer trail that intersected the new trail and frequently brought them eventually into more open terrain—interconnected fields and meadows. Cass was grateful that Noah, who had an extraordinary sense of direction, was with them. Otherwise, she would not have been able to be as exploratory as they were that day, for fear of getting lost.

Noah was leading the way as they followed what looked like ATV tracks through a thicket of raspberry bushes into yet another clearing. "Whoa," he said and stopped. Cass and Lori looked questioningly at one another and hustled to catch up. Lori whistled. Cass muttered, "Well, shit." And then all three stood silently together, surveying a vast field of obviously well-cultivated marijuana.

The fact that the remote woods of Quebec were studded with grow-ops was well known. Helicopters frequently seemed to be patrolling Lac Rouge, and Cass and Noah had speculated that they were hunting marijuana fields. Cass had often encountered small patches of weed on her treks, which she assumed various neighbors were cultivating for their own use. But this was clearly a big commercial operation. Posts on which cameras were mounted marked the perimeters. The silence and the stillness were tense, and Chuff and Zeke picked up on it. They were no longer dancing but instead standing with their heads raised at attention. Zeke whined,

Chuff rumbled. "You know what?" said Noah. "Discretion is the better part of valor. Let's get out of here."

Which is what they did. About-turn, and outta there. And they speculated, on their return trip, about whether what they had seen explained some of the inexplicables about Jean-Luc's behavior. No conclusions, and certainly no actions to be taken. If the Harwoods had somehow discovered a local crime syndicate that dealt hard drugs or sex-trafficked children, it would never have occurred to them to not immediately contact the provincial police—the *Sûreté du Québec*. It never occurred to them to initiate such contact under these circumstances. Their disquiet with their discovery was in no way grounded in disapproval of weed, which they all frequently indulged in. It was the scope of what they'd seen with its intimations of a criminal enterprise that had generated their unease.

So when a few days later, Cass and Lori took their last trek of her summer visit, they did not try to retrace the route they'd traveled with Noah. Instead, they stuck to the new trail until it connected to the more familiar trails they'd used for many years. While there had been no sign of it when they'd hiked with Noah a few days earlier, Lori experienced some of the paranoia that characterized the previous summer's visit. And Chuff and Zeke also seemed a bit hinky. Cass wanted to shake all three of them.

But she didn't need to because she saw from afar, through the trees, a flash of the orange backpack that Xavier often carried, and realized they were probably reacting to his eerily silent presence not all that far from them. She had told Lori about him and was eager to have him show himself, so she could introduce them. She wanted to know if Lori found him as intriguing as she did. And so she did something she'd never done before. She called him. "Xavier," she hollered. "Xavvy!"

They waited, and again Cass caught a glimpse of the orange backpack as Xavier bushwhacked his way through the undergrowth, eventually emerging onto their trail about one hundred yards ahead of them. "Go ahead," Cass said to the dogs, who ran to greet the boy, Chuff with dignity, and Zeke with none. Cass and Lori also advanced to greet him.

Xavier had always looked like a backwoods elf to Cass. His slim build and fine features would have appeared incompatible with the gear he carried had he not generated such an inflated sense of confidence. Typically, he carried a backpack, had a large hunting knife on one side of his belt and bear spray on the other, and binoculars around his neck. Today, she noticed that he'd experienced a significant growth spurt and looked larger and more robust than in the past. She also saw that he had some new gear. "What's that?" she said, pointing to the camera hanging around his neck above his binoculars.

"It's a digital camera," he responded. "I got it for my birthday."

Lori asked him when his birthday was and how old he was. He told her his birthday was in late April and that he had just turned thirteen.

Cass did the introductions. Lori immediately fell into a sweetly flirtatious mode that Cass thought was completely appropriate for a thirteen-year-old boy. Xavier handled it with far more *élan* than she expected. He didn't yet know how to flirt, but there was a glimmer of the future in the playfulness with which he accepted the attention of Cass's glamorous cousin. He agreed immediately when she suggested that she first take a picture of him, and then one of him and Cass together. Cass, whose instinct was to throw her arm around his shoulders, realized that might not work. Instead, she told the dogs to sit, and she adopted a tough-guy pose, arms akimbo behind Chuff, and suggested that Xavvy do the same thing with Zeke. He did. The kid then surprised Cass by asking if he could take a picture of Lori. While Chuff and Zeke held their stays, Lori posed behind them, but not in a tough-guy pose. Instead, she stood with her shoulders back, chest out, and chin lowered. Cass was sure that Xavier would be looking at that picture often.

That was the first time that Cass and Xavier didn't part paths shortly after meeting. He accompanied them part of the way back. Lori told him that Cass had told her about him and his penchant for observation. Familiar with fieldcraft from her work with special ops veterans, she asked probing questions about practices Xavvy used to stay hidden in the woods. Flattered by her attention, he provided insights, which revealed to Cass for the first time just how long and well he'd been observing her. At the point where their new trail intersected an older one, he bid them farewell. Playfully, Lori asked, "What, you're bored with us already?"

"No, no. But I have some chores to do for my dad, over there," he said, pointing in the general direction of the older trail. So Cass, Lori, and the dogs headed off in one direction, and Xavier in the other.

Lori left the next morning. As they hugged goodbye, both Cass and Noah urged her to be very careful in her dealings with Mike. They reminded her that she was always welcome if she wanted to visit before her already-scheduled New Year's visit.

13

XAVIER - SECRETS

I have secrets. So do you, don't you? I think we all do. Stefan surely does. He always talks about us being totally honest with each other, but I know he isn't that way with me. For example, when he goes to Ottawa for his "business meetings," I know he does more than business. He's usually away three or four nights, which he says is required to discuss important anarchist business, complete the "editorial process" for the journal he writes for, and see doctors and get medicine for his back.

I don't mind when he's away; in fact, I like it. It was a little scary when he started doing it a few years ago. He gave me all kinds of lists, and we practiced all kinds of "what ifs" before the first time he left. He'd describe a situation, and I'd have to tell him what I would do if that happened. We would talk about it, and he would help me so that I could handle it even better if it ever happened. He even gives me a phone number in Ottawa, where I can contact him in an emergency. But in our house, phones are very bad and are to be used only if your life is in danger. That's for me, of course. Stefan sometimes takes or makes calls when he thinks I'm asleep. That's how I know he does more than business when he's in Ottawa. A couple of times, I've heard him say stuff like, "So we'll have a night or two together after the meetings. I can't wait to be with you, baby." So I assume he has a girlfriend in Ottawa. I don't know why he thinks he has to keep that a secret.

But it's okay because as I said, I have secrets too. Some of them are about things I feel. For example, I never told Stefan how I felt about Katrinka. I think he kind of figured it out, but I never told him. Many of my secrets have to do with not sharing what I think and feel. That stuff is private. It is only mine. But I have other secrets about real things you can touch and see; things I don't want Stefan to know I have, which means I need a place to hide those things. I have a great place.

Our cabin doesn't have a basement. It is raised on cinderblocks and is only maybe a foot off the ground. But there's lots of important stuff that goes on under the cabin. If there is a problem with the plumbing, someone has to crawl under the house to deal with it—same thing when mice dislodge the insulation, which happens almost every year. Of course, at first, it was Stefan who had to go under the house. That was until a few years ago when his back got really bad. He'd be laid-up for days after a trip "down under"—that's what we call it. Sometimes it was so bad that he had to take these very powerful drugs, and when that happened, he would sleep for an entire day. I couldn't even wake him up to give him some soup like I wanted to. I was afraid he'd never wake up. So I told him I could do it. Even though I've grown a lot lately, I'm still smaller than he is, and back then, I was very little. Eventually, he instructed me in what had to be done and let me try it. He went under to see how I'd done. He said I did well, that like him, I knew that details matter. So for the last few years, I've done anything that needs to be done "down under."

This has allowed me to have an excellent place to hide things I don't want Stefan to know about. There are boards underneath where the kitchen is that I've had to explore when working with insulation. I now have my own special board, where I've hollowed out some space where I can hide stuff. My secret stuff includes extra notebooks with the drawings of Cass and the dogs, which would reveal how much time I spend observing them. But it also includes special stuff I've liberated that I don't want Stefan to know about.

Liberation is a game Stefan taught me when I was littlelittle. He told me that good equipment deserves to be well-cared for. When he taught me how to Just Watch, he'd find hunting stands, where we could watch campers, fishermen, and hunters. And he would explain when they did things right and when they didn't. Not looking after your equipment is not right. So when people were careless, particularly when they were careless and drunk, or even better, careless, drunk, and asleep—which happens pretty often—he taught me how to do a super-quiet leopard crawl, which means crawling low to the ground on your belly. And I would have to leopard crawl to liberate the good equipment. It was scary and very fun! I got us lots of good stuff. As far as Stefan knew, it all went into a big wooden chest in the book room.

But I have liberated some stuff on my own, things I never told Stefan about. And that stuff goes into my hiding space under the house. Most of it is small stuff. My favorite little liberation was a system for carrying water in a pack with a hose you can sip it through. But the main thing, the big thing in my hiding space, is the rifle I liberated a year ago when Stefan was away.

I was Just Watching a little clearing off the main road where hunters often met up with each other. It was early in the season, and I was there before anyone arrived. But as the sun rose, four SUVs showed up. They were big, expensive-looking vehicles. Six men got out, all dressed in in the kind of clothes that hunters from the city wear and that Stefan makes fun of. He calls those kinds of guys "dudes," which as far as he is concerned, is not a good thing. One of the men, who I think maybe was younger than the others, acted excited. He reminded me of how bullshit dogs like Zeke try to act tough but end up wagging their tails fast and low and licking the mouths of the no-bullshit dogs. He was the guy with the biggest SUV. While they were getting ready to go, he took two rifles out of the car and showed them to the other men. There was a lot of discussion. I'm sure they were deciding which one he should use that day. They agreed on the fancier, newer-looking one, with a powerful-looking scope. The guy put the other one back in the SUV. I recognized it was a Lee–Enfield from the magazines and catalogs I studied with Stefan, who had said it was a very good bolt-action rifle.

It never occurred to me to liberate it. Breaking into a car was not something Stefan had taught me to do. But the guy never locked his vehicle! I couldn't believe it! I waited until they left. And then I waited an hour after that, figuring the guy would eventually realize his mistake and return. But he didn't. I did a leopard crawl to the car because that's part of the drill, but I didn't need to. I took the rifle and the box of ammo that was right next to it and put them in the woods where I'd been watching. Then I went back and obscured my tracks. That wasn't necessary, either. These guys were dumb. But as Stefan always says, sticking with the details usually helps and never hurts.

The Lee-Enfield has been in my hiding place ever since. I've never used it for hunting. But every now and then, when Stefan is away, I take it out and do some target shooting with it. It is a nice piece. It may even be more accurate than the 3030 Winchester Lever Actions that both Stefan and I use for hunting. But the Winchesters are good, reliable, comfortable weapons. And knowing that I have the other one under the house, well, some secrets just make you feel good, don't they?

It works that way for me. That's why I never told Stefan about when I first met Jean-Luc. I made that happen very soon after Stefan told me about Katrinka's death. I didn't want Stefan to ask me any questions about how and why we met. One of the main reasons I wanted to keep this private was that after I heard what happened to Katrinka, I knew I wanted to meet Jean-Luc, but I wasn't sure why.

It was easy to do. I had already figured out that I could tell when Tessier was around by looking for smoke from his chimney and tracks leading to his outbuilding. So I waited and observed until I saw him starting the long trip from the outbuilding to his house. I came out through the woods with a compass, as though I was lost. When I got close to him, I called out, "Hey! *Bonjour! Attendez, s'il vous plait!*" He waited for me.

When I caught up with him, I introduced myself, continuing to speak only French. I said, "You're Jean-Luc Tessier, aren't you?" I said it real friendly-like, but I knew he would be suspicious. I was right.

"What's it to you?" he said, not friendly at all. So then I told him a story about how my dad and the guys at the auberge talked about him, about what an impressive guy he is, and how he is this great trapper and hunter. You know how a partridge gets all plumped up when he's courting? Well, that's what Jean-Luc did as I dealt him this bullshit. He bought it completely – a little kid who thought he was a hero! So, of course, he became really nice to me then.

I told him I was interested in trapping and wondered if he'd take me out with him some time when he checked his lines. "I don't have lines anymore," he said, and his voice was hard and mean when he said it. When I asked him why not, he said it was because some woman trespassed on his property and then wandered beyond it to where his traps were, and the "stupid bitch" got her dog killed in a marten trap. He said she called the police on him, and he didn't like the attention, so he'd taken out his trapline. But he said he'd show me the equipment if I was interested.

I said I was. That was the first time he took me into that big outbuilding where he spends so much time. There were two parts to it. The whole place smelled weird. The back part was walled off, and there was a big lock on the door. The front part was large, big enough for his truck to be there and still roomy enough for a couple of bunk beds, a hot-plate, and lots of shelves with all kinds of equipment, including some big scales and the traps, which he showed me. "This was the one that got the bitch's dog," he said proudly as he handed me one of them.

I felt like I was going to throw-up, but instead, I just said, "Oh, wow!" I checked out my hands as I gave it back to him. They weren't shaking, even though inside me, it felt like all the little atoms that make up me were vibrating like crazy.

So that was our first meeting. The whole time we were together, I acted like he was some kind of superhero. He liked that and invited me to come back and visit. Eventually, he started paying me to help him with odd jobs. By that time, I'd already told Stefan that I'd met Tessier. I figured that enough time had passed since Katrinka died, and Stefan wouldn't put it all together. Stefan seemed okay with it, but he told me to be careful. He said that the guys at the auberge said that Jean-Luc is weird, that he drinks alone, and seems to have no friends. Drinking alone at the auberge is unusual. Stefan's a pretty solitary person, but I gather that he knows a few guys there that he drinks with.

So just a few minutes ago, I said that some secrets make you feel good. True. But not all of them. I've learned that keeping secrets can become a habit and that those kinds of secrets can make you feel bad. I figured that out after I talked to Cass the first time after Trinka died.

The Harwoods didn't show up for a long time after Katrinka's death. I figured they didn't want to come back until they at least started to get over it. I knew from the way I felt that it could take a long time to do that. But I knew from Just Watching their cabin that they started coming back again in May. That's when I saw Noah, and that big guy Stefan said is their nephew, Paul, cutting a new trail so that they wouldn't have to go by Jean-Luc's place anymore. There was another guy who worked with them one day. He wasn't competent like Noah and Paul, but he tried hard. Cass and Chuff and Zeke never showed up over there to help them. Eventually, I figured out that she wasn't going into what she called the back bush any longer, which didn't surprise me. I figured she didn't know that the trapline was gone.

Eventually, I could observe enough to know that Cass was trekking now on the east side of the road. This area isn't as wild as the back bush, which means it is much harder to stay hidden from your subject. So I didn't. Once I observed which way Cass was headed, it was easy to get in front of her, and then I just waited in the bush near the trail I knew she was taking. When I heard the dogs' bells announcing they were getting close, I headed onto the trail and started walking toward them. As they came into view, I stopped and did some serious acting. First, I turned my head to look at Chuff and then at Zeke. Then I held my hands out as if to say, "But where is Katrinka?" I had tried that out in front of the mirror at home to see if it looked natural and would be understood. I'd also practiced "forgetting" to speak English to her, to show how upset I was.

When I joined Cass, I went through with what I'd planned for my acting. Almost everything went as planned. Except that when she told me about Katrinka, I cried. I hadn't planned that; I didn't think I could pull it off. Here's what I hadn't expected: that crying wasn't for Katrinka because I was already dry for her. It was that I felt so bad for Cass, who was trying so hard to tell me what happened in a way that would be as gentle as possible for me. It made me feel sort of the way Katrinka used to. And it made me feel bad about acting with Cass. One of the things I learned from watching her with the dogs is that she was always honest with them.

I felt very bad about being dishonest with Cass when I didn't have to. It would have been okay for me to let her know that I'd already heard the news. She knows how that sort of information spreads around Lac Rouge. But I had a plan, and I stuck to it, and that was wrong. I also learned that from watching Cass train. Sometimes I could tell what she was planning to work on. I had watched enough to recognize different activities she called drills that she worked on for different exercises. But it was easy to see that if something wasn't working well, she'd throw it out and try all kinds of other things until she found something that did work. Stefan called that sort of thing when we worked on problems around the house like plumbing "improvisation." I was good at planning, but so far, not good at all at improvising.

It was during this time in the spring that I found that observing Cass was harder for me in terms of how I felt than it had been before. Since we'd already met, I knew I could continue to observe her without staying hidden. But Just Watching had become kind of a habit, and habits are hard to break. So I didn't do it as much as I used to, but I still did it sometimes. And every now and then, I saw new stuff that I didn't understand. That spring, it had to do with the guy I saw working on the new trail with Noah and Paul.

He was around for maybe four days, and most of the time that Noah and Paul worked on the west side on cutting the trail, the other guy went on long walks with Cass. He didn't slow her down. Like her, he was one hell of a fast-walker. They talked—a lot. I couldn't hear what they were saying, but sometimes it seemed like it was very serious, and other times they were laughing. And sometimes they stopped when they were talking. And that guy touched her—a lot. He'd put his arms around her and hug her long and hard. He'd pull a piece of hair out of her face and tuck it behind her ear. He'd "help" her climb over and under things that I'd seen her manage on her own a dozen times. She didn't need any help.

The weird thing was that she clearly didn't mind this stuff. She touched him too. I didn't like what I was seeing, but I didn't know what it was. It wasn't like it was with Big Dude, who had been around during Lori's winter visit. He acted like a dog scenting a bitch in heat. Cass didn't like it, Noah didn't like it, and Chuff didn't like it. I seemed to be the only one who didn't like what went on between this other guy and Cass. I was Just Watching the Harwood cabin when the guy said goodbye to them. Both he and Cass acted the same way with Noah right there, and both Noah and Chuff seemed fine with it. I sketched the guy and Cass together and put them in my hiding place under the house. And I stored my uneasiness about Cass and this guy in my mind where I kept my secrets. I figured when Lori visited the next time, I'd do a lot of watching to see if I could figure out the difference between Big Dude and the guy who went walking with Cass.

But that didn't work out. Lori did come for a long visit during the summer, but Big Dude wasn't with her. Everyone seemed very happy to not have him around, including me. I finally got to meet Lori. It was easy; I just made sure Cass could see me in the woods and then figured I'd "meet" them at the next trail intersection. But you know what? Cass didn't want to wait. She hollered for me! Her big holler rolled through the woods the way it used to when she would call Trinka. And she used not just my formal name, she used my call name! I felt good when I heard her yell, "Xavvy!"

So that's how I met Lori. Notice that I don't call her Boobs anymore? That's because she is a real person, a very nice person, a terrific person, not just a kind of movie-star clothes hanger for big breasts. I had fun with her—a different kind of fun than with Cass, who is also fun. Most adults aren't, you know?

14

CASS - BALTIMORE IN SEPTEMBER

In mid-September, Cass drove to Baltimore to attend a large Freeman clan gathering for the Saturday afternoon wedding of the child of one of her first cousins. A trip back to the family was not an uncommon event for Cass; she generally undertook one every couple of years. These boisterous and unendingly social gatherings were way too much for Noah, for whom they generally pleaded work and dog commitments that precluded accompanying Cass. Because both of her sisters had adult children who drove from distant states for such events, the sisters' large suburban homes were crowded. So over the years, the practice had evolved for Cass to spend most of her visit quartered with Lori, about forty-five minutes away from older sister Louise's place. Then toward the end of the visit, once Louise's crew had decamped, Cass spent the last couple of days of her visit there.

Considerable time had been spent on the phone with Lori, nailing down dates, wardrobe, and other administrative details. Cass was particularly interested in the status of Lori's relationship with Mike. Lori reported it as ongoing but winding down, claiming that she was gradually weaning him off his obsession with her. She said she'd been clear on the relationship not being the forever one that Mike envisaged, had told him that she wanted and needed more alone time and thus, after several dramatic and slightly adrenal episodes, had reclaimed the house key she had given him and changed the locks. She had also adhered to the Harwoods' suggestion about getting an alarm system.

Lori said she wasn't being overly-vigilant about imposing a full-stop to the relationship. Mike was in the final stages of selling his business and would then be embarking on what he called his freedom road trip, having abandoned the idea of relocating his business in Mexico. Instead, he would undertake luxury travel through Mexico, the Caribbean, and South America. Eventually, he'd decide if he wanted to buy a place and settle down in one of the places he'd sampled, where he could live like a king on the proceeds of his business, or whether he simply wanted to continue to wander. Wherever and whenever he went, Lori looked forward to his departure as the natural end of their relationship. In the interim, she confessed to still enjoying his sexual mastery. But she assured Cass that she'd been forthright with Mike about wanting private time with Cass, and thus seeing him little or not at all during the time that Cass was with her. When Mike protested, citing his fondness for Cass and what a good relationship they had, Lori had suggested that they'd do a brunch together sometime during the visit.

Which was why Cass was both startled and displeased when she rolled into Lori's driveway on a Monday in the late afternoon after a ten-hour drive, to have Mike step out of the house before Lori, to welcome her. As he approached her, Cass looked inquiringly to Lori behind him, who gave her a clear body-language message, saying, "Sorry, couldn't help it." Some things don't change. Mike immediately folded Cass into a too long, too close, too intense hug. She failed to reciprocate, in the time-honored fashion learned from Noah and the reserved Harwood clan; she allowed herself to be hugged while standing stiffly, and put one arm half-heartedly on his back, tapping a "there, there," the way you would burp an infant. Mike then redoubled his efforts. He stepped back a pace, lifted her chin, and gave her a gentle and slightly lingering kiss on the lips. If she liked him, it would have been lovely. She didn't. It wasn't. "Sweetie," Mike boomed. "It's so good to see you! We've both really been looking forward to your visit."

There was no opportunity to find out what the hell was going on until ten that evening when Mike departed after taking them to an ostentatiously expensive restaurant. Cass, who had been sitting all day and had long ago lost any enthrallment with protracted fine dining, was treated to what seemed like an endless parade of only the finest wines, aperitifs, and artfully-arranged tiny foods, some of which Mike picked up and fed first to Lori, then to her. Cass was sure that he had requested the very prominent table they had and timed his attentions to maximize being observed by other diners who would be impressed by him being accompanied by two such "luscious babes," as he phrased it. Cass did not feel luscious. She would have killed for a big salad and a beer, but in the spirit of keeping the peace, pretended she was as thrilled with this "gift" as Mike wanted her to be.

Once back at Lori's, Cass was relieved when Mike appeared to graciously pick up her cues about being tired and looking forward to seeing him for brunch in a few days. After he left, Cass turned to Lori. "What the fuck?" she asked. Lori shrugged. She'd thought that the idea of getting together midway through the visit for brunch had been well-accepted. Then, maybe an hour before Cass arrived, Mike showed up. He claimed he'd been in the neighborhood and just wanted to say hello.

Lori, already well-versed in how things with Mike could quickly go south when he didn't get his way, did not get into an argument with him. Same thing when his brief hello morphed into the big dinner, for which they discovered he'd made reservations. She apologized to Cass about how the evening had evolved, and then she and Cass spent an hour gossiping and catching up as they had all their lives. When Cass again expressed concern about Mike, Lori emphasized that it was basically a cost/benefit analysis. Was it worth incurring the considerable discomfort that would be required to excise Mike completely from her life now, given that he'd be moving on by the end of the year? Neither she nor Cass liked it, but the result of the analysis seemed to make sense.

During the next few days, Cass and Lori shopped, saw movies, drank wine, worked out, and played scrabble. They visited at Louise's place with masses of Freemans who had arrived ahead of time for the wedding. They were supposed to meet Mike for brunch on Thursday at a trendy bistro that Cass and Lori always liked. An hour before they were going to leave, the phone rang. When Cass heard Lori say into the phone, "Oh, that's too bad; we were looking forward to it," she pumped an arm upward in victory. Not so fast. There was more conversation, and it ended with Lori saying, "Okay, great; we'll see you then." When she filled Lori in, it turned out that a problem had come up with the sale of his business that Mike had to attend to immediately. He'd apologized profusely and told her he'd already moved their reservation back to late afternoon when they could all have an early dinner together. Cass and Lori helplessly shrugged at one another. Okay.

At dinner, Mike regaled them with details—oh, so many details—about the sale of his business, how brilliantly he had just resolved the problem that had emerged, and how the fortune he was extracting from that was setting him up for a lavish lifestyle starting with his freedom tour. Though the dinner went longer than hoped for, Cass felt it had gone reasonably well when they bid farewell to Mike in the bistro parking lot before going their separate ways.

But Mike had other plans. He said that in the process of sorting stuff at his house, which he'd sold and was getting ready to vacate, he'd assembled a whole stash of Lori's stuff that needed to be returned. He said he'd just follow them back to her place. He appeared to not hear Cass's suggestion that instead, they transfer that stuff to Lori's car right there in the parking lot. Instead, he swung into his Cadillac, started the motor, and appeared to wait so that he could follow them. Though he'd ignored her suggestion, Cass could tell that he'd heard it from the tightening of his jaw and the pulsing of a large vein in his forehead before he turned away. Lori had told her that the pulsing vein was a precursor of trouble. She said, "When you see that vein moving, seriously back off." They both did.

At Lori's townhouse, Mike hauled in a couple of large tote bags of miscellaneous Lori gear. He set the last of the tote bags down and then said, "Okay, now for the *pièce de résistance*." Cass, used to living in a French culture, looked down and successfully swallowed the smirk that had surfaced as he pronounced it "peace dee resistance." Silently, she chastised herself for being a snot. There was plenty of reasons to dislike the guy without resorting to snobbery.

Mike returned to his vehicle and emerged holding a large, flat, wrapped parcel, perhaps three feet wide and four feet long. He was also brandishing a magnum of Dom Perignon. His face was flushed, he was grinning hugely, and his blue eyes were alight. It was the first time that Cass could see why Lori found him attractive. He looked excited, vibrant, and young. "Oh my God," breathed Lori *sotto voce*. Cass turned to her inquiringly. "You'll see," said Lori.

Mike stepped in front of them. He told them to wait where they were for a minute, then pushed open the front door of the townhouse, stepped in, and closed it. Cass and Lori waited in the parking lot. After about two minutes, he opened the door and gestured them in as a maître d'hotel would. "This way, ladies," he said and led them to Lori's living room.

There, sitting on the mantle of the fireplace, which he'd cleared of the many small Lori-like accessories it typically sported—now jumbled together in a corner on the floor—was a large, vivid painting of an impressionistic sunset. Cass gasped, not only at the surprise but at the beauty. Next to her, Lori whispered, "Oh, Jesus, it's the Edmondson!"

Mike explained that he had a few good paintings and that this was the one Lori had always loved. He said he was selling most of them, but he wanted Lori to have this one to remember him by. He'd placed a tray with the Dom Perignon and three glasses on the coffee table. He opened the champagne, poured with a flourish, and handed a glass to each woman. Raising his own glass, he said, "To old friends, new beginnings, and memories." He then gave Cass a mercifully brief hug and Lori a long, deep kiss, which she returned. Despite her misgivings, Cass got it. It was a beautiful painting, and the idea of Mike accepting that all of this would soon be relegated to memory was cheering indeed.

The evening wore on. All the talk was small, and Mike's stories were less self-conscious and grandiose than usual. He drank most of the champagne, and halfway through, Cass decided he was a reasonably pleasant drunk. Eventually, the magnum was emptied. It was about eleven. All three of them arose, as if by a common impulse. They were standing in the hallway that led both to the front door and to the stairway that ascended to Lori's second-floor bedroom. Cass looked inquiringly at Mike. "You're in no shape to drive," she said. "Should we call you a cab?"

Mike looked at Lori and replied, "Oh, I don't think I'm going anywhere, am I?"

Lori, looking acutely uncomfortable, said, "You remember I said that Cass and I want private time, right?"

"I do. But private time doesn't have to be alone, does it?" As he said it, he wrapped an arm snugly around Cass's waist. He turned to her, pulled her to him, and said, "Come join us, little girl. I'll take you places you've never been to before." Acutely uncomfortable but hoping to avoid a scene, Cass said lightly, "Oh, I'm really not much of a traveler. The only place I'm going tonight, Mike, is downstairs to my bedroom."

Mike's face reddened. The pulse is his forehead throbbed. He said, "Why do you always have to be such a bitch? We were having such a nice time, and then you had to spoil it by sounding like such a snot. But I'll give you another chance; otherwise, you'll never know what you're missing."

He grabbed her by both shoulders and started kissing her neck. When Cass struggled, he drove her back against the wall and started grinding against her. She could feel his erection straining against her. He was well over six feet tall, and she could feel the dull heat of his 220 pounds. She attempted to push him off, but her years of weight training gave her no advantage against his bulk. She managed to jab an elbow into his ribs. Though it was a weak blow, her bellow was not, "No! Get off me!" Cass howled.

She was amazed that her feeble effort accelerated him to rage so quickly. Mike kept her pinned to the wall with his body, wrapping both hands in her hair, close to the scalp, near each ear. He banged her head against the wall and said, fiercely, "Come on, bitch; say yes."

And Cass, who had somehow ascended to the ceiling to look down at the scene, again yelled, "No! Fuck off!" As Mike banged the small woman's head against the wall a second time, he continued to grind his pelvis into her. Cass-on-high thought, *"He could kill her."* An impartial observer, she noted Lori moving. Lori approached Mike from behind and wrapped her arms around him, rubbing her breasts into his back and her crotch against his ass. "Forget her, baby," she breathed at him. "You are making me so hot!" She reached around with one hand and started caressing his cock. She kept at it until his focus on his cock replaced his attention to Cass. "I told you she's an uptight bitch. I'm all you need," Lori breathed as she continued to caress him, making the kind of "ooh-ah" sighs that Cass had only heard in porno flicks.

Cass-on-high saw the small woman who was no longer pinned to the wall slump to the floor as Mike turned toward Lori, who took his hand and started to lead him upstairs. "You'll never know what you're missing," Lori called to her gaily, as if they'd all been playing a game. She and Mike went up the stairs together, Lori leading him while still holding his hand.

Lori kept a lamp on in her bedroom. Cass heard the door click shut and when she looked up the stairway, she saw a sliver of light leaking out from under the closed door. Shaking so badly she had trouble finding her feet again, Cass padded into Lori's kitchen and grabbed the largest knife she could find. She crouched on the first step, determined to intervene if she felt she had to. But the only sounds she heard sounded like pretty normal sex sighs and moans. There was a hoarse cry she assumed was Mike's orgasm. Moments passed. The light under the door disappeared. Cass retired to the sofa, still adrenalized and still listening. Nothing to hear. She wanted to call Noah but was afraid to do anything that might be heard upstairs, so she didn't. At about five in the morning, she finally went to her downstairs bedroom. Completely counter to her expectations, she fell asleep almost immediately.

She awoke as Lori, in a dressing gown, put a tray with two cups of hot coffee on her bedside table, pulled open the curtains to allow the bright sunlight to invade the room, and sat on the bed next to Cass. Cass looked at the clock. It was ten. "Mike?" she croaked to Lori. Lori told her he'd had an early meeting and had left uneventfully a few hours ago.

Each confirmed that the other was okay. Cass had only a small bump on the back of her head, which hurt only if probed. Lori, who was moving stiffly, acknowledged that the sex had been very rough indeed and that she had continued to play it as if she liked it. "You understood, right?" she asked Cass at one point. Cass did. She thanked Lori for intervening. And then urged her to call the police. A lengthy discussion went nowhere. Lori insisted that involving the police would only make things worse. An angry Mike was not what she wanted to deal with. "It'll all be over by January when he moves," she said.

The next night they went to the wedding. After that, Cass spent a night at Louise's. Neither she nor Lori talked about Thursday night again or mentioned it to anyone else. When they parted, their hug was longer and more intense than usual. They alluded to "the episode" only by confirming that they'd celebrate Lori's liberation when she arrived for her winter visit.

Cass drove home to Ottawa. She day-dreamed about Lac Rouge as she drove. She surprised herself when she realized that in addition to the long-standing charms of the place, she was also looking forward to her next encounter with Xavier. The kid was fun. And as she drove, she also planned how she would tell Noah about what had happened with Mike, readying her arguments for not having notified the police, knowing that would be the focus of Noah's response.

It was. The Harwoods seldom argued, but they did this time. Repeatedly. It took considerable time and effort before harmony was restored at the Harwood house. Chuff and Zeke, sensitive to human conflict, had to be relegated to the basement for long periods. Otherwise, they exacerbated the tension with their attempts to intervene, which generally consisted of them both endlessly circling Cass or interposing themselves between Cass and Noah. Noah, the most peaceful of men, never displayed threatening body language when they argued but appeared to incur their concern regardless, which Cass assumed was attributable to his larger size, deeper voice, and testosterone. When the storm had finally passed, Cass and Noah staged elaborate shows of physical affection for one another in front of the boys to persuade them that all was well. Not so, though. It was better than when the matter was under heated discussion between the Harwoods, but true equanimity was not restored until they got up to Lac Rouge again in October.

15

CASS – TRAINING IN OCTOBER

A mantle of red and gold welcomed the Harwoods back to the cabin. The cool crisp air had the copper burnish acquired only at that time of year. Autumn had always been Cass's favorite season, and when they bought the cabin, she'd thought this would be the very best time to be at Lac Rouge. But she hadn't reckoned on hunting season. The Harwoods were not and never would be hunters, and both had to make significant efforts to repress the aversion they felt about it. They had many friends and neighbors who hunted, and Cass and Noah were reasonably successful in their efforts to be accepting and non-judgmental, successfully invoking the axiomatic "different strokes" philosophy.

Over the years, Cass had come to accept that because of the hunt during the fall, they and the dogs had to avoid the back bush and limit their treks to the tamer terrain on the east side and to road walks. Cass regarded road walks as better than nothing, but just barely. Both the pleasure of the dogs and the pleasure she took in them was markedly inhibited by being on leash. They could, of course, run free on the various family properties. But those few acres felt meager compared to the many miles of freedom on offer in the back bush.

But being there was still better than being in Ottawa, and Cass hoped she would encounter Xavier at some point. She suspected that he was a hunter, and so wasn't surprised when on the first trip they made in October, she saw no sign of him, either by actually seeing him or by monitoring Chuff and Zeke, who she'd finally realized had long shown signs she'd missed when he was around but unseen. She was sure he did less of this covert surveillance than before. As time went on, she caught a glimpse of him in the woods more often than in the past. She suspected that while some small part of this might reflect an improved ability on her part to read the dogs and scan the woods, the larger part was that Xavier, whom she recognized as a truly skilled woodsman, was intentionally allowing himself to be seen. At that point, their refined "what next?" dance would play out. There would either be a discrete wave with no in-person interaction or body language that beckoned for either a short or increasingly longer walking-together visit. As time progressed, acknowledgment but no visit had gone extinct.

On their second visit in October, Cass did indeed catch a glimpse of the boy as she did a brief walk on the east side with Chuff and Zeke. She was planning on training, and so carried her heavy equipment backpack. The "what next?" dance required no thought on her part; she immediately beckoned Xavier to join her. Their greetings were as low-key as ever. Cass, generally a demonstrative human, had intuited from the start that with Xavier, she had to talk less and go soft and slow. This was the same kind of difference that characterized the much calmer, quieter persona she adopted with shy dogs, compared to the exuberance with which she worked her own dogs. She didn't think Xavier was shy but felt strongly that he was intensely private. With few boundaries of her own, this was a quality that had always fascinated Cass. Indeed, it was part of what had first drawn her to Noah and kept her there. She felt that intensely private beings required the same kind of soft, slow approach she accorded to shy ones.

Xavier was always considerably less muted in how he greeted Chuff and Zeke. This gave Cass an idea. She told him she was going to train and that Noah wouldn't be joining her until later. She wondered if Xavier might want to accompany her and help. Of course, Cass was perfectly capable of moving equipment on her own, but she thought Xavier would be more likely to accept a role as a helper than as a simple observer. She was correct. He readily accepted her offer.

As she trained and he moved equipment for her, she explained what she was working on. She started out being very general. But the astuteness of Xavier's questions and observations quickly led her to offer considerably more detail in her explanations. Cass and Noah had long disagreed about the extent to which some of her favorite training approaches were appropriate for their students. For example, Cass made considerable use of her eyes in training, and her boys were very sensitive to that. She could direct either of them either to the right or left by moving her eyes in that direction. And she thought that the skillful use of eye-contact and eye-movement could be a critical aid in resolving some issues, like getting a dog to come to front perfectly aligned with its handler. But when she injected this into coaching sessions, Noah objected. He thought it was simply too esoteric for their students to either understand or reproduce.

But Xavvy—clever, clever Xavvy—noticed it on his own and asked about it. "When you call Chuff to front, you look directly at him, but when you do it with Zeke, you look over him, not at him. Why is that?" He totally got her explanation about having a different way of interacting with each dog, depending on the dog's personality. He said that when he observed animals, he noticed there were often significant differences in how two members of the same species might react to the same stimulus. He actually used the word "stimulus," which Cass found remarkable. She repressed her desire to ask him about it, sticking with her go soft, go slow approach with the boy.

Xavier shared Cass's interest in the smallest nuance of posture and body language. She explained the simplicity and rigor of a dog and handler team in flawless heel position—the dog perfectly aligned on the handler's left side, with both dog and handler squarely facing front. While watching the very taxing, one-step drills Cass and Chuff were performing, Xavier was astute enough to wonder how she could tell if she and Chuff were getting it right. "You don't even look at him. Why not? How can you tell if he's got it right?" he asked.

Bingo! thought Cass. He had asked the perfect question. She commanded him to watch while she called Zeke—who was considerably more error-prone than Chuff—to heel position, which he did perfectly. While they stayed in position, she told Xavier to watch what happened when she looked to her left to check Zeke out.

"Holy shit!" Xavier crowed. He had instantly seen what she had done; she had moved her head and shoulders very subtly to the left to look down at Zeke, and this had resulted in Zeke slightly realigning himself because her left hip had also moved infinitesimally in the process. And as simply as that, they were no longer in perfect heel position.

"But then how do you both learn how to do it?" Xavier asked. Cass explained that when she trained indoors, she made considerable use of mirrors. She explained that once you see something, it is easier to feel it. She told him how Noah once told her she was doing something in the ring that was losing her points, but she was certain he was wrong. She simply couldn't feel it happening. He then showed her a video of her doing exactly what he'd said. And suddenly, after that, she could feel what she couldn't before. But she had to see it before she could feel it.

"Wanna try?" she offered. When he agreed, she asked him to get his camera, which she knew he usually carried in his pack.

Xavier handed her the camera, and she instructed him to call Zeke into heel position and then tell her when he thought they were both exactly right. When he told her, she snapped a shot, then showed it to him. On-screen, he saw that he was slightly twisted from the waist, head and shoulders cranked a bit to the left so that he could gauge the correctness of Zeke's position. He was amazed; he'd thought they were both absolutely square. Cass hung the camera around her neck, and without even thinking about it, took him by both shoulders and squared him up. It was the first time she'd ever touched him, but it was done so unconsciously that neither of them noticed. "There," she said and took another picture. She urged him to not move as she showed it to him. "Can you see the difference?" she asked. He said he could. "Now you've gotta feel it," she told him. She coached him to maintain his position and concentrate all his senses on feeling how he and Zeke were positioned in relationship to one another. She had him turn his head to look at Zeke while keeping his shoulders and hips completely square. She had him caress Zeke with his left hand and tell him, "Good. Heel." She assured him that over time, skilled trainers develop the ability to feel their dog's proximity and position when they're close, even though they're not touching.

They went through the drill—action, picture, re-position exercise several times. Cass either straightened his shoulders or turned them slightly to help him memorize how each position felt. Right or wrong. It was obvious to Cass that though many of her adult students found this kind of approach tedious, Xavier was enthralled with it. When she asked him about that, he told her that as both a naturalist—Cass was again amazed at his use of the word—and a hunter, being able to recognize and control even the smallest of his movements was a critical element of success.

Cass suggested that they review the pictures one more time before knocking off. Not recognizing that they'd already seen all the shots she'd taken, she hit the back button another time, revealing the preceding image on the camera. It was a shot of Xavier, bare-chested, looking up at the camera as if startled. Cass was stunned by the picture. The boy's torso was lean and well-muscled, a hairless column that was quickly becoming more adult than boyish in the width of his shoulders and depth of his chest. Sweat trickled down his chest and disappeared into the baggy jeans he'd cinched high and tight around his waist with a belt, as opposite the hip-hop low-slung, underwear-revealing style of young macho-men as was possible. It was a beautiful, spontaneous portrait that immediately stirred unease in Cass. She flicked back for another shot. This one looked like it had been taken seconds before the other, while the boy was unaware. He was wielding a shovel, the muscles of his arms and back bunched impressively. She flicked back one more shot to a robustly built man in his forties, with a big mustache and matching gut. In the background was what Cass thought was the large outbuilding on Jean-Luc's property.

Very casually, she showed Xavier the pictures of himself. "Nice shots," she said. "Who was the photographer?"

"Shit," he said and then explained that he'd recently been doing some work for Jean-Luc, who took the pictures.

Cass, unable to hide her surprise, interrupted to ask, "Really? You're working for Jean-Luc?" She immediately regretted the interjection, recognizing the possibility that her tone betrayed both her surprise and disapproval.

Xavier probably heard it too. He responded, "Well, I can use the money," then added, "but I didn't sign up to be his model." He explained that sometimes when he was working, Jean-Luc borrowed his camera and took pictures, including some of Xavier working. Xavier added that he didn't like the practice or the pictures, and he usually deleted them. He must have just forgotten to do so for these few. Cass observed that he had seemed okay with having his picture taken when Lori was there, and the camera was new. "Well, it depends," Xavier said. "I was okay with those pictures. But it feels creepy when Jean-Luc does it."

Given Cass's visceral response when first viewing the shots, she was not surprised by Xavvy's reaction, and was eager to explore it further. But wary of the uncertain ground under her feet, she girded herself to restraint. So she simply remarked, "You know, I've only met the guy a couple of times. I don't even know if I'd recognize him if I saw him on the street." She flipped to the picture of the big-bellied mustache-man, and asked, "Is that him?"

Xavier looked surprised. "Not even close," he replied. "I don't even know who that is. One of Jean-Luc's guys, I guess."

"Jean-Luc's guys?" Cass queried. Xavier told her that occasionally, a guy in a truck would show up and that as soon as that happened, Jean-Luc would quickly pay Xavvy and get rid of him. He never introduced whoever had shown up. He'd just get him to drive into the utility building, go in with him, and close the door. As Xavier shrugged, Chuff and Zeke went wild. Noah, carrying a small backpack, had arrived.

He and Xavier greeted one another casually with mini-waves. No handshakes. Noah announced that it was a warm day, and he'd figured a break would be appropriate. He took a small tarp out of the pack and then extracted a large bunch of grapes, chunks of cheese, a box of crackers, and a couple of bottles of water. He set them all on the tarp and threw himself down next to it, saying to Xavier, "Come on, buddy, join us." Cass held her breath. Xavier did not.

"Sure," he said and then set to enjoying the food as only a thirteen-year-old boy can.

When the food was gone, Xavier continued to lounge with Cass as they both watched Noah go through a brief practice session with Zeke. This was the first time she'd ever visited with Xavier when they weren't walking. She was pleased with how naturally it had happened and how comfortable it felt. Xavier asked Cass questions about what Noah was doing, and several times noted small miscommunications between Noah and Zeke that Cass had missed. Each time, she told Noah that Xavvy had noticed something interesting and then invited the boy to explain. And each time, he did. His explanations were based purely on what he observed. They were devoid of judgment. They were brief and cogent. Each time, Noah nodded, thanked him, and then integrated the input into what he did next.

As Noah was finishing up, Xavier asked Cass if she needed him to help put the equipment away. When she said that she didn't, he said he'd be on his way. He called goodbye to Noah, shrugged on his pack, and left, walking in the opposite direction to the way they'd head home. Not much later, Cass, Noah, and the dogs headed for home.

"What a smart lad!" Noah commented.

"No shit," Cass responded.

16

XAVIER – EARLY AUTUMN: A NEW PROJECT

Stefan's back has been very bad lately. He no longer tries so hard to move as if everything is okay. It's obvious that it hurts. He doesn't like it if I ask him about it, though. But he did tell me that the drugs he's been taking don't seem to be working anymore. I feel bad for him, but it does have some advantages for me. Stefan doesn't spend as much time on our lessons together as he used to. I think sitting hurts him, but it also seems that he can't concentrate for very long without getting mean. He doesn't like getting mean; I've always known that. So he is giving me more assignments to do on my own, and he just reviews them with me. I sort of miss having more lesson time with him because Stefan is a very good teacher. He asks lots of questions and then shuts up and lets me work on the answers in my head before I start talking. Well, that's what he does when he feels fine. I think waiting is harder when you're in pain.

But you know what? Cass is also a very good teacher. I learned that about her the day she asked me to help her when she was training the boys in the fall. I knew that helping her was kind of an excuse, that she wanted me to experience training up-close to see what I thought about it. I liked it, and I liked the way she taught me stuff. That was the day she found out that I knew Jean-Luc and was working for him. I was pretty pissed at myself for leaving those pictures on my camera and letting her see them. But she didn't ask too much about it, and I didn't tell her too much either.

I think she would have been upset if she'd known how much time I've spent with Jean-Luc when he's around. Now that I can learn so much about the Harwoods in person, I have kind of made Jean-Luc my big observation project. Stefan always talks about how important observation is. The more you know about your subjects, the more you respect them. And knowledge and respect are essential if you want to understand the world around you. But it is even more important if you want to hunt the subjects you've been observing. When he said all of that, he was talking about observing animals. But I think mostly it is also true when you observe human subjects except for the respect part. What I learned about Cass, Noah, Lori, Chuff, and Zeke made me respect them. But it hasn't worked that way with Jean-Luc.

I don't want you to think that whatever Stefan says, I automatically accept. I think about stuff. I don't necessarily tell him when I disagree with what he thinks, but it isn't a big deal because it doesn't happen often. I usually agree with the things he says. For example, I agree that thinking, working hard, and paying attention to details is important. Jean-Luc is not that way. The guy is lazy and sloppy. That's why Katrinka died — because he didn't take good care of his trapline. But it isn't just that. It shows up in almost everything he does or doesn't do.

It's worked out great for me because he pays me to do stuff that he is too lazy to do himself. I put out apples, hay, and salt licks for deer at various places far back on his property, and then in the back bush in places that could be easily observed from deer stands. And when vines started to climb up around the cameras posted all over the place, I tore them down so that the cameras could continue to work. And when he had a fence that needed to be repaired, with new posts dug, he got me to do that. I'm a good size for a kid my age, and I'm very strong, so I could do it. But he's an adult, and he shouldn't have assumed that a kid my age was okay doing that kind of hard work.

That was when he took those pictures Cass saw, when I was hot, sweating, and hungry after working all morning. I just looked up and *click!* I was kind of pissed. He hadn't even asked if he could go into my pack and take my camera; he just did it. And it wasn't the first time. After that incident, I realized that every time I took my shirt off, *click,* there he was. Of course, once I realized this, my shirt stayed on no matter how hot it was; it just took me a while to get it. But there was more creepiness than just the pictures. A couple of times, he kind of ran his finger down where I was sweating and said something like, "You must be really hot. Do you want to come inside the house and take a shower?" And I completely didn't and told him so. He also put the finger he'd touched me with into his mouth and sucked it. Which, combined with the way he touched me, made me want to throw up. But I disciplined myself the way Stefan had taught me to when I'm scared or want to heave, like when I learned to butcher a deer. You kind of go away from yourself, you stay calm, you hang in there, and you don't let anyone know how you really feel.

So here's the thing about Jean-Luc touching me. It felt like he was leaving the kind of trail that a slug would. I checked, and there wasn't anything there on me, even though I felt like I had slimy boogers on me. I think he must have bad hands. I assume there is such a thing as bad hands because the day I helped Cass with training, she taught me about good hands. She said that often, you can communicate better with a dog by touching him with your hands instead of giving him a command. For example, with Zeke, he gets over-excited and he needs to calm down before he can do stuff right. We did it like an experiment. She told me to stand next to him, and to think, *Zeke, you are a very good boy, but I need you to calm down.* Then she told me to take a couple of deep breaths so that Zeke could feel how calm I was. And then she told me to try and tell him to be calm just with my hands. She didn't tell me how to do it; she let me figure it out. I kind of pressed him to me and sort of held the back of his neck firmly but with no meanness. It sounds very creepy, but I felt like I was holding him calm with love. And you know what? It worked. Zeke quieted right down. And Cass said to me, "Hey, my man, you have very good hands." That made me feel great.

Cass has good hands too. I generally don't like it when people touch me. But during our lesson, Cass did, and it didn't bother me at all. It just felt like communication. That surprised me, since the only other person who has touched me recently, except Stefan, has been Jean-Luc. And you know how I feel about that. I guess that was communication too, but not the kind I wanted to have.

Now that I think about it, that is kind of a pattern when I'm with Jean-Luc. I observe while he acts like himself, without ever knowing that he's communicating all sorts of extra stuff to me. That's the way it was when the guys with the trucks showed up. Jean-Luc always looked at his watch, and I could tell that whatever time it was, it wasn't the time he wanted the guy to arrive. Or that he didn't want me to be around when the guy showed up. Each time it happened, he got rid of me fast and then took the guy into the utility building. I don't know what goes on in there, but it must be interesting because Jean-Luc doesn't want me to know what it is. I make him believe that I don't have any interest in it, and that I'm not very smart. Jean-Luc is not very smart. He believes my acting. Although, maybe I'm not being fair. It seems that I am a good actor. It worked when I acted with Cass also.

Remember when I told you that when I met Jean-Luc, I acted like he was a hunting and trapping superhero? That was because I wanted to see what kind of hunter and trapper he really was. I didn't have a plan at that point. I was just collecting information, and it felt important to me to know more about him as a hunter and trapper. Probably because of Katrinka, right? Well, as you know, I couldn't find out much about him as a trapper because he had taken up his traplines. But even so, I could still see Jean-Luc's sloppiness and laziness because the traps he showed me that very first day were not well-maintained. They were rusty, and the one that killed Katrinka still had blood on it.

So even though I couldn't see him in action as a trapper, I figured I could gather some intelligence about him as a hunter. From what I've read and seen in movies, "gathering some intelligence" is how spies talk. And it wasn't until just now when I said it that I realized that before, I'd always observed as a naturalist and maybe a hunter. But with Jean-Luc, it felt more like I was a spy and maybe a hunter. It didn't affect how I observed; it had more to do with why I was observing. I wasn't very clear with myself about why Jean-Luc had become such an important project to me. But I knew that my reasons were very different than they'd ever been before. Even though I think deep thoughts about a lot of stuff, I didn't in this case. I didn't want to, and I didn't let myself. I just did what I was doing.

And one of the things I was doing was getting a handle on what kind of hunter Jean-Luc was. All I had to do was ask a couple of questions, and before I knew it, he was showing me his rifle. Very fancy. I didn't have to act like I was impressed. He had a 6.5 Creedmoor, which I knew from Stefan's catalogs is a very expensive custom rifle. "Wow, I would love to try that sometime," I said. I wasn't acting; I'd never had an opportunity to try this kind of gun before. Jean-Luc asked me what kind of rifle I had and when I told him, he suggested I get my "popgun," and we'd do some target shooting. Okay.

By the time I returned with my Winchester, he'd set up some hay bales with targets in the meadow, where his utility building is tucked away. We took turns with our own rifles. First, I discovered that Tessier was not much of a shot despite the Creedmoor. Second, he got nasty very fast when he started to suspect that I am what I am, which is a very good marksman. Stefan made sure of that.

And I made sure, very quickly, to first act excited when I shot well, as though it was unusual good luck, and second to intentionally blow enough of my shots so that it looked like he was the expert.

Once I had again given him the superhero routine, he let me try the Creedmoor. It was a sweet rifle, but I knew I couldn't perform well with it for my purposes. And I didn't. But I kind of set the stage for hunting with him by talking about how awesome it would be to go out with him during deer season and see him take down a big buck with the Creedmoor. It was like baiting a hook. He bit hard. He told me that he'd be there for the final days of the deer hunt in November and that we should hunt together then. He said the invitation was special because he usually hunts alone. He kind of ruffled my hair and touched my face, leaving his touch-slime track on my cheek, while he stood too close to me and suggested that maybe I should sleep at his place that weekend since we'd be starting out early. "Maybe," I said while my gut churned.

It was funny. Right up until then, I didn't have a plan. I just had loose pieces of ideas here and there, almost like day-dreams. And then just like that—*click*—they came together into The Plan. It was like magic. Like I hadn't made The Plan, but that instead, it had happened to me.

So that night, I asked Stefan about our plans for the hunt. This has always been an important time for the two of us together. My whole life, Stefan's been teaching me how to observe, how to avoid being observed, how to withstand cold and boredom, and how to treat animals with respect. And so the deer hunt is kind of like a final exam each year. But while I am not crazy about the tests I have to take for homeschooling, the hunt is a test I look forward to every year. I like the excitement of testing my skills and seeing if I can make Stefan proud of me. But there's a lot more to the hunt than that for us. It is a time when we feel connected, like the two of us are a unit, but a unit that is not isolated, a unit that is part of the woods and the wind and the world. We never talk about that stuff. But when I hunt with Stefan, it feels as though we share our brains, blood, and bones.

I could tell Stefan was uncomfortable as soon as I brought up the subject of the hunt. He said, "I've meant to talk to you about that. Do you want some hot chocolate?"

Uh-oh. Stefan's approach to food treats is kinda opposite to Cass's. She gives the dogs cookies when she wants to reward them. Stefan offers them to me when he's going to give me some bad news. So I took the hot chocolate and waited.

"You know I don't like to talk about it, but my back has been getting worse, and there are more and more things I can't do like I used to," he said. And then he told me that because of his back, we wouldn't be hunting this year. Notice I said "we"? That's because I'm too young to hunt on my own. The law is that kids my age can only hunt with an adult.

Little pieces of my plan were clicking into place in the background, and I was just like magic, dealing with them. I was improvising! So even though I knew what the answer would be, I asked Stefan if I could go without him. He reminded me that I needed to be with an adult and then said, "We pretty well keep to ourselves, right? I can't think of anyone else you could hunt with, can you?" I quickly decided that mentioning Jean-Luc would not be smart, given my plan. So I just looked down, really sad, and shook my head, "No."

Stefan said the good thing was that hunting licenses are costly, so we would save money by not buying them this year, which meant he could use the extra money for a great birthday gift for me in the spring. Cass taught me that there's nothing wrong with bribing a dog, though rewards are better. But, hey, he was trying, right? And then he told me that we'd have a great season next year because he had an appointment with a new specialist in Ottawa, who had good success with cases like his, and he was hoping that meant that soon he'd be back to normal. I told him I was hoping so also. I was telling the truth, even though I was secretly happy to hear his news since us not hunting together this year made The Plan much easier to operationalize. I'd heard that word used by spies in movies; it means "make it happen."

I asked Stefan when his appointment was, and he told me. He went to the drawer where we keep all kinds of important papers and got out a calendar to show me that he'd be gone for four nights in November because in addition to seeing the doctor, he'd do his regular anarchist business. Later, I went to the same drawer and looked at the schedule for hunting deer with antlers in our zone. Bucks are all we hunt. Stefan says you get a license and hunt does or fawns only if you're desperate. I guess we've never been desperate, which is fine by me. I don't like the idea of killing does and fawns. Anyway, here's what I discovered: Stefan was going to be away during the last few days of the season.

You know how sometimes everything is hard? If you are superstitious—and I'm not—it would be easy to think it means that whatever it is you're thinking about, you shouldn't do it. It works the other way also. When everything is easy, when all the little details just kind of fall into place on their own, it's easy to think it's meant to happen. I'm not superstitious. Not really. But in my heart, it felt like The Plan was kind of my fate. Stefan would be away during the weekend that I had told Jean-Luc I'd hunt with him.

It was October when Stefan and I talked about the hunt. Over the course of the next couple of weeks, I did a lot of scouting in the back bush, looking for the best place. Each time, I started from Jean-Luc's place and went in different directions. Eventually, I found the perfect place.

17

XAVIER – THE HUNT IN LATE AUTUMN

Stefan left on a Thursday and was supposed to get back on a Monday. After he left, I did a little bit of preparation. I retrieved the Lee-Enfield and ammunition from my hiding place under the house. Then I cleaned it, loaded it, wrapped it in a blanket, and hid it under my bed, just in case something weird happened on Stefan's trip and he decided to turn back. I knew that wasn't likely, but I agree with what Stefan has taught me; this is what he calls contingency thinking, and contingency thinking is part of paying attention to the details. I also found my last-year's hunting license in the drawer with the calendars. I figured a really responsible adult would ask to see it, and in light of that, that Jean-Luc wouldn't. But because details count I wanted to be prepared. I had to first hope no one asked to see my license and that if they did, they'd look fast and not notice the date. It was kind of smudged anyway – good! I tucked it into the wallet I got for my tenth birthday and headed over to Jean-Luc's place in the late afternoon.

It was a nice walk over. The season's first snow had fallen on Wednesday night, just a couple of centimeters that kind of frosted the ferns that turn brown and smell so spicy in the fall. I practiced walking as silently as possible. The air had that crisp dark-soon quality it gets only at that time of year. As with just about everything about The Plan, it worked out as I'd hoped. I could tell that Jean-Luc had arrived just shortly before I showed up, because he was unloading his truck in the front lot – hadn't yet put it in the utility building where he usually parks it. Or hides it. He really doesn't like people knowing when he's around. I knew it was special that he'd told me when he'd be coming to Lac Rouge to hunt. I didn't like being special to him, but that doesn't really matter, does it?

Right away, I did some acting. I made believe I was very happy to see him. He acted like he was really happy to see me too, except in his case I think it was real. Keeping a good distance from his hands, I told him that my dad (I always called Stefan that when I was with Jean-Luc) said I could hunt with him on Saturday, and maybe on Sunday, but that he wouldn't let me stay the night with him. I pretended to be pretty disappointed about that. But I told Jean-Luc the truth - that I am a very early riser, and would arrive at his place before dawn on Saturday morning.

And I did. I was there at four-thirty and was not even a little surprised to see his lights didn't go on until after five-thirty and that it was almost six-thirty before Jean-Luc came out. Lazy, right? Serious hunters should be in place by daybreak. That's what Stefan and I always did.

Even though his timing was poor, Jean-Luc looked the part. It was a very cold day, and he was wearing heavy-duty winter camouflage. He had on camo-everything except for his big black gloves. They looked like snowmobile gloves to me—very clumsy for hunting. But he showed me that he was wearing much smaller, fitted, good-quality hunting gloves underneath. I nodded but thought it was kind of dumb; it just meant there would be extra movement required to take off the big gloves before taking a shot. Notice I mentioned "camo-everything?" Jean-Luc wasn't wearing an orange vest. That's illegal, but it didn't surprise me. But I acted surprised. "Hey, you forgot your vest!" I exclaimed. He pretended that he'd just forgotten, went back into the house, and came out wearing a vest.

We talked for a minute before heading off. Jean-Luc asked why I had the Lee-Enfield instead of the Winchester. I told him it was my father's rifle, and it was a big deal that he was letting me use it. I asked him which way he wanted to go. It didn't sound to me like he had any kind of plan, but I didn't care. I was just going to go wherever he wanted. So we set off. Fortunately for me, he didn't head in the direction I'd already scoped out for Sunday. That was one of the reasons it was perfect. It was in an area that was not all that accessible by snowmobile or ATV, and since Jean-Luc is not much of a walker, I figured he wouldn't be all that familiar with it.

So we headed off, me walking behind him so that he could choose the route. At first, he wanted to chat. But even though I was just pretending to hunt that day, there are still some things that are right and others that are wrong. You're supposed to be quiet when you hunt. When I either didn't respond to what he said or just whispered a word or two, he got the hint and shut up for the most part. But that wouldn't have made much difference if this had been a serious hunt. Jean-Luc is a big guy, and he obviously had never learned how to move soft and silent in the woods. Any self-respecting deer would have heard him kilometers away. As would other hunters. But we didn't encounter any of either of them.

We eventually ended up in a stand where we could watch the woods and a neighboring field. We stayed there for a couple of hours. Once, I saw a small buck a long way from us in the woods. Jean-Luc didn't see him, and I didn't point him out. If he'd snagged a buck that day, The Plan would have died along with the buck. It didn't. As far as Jean-Luc was concerned, the day was a bust.

We headed back at about two in the afternoon and were back at Jean-Luc's by three-thirty. He invited me in for a hot chocolate. I was cold and would have liked one, but there was no way I wanted to go into his house. So I told him I'd promised my dad I'd be home before dusk and needed to get going. And then I baited my hook again. I told him there was a place where my dad and I hunted before, and we had always bagged a buck there. I told him that if my dad let me go hunting again tomorrow, I'd show it to him. As expected, he bit—hook, line, and sinker. He said he'd like to go there tomorrow, even if I couldn't, and asked if I could explain where this great spot was. I told him to get some paper and a pencil, and then I drew a map and explained how to get to the perfect place I'd found. I told him I wanted to go with him and that once again, I'd be there at dawn if my dad let me go. And I told him that if I wasn't there, he could just find his way there with my map.

I suspect you've figured out that I never intended to show up on Sunday. At least not as far as Jean-Luc knew. But I was there, in position, hidden in the woods where I could observe his place by four-thirty. It wasn't as cold as the day before, which was not surprising. I had checked the weather radio, and snow was forecast to start at some point that morning and get very heavy later in the day and throughout Monday. It usually gets a bit warmer when snow is on the way.

I was happy about the forecast for several reasons. First, the warmer temperatures meant that I wouldn't have to convince myself to not shiver like I did all day Saturday. Second, the snow would probably persuade many people who planned to hunt on the last day of the season to sleep in instead. And finally, snow would likely hide the outcome of The Plan for a long time. So it was all good, just another piece of the puzzle falling into place.

Jean-Luc stepped out of his house at six. He was carrying the Creedmoor and wearing the same stuff as yesterday, but not the vest. No surprise. He took something, which I assume was my map, out of his pocket, looked at it briefly, and headed off in exactly the direction I'd indicated—all good. I used my best woodcraft skills to track him as he made the trip, ensuring that I could be neither seen nor heard. This was pretty well just for the fun of it since Jean-Luc made so much noise himself, he'd never hear me, and I had confirmed throughout the day yesterday that his observation skills were no better than his silent stealth. That's what Stefan calls walking like a ghost in the woods.

It took him about an hour and a half to get to the landmarks I'd explained to him. He climbed a well-hidden stand I had drawn and then used his binoculars to look around. He smoked a cigarette. I kind of celebrated because this meant that no buck was going to lose his life to Jean-Luc Tessier that day. He might as well have posted a huge sign saying: Stupid Human Aloft. He stayed there for about an hour. Then the snow started, and Jean-Luc became impatient. I saw him get the map out of his pocket again. He looked at it, put it down, and then trained the binoculars in the direction of the ravine I'd told him about. It is steep and ends in a creek. I told him I'd put salt licks nearby so that in the spring and summer, deer could have a nice salt treat and then follow it up with a drink. They're not all that into salt at this time of year, but like most critters, including humans, they tend to go to places where they've been before.

I got into position exactly where I'd scoped it out when I was scouting the location, lying on my belly behind a log that I could rest the Lee-Enfield on so that my arms wouldn't get tired while waiting for exactly the right shot. If there had been any indications that there were other hunters around, I would have been scared because I had darkened my face and wasn't wearing my vest and figured I was so well camouflaged that a careless hunter might only see movement and shoot me. But just like yesterday, there was no evidence of other hunters by either sound or sight.

I sighted on Jean-Luc as he worked his way down the ravine. It was hard because the snow was coming down steadily. But snow is kind of like darkness. You know how, when you first go into the dark, and you can't see anything, but then your eyes adjust? Well, it felt kind of the same to me, trying to keep my eyes on a moving target in the snow. My eyes did adjust, but I thought it would be a surer shot if he'd just stay still for a minute. He did. He was on alert, but not because of me. His back was to me. I settled the Lee-Enfield firmly into my shoulder, took a deep breath, and pulled the trigger. The sound of the shot cut through the air. I suspect Jean-Luc didn't hear it until he was already falling forward, like a tree felled by a pro like Stefan. I felt that rush that you always get when you've hit your living target.

And then, nothing. A stillness as thick as snow fell on us. No wind. No birds. No movement from Jean-Luc. And no awe. When I've shot a buck before with Stefan, there had always been that moment when you're so full of life and joy, you think you'll explode. But for Stefan and me, that is always quickly followed by a feeling that Stefan has told me is awe, where you feel small and grateful to and sorry for the beautiful animal that will feed you in the coming months, and where you hope he had had a good life and would be happy to die this way instead of getting old and sick and dying of starvation. This was different. At the moment I would have expected to feel awe, instead I just had a feeling of…. rightness. Stefan and I have been reading stories by Edgar Allen Poe, and I had been afraid that I'd feel the terrible guilt he wrote about. I didn't. I felt peaceful.

When it comes to deer, you need to watch and wait a long time before you check to make sure he's dead. I was not going to go anywhere near Jean-Luc, but I did watch for a long time. He never moved after I hit him. He lay face-down at the bottom of the ravine in deep undergrowth. The snow fell. He was well covered by the time I left, about an hour and a half later. I traveled cross country rather than using the trails, and I was very careful. Probably much more so than I needed to be, given the snow, which was accumulating quickly. It took me a good couple of hours to work my way home, but I was confident that no one had seen me at any point in my journey.

When I got home, I started shaking. I shook the whole time I cleaned the Lee-Enfield, and then stowed it and the ammo back under the house. By that time, the snow had soaked through my clothes. I hung them where they could dry near the wood stove, and then I took a hot bath. I kept shivering, though, until I made myself some dinner. I cut up a bunch of hot dogs and put them in a pan with a can of beans. I cut a couple of big hunks of bread off the loaf and loaded them with peanut butter, and made some hot chocolate. I stopped shivering with the first bite of dinner. It was a great meal.

The next morning, my clothes were dry, and I put them away. Almost half-a-meter of snow had come down, and it was still snowing. I was a little worried about Stefan, who was supposed to be coming home that day. But I didn't worry too much. He's a good driver, and the truck is super-equipped for the winter. He arrived as planned mid-afternoon and seemed to be in a good mood. He said the doctor had given him some new exercises and drugs, and he was hopeful that they'd help. And he said his other business had gone well also. I suspected he had seen his girlfriend. I figured out a while ago that when he came back from a trip happy, those turned out to be the ones where there'd be a phone call when he got back. Sure enough, after I went to bed that night, I heard the phone ring and heard him using the whispering voice he only uses for talking to her.

On Tuesday, the snow stopped. Stefan asked if I wanted to do a lesson, and when I agreed, he told me to choose what we'd talk about. I suggested we start with an Edgar Allan Poe story, *The Telltale Heart*. I was curious to see whether he thought the kind of guilt described there was inevitable if you'd committed a serious crime. I still felt fine.

18

CASS – NOVEMBER AND DECEMBER

The Harwoods adhered to their long-established schedule for November that year, bypassing Lac Rouge and the limitations imposed by hunting season to stay in Ottawa and focus more on training and competition. Cass was particularly keen on that this year. Chuff, an obedience legend, and even more than that, her "heart dog," had turned ten. Cass wanted the gratification of working with him as long as possible. At the same time, she was committed to taking him out of the ring while he was still a stellar competitor. It would break her heart to think that spectators might feel sorry for him. So she had to find that fine line and felt it steadily approaching. Though Chuff was still the joyful boy he'd always been, the white mask he'd been sporting since he was seven had now blended into a heavy white stripe running down the back of his once-auburn coat, and his step was observably less quick and sure than in his younger days. On the other hand, slowing down a bit had improved his always-good precision.

The most significant challenge for Cass under these circumstances was developing a program for Chuff that would maintain his zeal and precision but not over-extend him. And she needed to time it so that he'd peak for the premier event of the year—a prestigious national invitational event with significant prize money—held in Ottawa in mid-November. Unlike "regular" trials, which were held during the day, presided over by a single judge, and comprised a series of exercises the teams could watch ahead of time, this was a night-time, dress-up event with a three-judge panel and media coverage, and teams were sequestered so no one knew what routine they'd be asked to perform once they entered the ring. Surprise! Cass and Chuff had been invited and participated in each of the nine preceding years, and they'd won when he was a five-year-old. It was a very big deal. Getting a second win when he was a senior would be a wonderful cap to his career and add luster to his legend.

Cass thoroughly enjoyed the iterative process of planning, monitoring, and making changes as required as she and Chuff readied themselves for this competition. Meanwhile, Zeke and Noah, who were also invitees, were gelling as a team, one that Cass suspected might outperform her and Chuff. This was not a problem for the Harwoods. They'd been competing against one another for many years, had participated in countless run-offs against one another, and did so without any conflict, to the great delight of spectators. It was a win-win situation as far as they were concerned.

Cass had learned over the years that meticulous planning and practice and considerable mental preparation was a good formula for success but far from bulletproof. But for this particular competition on this particular evening, it worked. Chuff, always the most intuitive of dogs and exquisitely attuned to Cass's emotions, picked up on her excitement as they waited for their summons, and once they got it, the lad exploded into the ring. This obviously senior boy's high spirits won the crowd over immediately, and Chuff was that rare canine performer who fed off the crowd to perform his best—which he did. As they exited the ring, Cass didn't give a damn what the outcome would be. She felt like she'd been riding Chuff's joy the whole time they'd been performing and was so suffused with the high of that communion that the outcome seemed irrelevant.

This didn't mean that she was oblivious to the outstanding performance that Noah and Zeke put in a few minutes later. She thought they had a fair shot, and so did the judges. When the results were announced, Cass and Chuff had won, with only a three-point margin over Noah and Zeke. However, as welcome as they were, the trophies, the money, and the congratulations still paled when compared to the exquisite "we-ness" Cass experienced as she and Chuff exited the ring, and then later posed on a dais, shoulder to shoulder, for their formal portrait. She could feel this dog so fully that she couldn't tell where she ended and he began.

With that experience fresh in her mind, the other consuming dog-activity in which Cass was engaged that fall was bittersweet. Katrinka's death had put a sizeable dent in the Harwood's succession planning. Zeke had been trained by Cass to be her principal partner once Chuff retired. They expected Katrinka, only six years old when she died, to be able to compete for another four or five years. So a new puppy had not been on the horizon. But now, with Chuff's retirement looming and Zeke repurposed for Noah, Cass needed to start a new puppy. Typically, a competitive trainer works with a puppy for a good two years before undertaking actual competition. Chuff, who started competing and winning when he was only a year old, was the rare exception to the rule.

Cass, the least maternal of women as far as babies were concerned, was the extreme opposite with puppies. She was besotted with them and never begrudged the broken sleep and constant vigilance that came with each new puppy that entered the Harwood household. But she anguished over each new bonding process, feeling that she was unfaithful to her previous partner. This had been disconcerting in the past, but now, the morass of projected guilt she experienced was directly proportionate to the intensity of her relationship with Chuff. He was in her blood, and though she knew she shouldn't, Cass felt she was getting ready to betray him. She struggled. But she continued to conduct frequent consultations with her breeder, figuring out which bitch and sire were most likely to produce a dog with the qualities she sought.

There were also non-canine challenges confronting the Harwoods. Noah was the chief software designer for a long-time client in Calgary for whom he'd developed a vast array of e-learning, testing, and certification programs over a ten-year time span. Recently, at the client's request, he'd renovated the whole suite. A hardcore hater of travel, Noah had accomplished all of this without ever leaving Ottawa. But now, the client planned to launch the revised suite of programs at the start of the new year. And though they understood and had respected Noah's reluctance to travel, in this case, they insisted that he be on-site in Calgary. They offered a considerable financial incentive for him to overcome his reluctance.

The Harwoods were happily concordant in their attitude toward money. It was what they needed to have the lifestyle they loved. They didn't require extravagant amounts, given that they were neither fine-diners, world-travelers nor domestic big-spenders. The dogs were probably their biggest expenses, and they made enough as coaches to cover those costs. At the same time, they were both self-employed, and the specter of financial need is never far from the heels of those that run that race. Losing this client would be most unfortunate for them.

And so they succumbed, even though they would lose at least a week together in their traditional winter month at the cabin. They decided they would spend about a week at the cabin in late December and then head back to Ottawa so that Noah could make his way to Calgary on December 29th. At first, they thought Cass would simply wait for him in Ottawa, and then they'd return to the cabin together when he got back from Calgary. But that was before the issues around Lori's visit came into focus.

Despite a restraining order, Lori had been to the emergency room in early November after Mike caught up with her in the parking lot of her gym. The intervention of some other gym members prevented more serious injuries, but even so, she had been kept overnight for observation because of concern about the potential spinal implications of whiplash-like symptoms brought on by the way she'd been shaken. Questioned by the police, Lori refused to press charges, figuring that would only delay Mike's departure. Only days later, Mike attempted to stage a dramatic apology by barging into her workplace, carrying magnificent floral offerings. Never the sharpest knife in the drawer, Mike had once again picked a location likely to contain able-bodied male protectors. Lori worked for a government agency that provided a range of services to veterans. When a few of those who witnessed and intervened at the workplace incident took Lori to coffee and got the full background on what was going on, they organized ongoing informal surveillance, where there was always at least one "watcher" posted outside Lori's townhouse. There were benefits to being Lori.

The veterans' surveillance seemed to have provided a much better margin of safety than the restraining order had. And because Mike was now in the final stages of selling his house and settling his business before taking off for his encounter with unlimited freedom, Lori felt optimistic that the ordeal would end in late December when Mike would leave for the first stage of his freedom tour, starting in Mexico.

But that didn't alter her concern about how the tumult in her life might be perceived in the workplace. She had requested her traditional winter vacation week the previous year, and after making discrete inquiries, she felt hesitant to ask if she could change the dates. Lori's role at the agency was long-established, and much relied upon, and finding a replacement when she was away was always difficult. So even though Noah would be away, Lori's cabin visit was still scheduled for the first week of January.

Cass and Noah decided that she'd run him to the airport for his flight, keep the car so that she and the boys could pick Lori up at the airport, and then make their way to the cabin. She'd hook up with Noah again when she brought Lori back. Though both women would miss Noah, they also looked forward to that rare treat for women with both girlfriends and men in their lives: a girls-only visit.

YEAR THREE OF THE STORY

19

CASS – THE START OF LORI'S JANUARY VISIT

Cass and Lori arrived at the cabin on the last day of December, during a rare two-or-three-day period when it didn't snow that winter. Cass was relieved since she had not been looking forward to the amount of shoveling she and Lori would have had to do to simply make their way down the long flight of stairs to the front door if there had been a substantial snowfall since she and Noah left.

They arrived in the afternoon, and after being released from their seatbelts, Chuff and Zeke exploded out of the car, and the women took a few minutes to watch the boys leaping into and out of the huge drifts already lining the road. Sprays of snow erupted into the air, shining like diamond dust as it fell again on the maniacally grinning Golden Retrievers. Welcome, ladies. Opening the cabin that Cass and Noah had left just a few days earlier went without incident. But it included a step that Lori had never seen before: the placement of weapons.

Cass, who frequently and confidently traveled on her own for business, was used to being with Noah all the time when they were at home, whether that was Ottawa or the cabin. She was embarrassed to admit it, but because of this, she was decidedly paranoid about being at the cabin when he wasn't there. And this resulted in her practice, on the rare occasions she'd been at the cabin without him, of placing potential weapons where they'd be in easy reach, regardless of where she was. A cavalry sword that Noah won as the top graduate of a young officers' training program for the Canadian Armed Forces was long, terrifyingly sharp, and snugly encased in a heavy, steel scabbard. It was placed in the closet nearest the front door. A baseball bat was slipped under the sofa in the living room, metal fireplace tools were always next to the woodstove, and, upstairs, an ebony walking stick was placed under her side of the bed.

Lori, who had lived comfortably on her own for most of her adult life and had never been exposed to this habit of Cass's, was amazed. In her own defense, Cass told her about how, some ten years earlier, a middle-aged couple, much like the Harwoods, had been at their nearby chalet. They made love in front of the fireplace, unaware that two men who'd been scoping out places for robberies were watching through the window. The scene had aroused the blood-lust of the potential thieves, who broke into the chalet and slaughtered the post-coital owners. The story was true. What Cass didn't add, however, was that she'd established her weapons placement routine well before her neighbors were murdered. The story, of course, did provide whatever rationalization she felt she needed.

However, it didn't intrude on the New Year's Eve dinner that she and Lori prepared together and consumed along with a nice bottle of red that they nursed through dinner and the long Scrabble games that followed. And throughout, they chatted. Family developments and politics were, of course, covered. And Cass was always eager to hear the stories Lori told about her clients and their brave efforts to reintegrate into civilian society. But she was also focused on her queries about Mike. Lori brought her up to date. She hadn't seen him since his apology attempt at her workplace had been thwarted. As an additional precaution to the restraining order and her veterans' honor guard, she had changed her email address. Despite that, somehow Mike had obtained her new address and had launched a barrage of emailed imprecations. Though Lori designated his address as SPAM, she occasionally monitored but never responded to his pleas. But she knew from her monitoring that the sale of both his business and house had been finalized, that he'd joined AA, and that he had started counseling to get help with his "anger issues." He had pledged that if she'd give him another chance, he'd continue therapy even while he was in travel mode since a condition he'd imposed when searching for counseling was a willingness to conduct telephone sessions.

As an incentive for another chance, Mike also offered to cover all of Lori's costs to join him on his freedom tour. He'd fly her to wherever she chose as their meet-up point, and from then on, they'd wallow together in money, margaritas, endless beaches, fine food, and dancing in the moonlight. Lori showed Cass one of Mike's many missives. If she didn't know Mike, Cass would have found his concept of a romantic idyll, presented with spelling errors and hope, to be naïve and charming. But she knew Mike, and his persistence troubled her. When that became apparent to Lori, she reassured Cass. She'd inveigled one of her veterans to also surveil Mike's place. He reported that on the day the sale of his home was finalized, just a few days ago, Mike had packed the Cadillac with a substantial amount of luggage and headed onto the freeway. Enjoying his role as an informal agent, the veteran had followed Mike at a discreet distance, halfway through Virginia. The man was indeed headed south. Lori was confident that her life was her own again.

So they celebrated, toasted the New Year, and tromped to the gazebo through the snow that had started falling. Bundled warm in parkas and boots, they sat in the gazebo, watching the boys play, bathed in moon shadows, as the snow fell.

The next morning, they skied. It was cold but not painful, and the day was clear and crisp. The snow conditions were perfect—about eight inches of new snow covered the trails Cass had already created. Cass introduced Lori to skiing the new trail that Noah, Paul, and Yates had created so that they could all avoid Jean-Luc's place and the area where Katrinka had perished. It was a perfect morning, except for Lori's disappointment at not encountering Xavier. Cass had briefed her on how the relationship had been developing, and both were hoping he'd find them while Lori was visiting. But it didn't happen that first day.

Before noon, the signs of more snow coming were unmistakable. It was just starting when they got back to the cabin. Cass checked the weather. Evidently, what they were seeing was the start of a major snow event. The forecast called for heavy snow for the next forty-eight hours. Because temperatures were supposed to stay cold and no gale winds were anticipated, Cass was optimistic that they would not lose power. It wasn't a big deal if they did; she knew how to start the generator. But in a Noah-less environment, she hoped she wouldn't have to.

In the late afternoon, after both women had showered and were relaxing with a joint while listening to old musical favorites, the dogs suddenly went berserk. Dark was encroaching, so Cass flipped on the porch light as she went to peer out the door, the top half of which was glass-paned, to see if she could see what had aroused them. Startled, she jumped back with a shriek when she spied a large parka-covered human about to knock. "Shit," she said as she took a deep breath to calm herself and take a second look, assuming it was a neighbor. Lori looked up from her magazine, and Cass took her second look. The world stilled. "Fuck," said Cass. Lori's eyebrows arched in inquiry. "It's Mike," said Cass, very quietly. She felt a cold calm descend upon her.

She motioned through the door for him to wait. Then she turned to Lori, and pointing to the front cupboard housing their parkas, said very quietly, "Suit up. I don't want to let him in, so we'll go out to talk to him. Grab the bat under the sofa. And let me take the lead to start with." Lori nodded her agreement. They both put on their parkas and boots while the boys continued to howl. Once they were ready to go outside, Cass commanded the dogs to hush and then signaled, "With me." She picked up the sword in its scabbard from the closet. Then they all stepped outside. Chuff immediately displayed his historic and unprecedented distrust of Mike, grumbling with his hackles up as he sniffed him to determine that it was, indeed, the big guy he disliked. Cass told both boys to sit and stay, and then she joined Lori to face Mike. The snow was falling. Dusk was upon them.

Cass's tone was quiet and neutral, as though she was encountering a work colleague with whom she had a minimal relationship. "Mike, what are you doing here?" she asked.

Rather than responding directly to her question, he immediately responded, "I've been driving for the last sixteen hours, and you're not going to let me come in?"

"Since first, you are uninvited, and second, the last time you saw Lori, she ended up in the hospital, no, you're not coming in. Let's talk, and then we'll figure out what to do." Lori reached out as if to touch his arm, but Cass intercepted the move. Lori then repeated Cass's question,

"Mike, I thought you had left for Mexico. What are you doing here?"

Mike took a deep breath. He appeared to be working hard and relatively successfully at maintaining his composure as he responded, "I was on my way, driving south. And as I drove, I realized that I could never live with myself if I didn't give getting back with you one last try. You are the only woman I've ever loved. I've changed my life for you, but you don't know about that since you won't see me, or take my calls, or answer my emails. I knew you'd be up here. I knew I had to try one more time to convince you. So I turned around and drove all the way back up here from North Carolina to give it one more try. Please, Lori, please." His composure held until the very end, at which point he broke into tears. He held his arms open to Lori, inviting her to enter his embrace. She did not. Instead, she and Cass exchanged looks.

Cass took charge again. "So tell us about the changes you've made," she said. She then released the boys from their stay, assuring Mike that they wouldn't give him any trouble if he kept his distance.

Mike, sniffling but no longer weeping, responded with a smirk, "Come on, Cass, stop with the bullshit. They're Golden Retrievers. They're not gonna do anything." Cass acknowledged that Goldens are not designed to be watchdogs. But she added that neither she nor anyone else knew how they would respond to a perceived threat.

"And since I don't think any of us want to find out, let's just talk calmly and keep our distance. So tell us about the changes you made."

Mike explained. He said he'd always had a problem with his temper, but it had never gotten out of control the way it had with Lori. He attributed this to two things: the ongoing stresses of selling his business, and realizing how much he wanted to be with Lori. He said that in the past, he'd always had the upper hand in all his relationships. He'd never encountered a woman as elusive as Lori, and his inability to control her had made him both afraid and angry.

Cass, professionally familiar with the impact that issues related to control had on domestic abuse, chose to explore this a bit. She asked how he had come to this realization. He explained that the last incident with Lori had shaken him, as had the visit the police paid him based on reports from the hospital where Lori had been treated. He got busy with Google and found a counselor he thought he could relate to. He had been seeing the guy three times a week, which was very expensive and which he contended demonstrated his commitment. The guy was putting him through an intensive program of cognitive-behavioral therapy, and when it quickly became apparent that Mike's dependence on alcohol was a significant factor in his explosions of anger, his counselor had urged him to join AA, which he had done.

The snow was still falling. It was cold. Things seemed to be under control. Cass asked Mike to give them a minute, and she and Lori stepped inside to talk, leaving Chuff and Zeke on the doorstep with Mike. After a quick indoor consultation, the women went outside again. Lori took the lead this time. She explained that they would not make Mike leave that evening, saying it would be too dangerous given the weather, roads, and his exhaustion. He could come in and spend a civilized evening with them and then get back on the road tomorrow morning. Cass then added that there were, however, conditions. There would be no drinking or toking—for any of them, he would have to keep his distance from them, and there would be no displays of anger. Any deviations from this would result in an immediate call to the police, which would completely fuck his freedom tour.

Mike was impressively mild as he accepted their conditions. When he entered the cabin, he looked around and immediately asked, "Where's Noah?" Cass heard an intake of breath from Lori and quickly responded before Lori could. She told him that Noah had a piece of programming he'd had to finish before he left Ottawa but that he'd be joining them later in the evening. To which Mike responded, "How's he gonna do that? I thought you guys had only one car?" Cass told him they'd recently purchased a second vehicle. Discussion over. But she was quietly alarmed at what she interpreted as Mike's skepticism. The cold and wary calm she'd experienced since he arrived deepened.

Dinner had already been in the oven when Mike appeared, so they ate shortly after re-entering the cabin. Cass indicated who should sit where at the long maple dining table inherited from Noah's grandfather. She sat at one end, Lori at the other, and Mike was midway between them. Cass kept the sword and scabbard very visibly leaning against her chair, and Lori did the same thing with the bat. Cass had Chuff do a down at her feet, and she put Zeke in a down by Lori. There was nothing relaxed or casual about the seating arrangement, by design. Cass was thinking with the same kind of calm clarity she often experienced when setting up a classroom for and then instructing federal offenders, one of the areas in which she specialized as a consultant. She felt like every fiber of her being was alert, aroused, and ready. It was the same way she used to feel when she rode her bicycle in heavy downtown traffic—a fusion of fear, hyper-awareness, and exhilaration.

This version of Cass was well-known to her competitors at obedience trials. In a competition venue, the ordinarily exuberant and gregarious Cass became very still. She was completely focused on what she had to do to get the best possible performance from her partner when they entered the ring. Once in the ring, she was totally unaware of spectators or any action outside the ring. In her mental image, there was a spotlight on Cass and her canine partner, and everything else was in darkness. It was why she loved to compete. She loved the way her focus narrowed so that for that period, she was free from the many strands of the competing thoughts usually weaving their way through her consciousness.

And this exquisite narrowness of focus prevailed throughout their dinner. It was a ragged imitation of a relaxed evening with friends. The conversation was social and considerably less interruptive than more spontaneous conversation is. Mike was asked about his trip to the cabin. He responded by providing what he thought was an amusing description of his stop in the village to buy gas, where the locals were "too ignorant" to answer even the simplest questions. He appeared doubtful when Cass pointed out that he was in a French-speaking province where his questions were probably not understood. "Oh come on; it's not that hard," he said. Mike was asked about his upcoming travels and briefed them on his plans. He worked hard at drawing a picture of unending sun-splashed luxury, obviously still hoping to change Lori's mind.

Per usual, but also in line with Cass's design, Mike remained the center of attention during the meal. Cass played the part of the cordial interviewer as she had done thousands of times throughout her consulting career, working hard to control her breathing and muscular tension to prevent Mike from picking up on and perhaps being abraded by her watchfulness. Lori, who reached often and reflexively for her wine-glass, which held only water this evening, worked hard at offering praise for Mike's plans without ever implying a personal interest in them. Though reasonably disguised, it was a tense and wary hour and a half for Cass and Lori. Cass couldn't tell if Mike was catching the undercurrents or not. Neither was she confident that she was reading him accurately. But she thought that things appeared to be under control.

Mike was a smoker. As dinner was completed, he reached into his pocket to extract his smokes. Lori reminded him that the cabin was a tobacco-free zone. Mike looked exasperated as he replaced his smokes and headed for the closet. Pulling on his parka, boots, and gloves, he huffed that he'd have a smoke outside. Not liking his tone, Chuff chuffed. Cass ignored the mildly inappropriate response of both man and dog. "Good idea," said Cass to Mike. "It's a beautiful night. It's probably gonna be a long time before you get to enjoy winter again. Why not go to the gazebo? You can be comfortable and watch the snow falling without getting wet."

20

CASS – THE END OF LORI'S JANUARY VISIT

Cass flipped on the outside floodlights for Mike as he exited, and she and Lori watched as he plowed his way through the accumulating snow on the trail to the gazebo. It was cold, but not brutally so—about negative fifteen degrees Celsius, and his parka, boots, and snowmobile gloves were, of course, only the best available. He'd be fine. They then quickly consulted and agreed on a plan for handling the situation at the cabin until they could get rid of Mike in the morning. They decided that the guest room where Lori usually slept would be abandoned for the evening. It was too tucked-away private to be easily monitored. Instead, Lori would sleep upstairs in the bedroom loft with Cass. Sharing a bed would be nothing new or uncomfortable for the cousins. They'd put Mike on the sofa in the living room, where he'd be easy to monitor from the loft bedroom, which had windows overlooking the whole of the cabin's first floor. Chuff and Zeke would sleep outside the loft bedroom, where they would hear and see any moves made by Mike downstairs.

They quickly made up the sofa as a bed. It was the first thing that Mike saw as he pulled open the front door, about a half-hour later. He stopped in the open doorway. "What is this?" he asked, pointing toward the sofa. The change in his previously mild demeanor when he'd headed for the gazebo was evident. There was an edge now that immediately raised goosebumps on Cass and hackles on Chuff.

Cass explained the sleeping arrangements she and Lori had agreed upon. Mike advanced toward Lori, aggression evident in his voice and posture as he asked, "And you're okay with this? You don't want me to spend the night with you?"

Cass, whom he'd passed in the process, stepped in front of him with her hands on her hips, leaning slightly toward him. Her voice was hard and cold, with no yelling or shrillness. "You agreed that we would all keep our distance and that there would be no displays of anger. Either chill and honor the agreement, or we call the cops."

"Fuck off, you cunt," he snarled as he backhanded her across the face, sending her crashing into the dining room table.

Chuff and Zeke ran to Cass, Zeke barking, and Chuff howling in anxiety. Cass acknowledged them as she scrambled to her feet and grabbed the sword and scabbard, which had been left at the table. "With me," she commanded them as she advanced toward Lori, who had grabbed the baseball bat and was swinging it at Mike, not to hit him, but to simply keep him at bay. And with each swing, she was screaming with a volume worthy of Fay Wray, "Stay Away!" *Swing!* "I'll kill you, you cocksucker." *Swing!* "Get the fuck away from me!"

Mike was facing Lori, his back to Cass and the boys, who were further aroused by Lori's screams. Chuff seized the moment, attempting to grab the back of Mike's thigh, but instead getting a mouthful of his parka. Zeke came in lower and grabbed the back of Mike's shin. As Mike stopped and howled, Cass swung in front of him, and using the scabbard like a spear, jabbed it repeatedly hard into his diaphragm as he twisted and attempted to dislodge the boys. Lori stood next to Cass, also using the bat to jab him backward. "Leave it! With me!" Cass yelled to the dogs so that there were then two women, and two dogs all fiercely concentrated on driving Mike back. The no-longer mild-mannered Golden Retrievers appeared to intuitively understand that the objective of this exercise was to drive Mike backward and out of the still-open door.

All five of them spilled out into the falling snow, with the appearance of stage lighting created by the floodlights Cass had turned on for Mike in the gazebo. Mike, driven back against a large woodpile, responded like a cornered animal. He charged forward, bellowing. Zeke was the first to recoup. Snarling, he grabbed Mike's thigh and shook and tore at it. Mike screamed, and as he did so, Chuff launched, clearly attempting to go for the throat and almost making it. Mike saw the leap and caught the seventy-pound dog in the air, both hands grabbing the ruff of Chuff's neck. Without even pausing, he twisted to hurl Chuff through the air toward the woodpile, which was when time and sound went slo-mo for Cass as she ascended.

From on high, she watched Chuff sail through the air, landing against the woodpile with a thud, and a protracted yelp that hung on the wind like an echo. It mingled with the refrain to "Peaceful Easy Feeling," leaking out of the still-open door to the house. At the same time, she saw the small woman holding the sword and scabbard, grasp it by the scabbard in the automatic stance from Cass Harwood's days as a softball player. As she wound up, she heard a cool coach's voice, "Not the head!" And still, at the same time, she heard another, much louder voice bellow in slow motion, "Motherfucker!" It appeared to be coming from the small woman as she delivered her blow to Mike's ribs. The coach commented amiably, "Base hit!" The Eagles sang that they'd like to get to know her as both a lover and a friend. Each of the soundtracks was perfectly distinct.

Time and space and Cass returned to their normal relationships, as she connected with her blow to Mike. *What the fuck?* There was a distinct shattering sensation as she connected before she encountered the solid chunk of muscle and bone that she expected. And Mike fell, screaming like a banshee as he clutched his side. Though unable to regain his feet, he was trying, intermingling his screams with promises, "I will kill you, cunts!" Out of the corner of her eye, Cass saw Lori embracing Chuff, who had staggered to his feet.

Without conscious thought, Cass attempted to withdraw the sword from its scabbard. It was a very tight fit, and she struggled. "Fuck!" she howled as she saw Mike making progress in regaining control of his body. "Keep him down!" she yelled to Lori, who quickly left Chuff and delivered a solid soccer kick—her sport—to Mike's testicles. Mike howled, turned onto his side, and started gagging. And Cass, happy Cass, had finally extricated the long gleaming cavalry sword from its scabbard.

Mike was still on the ground. Cass approached him and, without hesitation, placed the tip of the sword under his chin. Mike stilled. The Eagles sang on. Cass signaled Lori and both dogs to stand right behind her. "Mike," she said, speaking firmly but not yelling. "You are going to leave here now. If you don't, I will kill you. It would be completely justified." She did a visual check with Lori to see if she was okay with this approach. Lori put her head down for a moment, then raised it, took a deep breath, and nodded.

"I can't do it! You've broken me up," Mike moaned. As he did so, he reached for his crotch with one hand and his ribs with the other. The strong, astringent odor of scotch wafted through the air as he touched his ribs and whimpered. His dark parka was soaked on that side. Cass had feared it was blood but now suspected that it, or most of it, had come from whatever bottle he had hidden in his parka. She now understood the change in his post-gazebo behavior and the shattering sensation she'd experienced when she struck him.

Keeping the sword in place, Cass told Lori to get one of the ski poles from the collection of walking sticks and ski poles on the porch and toss it to him. "This will help," she said to him. "Get up." She, Lori, and the dogs watched impassively as Mike first rolled onto all fours, and then laboriously staggered to his feet. It took him several tries, but he eventually stood unsteadily before them, blinking dazedly through the still-falling snow.

"I can't," he moaned.

"You can," said Cass, moving behind him and now placing the tip of the sword in the small of his back. "Go!" she said. He took a couple of steps forward and then fell. "Get going," said Cass. He crawled. "Good!" she applauded him. Zeke, recognizing the praise in her tone of voice, immediately cavorted to the crawling man, circling and sniffing, tail wagging.

That appeared to be the incentive Mike needed. "Keep him the fuck away from me!" he yelled. He got to his feet again, grabbed the ski pole, and started staggering up the road.

It was a long way to where the Caddy was parked. Cass and crew only followed until he got to the sharp turn in the road. "What if he can't make it?" Lori asked.

"He can," responded Cass. "I didn't hit him all that hard. But he's been drinking. There was a bottle in his parka."

"Can he drive?" asked Lori.

Cass just looked at her and shrugged, then said, "He's got a full tank of gas. He's dressed warm, and it's not so cold that he won't be able to survive in the car tonight if he can't get his shit together to drive out of here now." She asked Lori if she was okay with that approach.

Still standing in the falling snow, they briefly discussed possible alternatives and implications. They concluded that if they called the police, it would take hours to get a response, they might have to deal with language difficulties, and the odds of being tied up for a long, long time in investigations and perhaps charges and trials were high. If they left things as they were, odds were that Mike would make it out either that night or the next morning, and the incident would be over. If he had an accident, not all that unlikely, given the road conditions and drunkenness, too bad so sad. And so they decided to leave things as they were. Shivering, without their parkas and gloves and still in their slippers, they went further up the road, past the sharp turn, and ahead of them saw Mike on his knees, struggling to arise. Which he did, using the ski pole for help. He then continued to stagger through the snow. He was making progress, albeit slowly. Cass, Lori, and Zeke returned to the cabin, where they found Chuff had regained his feet.

Chuff was walking slowly and favoring one side. When they got into the cabin, and Cass checked him over carefully, she concluded that he was bruised but unbroken. She administered an anti-inflammatory kept as part of the cabin stash of veterinary supplies. And though there was no longer any need to adhere to the sleeping plans they'd made earlier, without even discussing it, both women headed upstairs to share the bed in which neither of them would sleep more than a few minutes at a time throughout the night. Chuff and Zeke remained downstairs, and Cass was confident that they would sound the alarm if Mike returned.

He didn't. After a largely sleepless night, the women arose with the sun. They immediately agreed to check on the parking place up the road before they even thought about breakfast. Moments later, suited up for full winter, carrying their preferred weapons and accompanied by Zeke and a limping but mobile Chuff, they stepped outside. It was still snowing, and the dogs celebrated this, though less exuberantly than usual, sensing the tension around them. A good foot of snow had fallen since the storm had started yesterday afternoon. That was not enough to induce a stagger, but it was slow going indeed since it was almost knee-deep.

So they trudged. Cass, with no training as a tracker, was unable to see any sign of previous traffic. She suspected that even Xavier, with his skills, wouldn't be able to garner much through a foot of newly-fallen snow. She figured that was not so for the dogs, who trotted along with their noses frequently buried in the snow and zigzagged a crooked path, not unlike what she'd expect from the staggering Mike. They passed the sharp turn in the road. As they neared the parking area, Cass motioned them all into the woods that bordered the road. Keeping to the woods, they moved very slowly, inch by inch, toward where the car would be if Mike hadn't left. Cass controlled the dogs by signaling them to stay while she and Lori advanced to their next station and then signaling them to come, sit, and stay while she repeated the process. It was a training game they played often.

Though she didn't say anything about it to Lori, during this whole prolonged reconnoiter, Cass focused intensely on the road, hoping against hope that Mike hadn't fallen and failed to get up. Though she had not mentioned this possibility to Lori, she was acutely aware of stories about drunks who fell and then froze in a blizzard, only short distances from their doorsteps, which they couldn't see through the blinding snow. On the plus side, this was not a blizzard. It was a heavy but sedate snowfall with no high winds. And she had already decided that if she was ever questioned, she would never acknowledge having considered this possibility. Mike was not that badly injured. He was not that drunk. He was a large able-bodied human. That was her story, and she was sticking with it. She had no idea if Lori had gone through the same thought process and regretted that the odds were they'd never get to compare notes. Even between the two of them, some things are too private to share.

They got closer to the parking area and saw no sign of any vehicle parked there. They kept to the woods and continued what they considered their stealthy progress until they were directly next to the parking space. Nothing. Still quiet, they emerged from the woods. Cass pointed out a slight car-sized indentation in the snow that she thought likely indicated that it had been covered for a time so that there was less snow there than in the surrounding. Lori nodded; she got it. Both exhaled shakily and gave each other a subdued high-five. They continued their slow progress up the cottage service road until it intersected the road from the village.

Nothing. The cousins embraced, and Cass could feel that Lori was shaking as much as she was. They silently turned and started the long trudge back. They stayed on the road this time.

Their breakfast was subdued. Lori, who'd been briefed on Noah's displeasure with their failure to call the police when Cass had visited her in Baltimore, asked what Cass was planning to tell him. Cass replied that she would tell him exactly what either or both of them should tell anyone else if they were ever questioned about that evening: Mike showed up uninvited. Given the late hour and bad weather, they allowed him to come in on the condition that he remain civilized throughout. He did not, and when Cass brought this to his attention, he struck her, which induced the dogs to go for him. He was bitten on the leg several times, and Cass landed a feeble blow to his ribs as the women and the dogs ejected him from the premises. It was dark and it was snowing and as far as they were concerned, tough shit. He had a full tank of gas and should have been able to make it to the village where he could find lodging for the night. They checked in the morning, and he had made it safely onto the road to the village.

Cass asked if there was anyone Mike was in constant touch with—family or friends—who might call Lori if there was a problem, or who she might contact. Lori reported that Mike professed to have no family, had never been married, and had no friends that she'd ever heard mentioned or met. He seemed to have only business colleagues, with whom they occasionally dined. Lori's perception was that the objective of these encounters was primarily for Mike to show off his "luscious babe." She said that as far as she knew, Mike had estranged all these colleagues in the acrimonious process of divesting himself of his business. So, it seemed that the garrulous Mike was a well-disguised loner. There was no way of checking where he was and how he was other than calling him directly. Which they would not do. There were more benefits in not knowing.

They felt hungover from the tension of the last fourteen hours and spent the rest of the day snuggled in blankets on the couch, nursing coffees, watching old movies, and playing scrabble as the fireplace crackled cheerily. They did not drink wine or smoke dope. In the evening, Cass called Noah, three hours behind them in Calgary. As expected, despite the way Cass minimized the incident, Noah was thoroughly alarmed. "I'll come back right away," he said. Cass told him he was overreacting. It was over. They were fine. He should finish up his project as planned, and they would meet him back in Ottawa in a few days, also as planned. Though clearly uneasy, Noah eventually agreed.

So the day crept by. In the afternoon, the snowfall ended, and they both felt much better after a couple of hours, clearing the walkways and the deck. That evening, despite their nervousness, the cousins agreed they had to reassert normalcy. Lori returned to the guest room and Cass to the loft bedroom. Both were surprised to find that they fell asleep quickly and slept well.

The next day dawned crisp and clear, with no snow falling. Given the two feet that had come down since they last skied, the cousins opted to snowshoe instead. Their departure that morning was difficult because Chuff was still too stiff to accompany them through deep snow, and his mournful countenance as they bid him farewell was heart-rending. But they went anyway, and there was considerable hilarity as they set out. Neither woman was remotely as adept on snowshoes as on skis, and each agreed that the wide-legged shuffle both adopted made them look like weary cowboys with full diapers. But Zeke was delighted to be an only dog, and they made good progress, again taking the new Katrinka bypass trail. Not feeling terribly ambitious, they reversed direction and headed for home after about an hour.

Not long into the return trip, they heard shouts from behind them, "Cass! Lori!" Turning, they saw Xavier waving as he jogged toward them on his snowshoes.

"Look at that! Isn't that lovely?" Lori asked as impressed as Cass always was when she saw the way Xavvy moved on snowshoes. But Cass was too gobsmacked to respond. This was the first time Xavier was obviously following her, eager to catch up. This was a remarkable contrast to the nuance of all their previous meetings, which he had always staged to appear incidental. She was delighted, feeling that this enigmatic and compelling relationship had turned some sort of corner. Lori was delighted since she'd been hoping to see him again.

The atypical behavior continued once he caught up with them. The customarily reserved Xavier, who responded well to conversational forays but seldom initiated them, was very different during this encounter. Immediately upon joining them, he asked with a noticeable undertone of anxiety, "Where is Chuff? Is he okay?"

Cass, assuming his concern was predicated on Chuff being an old dog or anxiety because of the Katrinka story, reassured him. "He had a bit of a fall, so he's stiff. But he's fine. I just didn't think deep snow would be good for him right now."

Xavier breathed a visible sigh of relief. "That's good. I've never seen you without him before." He then asked about Noah and didn't seem surprised to hear that Cass and Lori were on their own this trip.

They chatted amiably as he accompanied them until they got to the road that separated the wild terrain of the west from the tamer world on the east side of the road. At one point, Lori mentioned something about going back to Baltimore. "You're from Baltimore?" Xavier asked brightly as if that was something special. Lori assured him that both she and Cass were from there. To which he responded, "I know someone from Baltimore; Edgar Allen Poe. Do you know him?" Laughing, they assured him they did. Poe was a famous Baltimorean. But he was long-dead; did Xavier know that? Xavier replied, a bit huffily, "Of course, I know that. They think he died of addiction." When they asked about his interest in Poe, he told them he was studying him in school and that Poe's stories were some of his favorites.

After they parted, Lori again talked about what a strange and charming kid Xavier was. Cass told her how different his behavior had been this time than all previous encounters and attributed the difference to Lori being there. "I think your appeal is ageless, baby," she said. Lori laughed and preened, comfortable with this assessment, given a lifetime of fervent male attention.

This encounter catalyzed the emerging sense of normalcy after the incident with Mike. Two days later, as they packed to return to Ottawa, Cass marveled to Lori, "Well, we're either very resilient or very insensitive. Or else, it wasn't such a big deal. Any way you cut it, we're okay." Lori agreed. They sang together as they drove back to Ottawa, bypassing without discussion, one of their long-time favorites, "Peaceful Easy Feeling."

21

XAVIER – UNEXPECTED ENCOUNTERS

You remember how I talked about how things just fall into place when they are meant to be? Well, that was at work again on that evening in January that I'm about to describe for you.

There'd been a lot of snow already by then. I was like a shoveling machine keeping our stairs and walkways clear enough for Stefan to manage when his back was troubling him. His trip to Ottawa had helped, but sometimes with Stefan, that makes things worse. When his back feels okay, he tries to do all the stuff he can't do when his back hurts. But he often overdoes it, and then the pain is so bad that he needs to take one of the new pills he got. That works. Except that the pills also make him sleepy. And when he's in awful pain, he takes two, and then he's out of it for a good eighteen hours.

That's what happened that day. After breakfast, we went out together to move two of our woodpiles. Stefan said there was a big storm coming, and he wanted to get them into our woodshed, so we wouldn't have to dig for them later. So that's what we did. It took a couple of hours of hard work. Afterward, we had a big lunch of grilled cheese and bacon sandwiches and lots of hot beans. Stefan was in a great mood and wanted to talk about my birthday in the spring. He asked if my list still included a crossbow and a dog. I said it did. He asked if there was anything else I wanted more than either of those two things. I told him there wasn't. Then he told me that this gift was too expensive to be a surprise. I had to decide which of those two things I wanted, so he could start making plans about getting what I decided on.

A long time ago, when I was littlelittle, Stefan taught me to make a pros and cons list. Whenever you have a decision to make, you take each possible choice and list the good things about it—the pros, and the bad things about it—the cons. Eventually, you compare your pros and cons for each choice, which can also be called an option, and it helps you decide on the best choice. So that's what seemed like the best way to handle making this decision, and I got some paper and started the list. But Stefan stopped me, and I could tell right away that the pain was starting. He told me I should take a lot of time to "perform my analysis" since it was an important decision that I should make independently, taking a lot of time to consider and re-consider. I was eager to get started, but I knew he was right. He told me to take my stuff off the table and put it in my room. As I went into my room, I looked back into the kitchen and saw him taking one of his pills. Then he kind of hobbled to his easy chair and sat down with his eyes closed. He looked bad.

And he looked even worse when I came out to check on him a while later. He was still in his chair, and his face was kind of gray and scrunched up in pain. He asked me to get him a pill. I could tell that he didn't know I'd seen him already take one. But I wouldn't have said anything anyway. They make him feel better, and I can take care of us when he does the big sleep after taking two. So I got him one and then told him I would put on my snowshoes and do some observing. He nodded his head, but he was already half-asleep. I grabbed my backpack, and out I went.

I knew that this was about the time that Cass, Noah, and Lori usually arrived for their winter stay. So I worked my way through the woods to their place to check it out, established a good Just Watching spot overlooking the sharp turn in the road and their cabin, and saw that their van was already there and that there were lights on in the cabin. I used my binoculars, and through the light snow that had started to fall, I could see ski tracks both coming and going. But there were signs of only two skiers. One of them had to be Cass; she never stays back when there's skiing to do. So the other track could mean that it was Noah with Cass and that Lori wasn't going to be there this year, which would make me a little sad. Or it could mean that Lori was there and had gone with Cass while Noah had stayed home. He often does that. There was no way for me to know at this point. The falling snow prevented me from telling if the tracks were made by two people of about the same weight or by one heavier and one lighter person.

I watched the cabin for a while, but there was little to see. The door opened once, and Cass came out to grab some firewood. Some nice music drifted out until she closed the door. I've never been inside the Harwood cabin, but I imagined it like in some movies I'd seen: a bright fireplace with Chuff and Zeke sleeping in front of it, and people talking and drinking coffee or wine while soft music played. That's the way I imagined it. That's the way I hoped it would be for me someday when I'm grown up.

There wasn't much to observe at the cabin. Given the ski-tracks and the falling snow, I figured whoever was in the cabin was probably in for the rest of the day. But I wanted some action, so I decided to head over to Cass's back bush to scope out the best places to intercept them when they skied the next day. I didn't make much effort to remain hidden; I was just a kid on snowshoes. But the habit of hiding is automatic with me, so I was still tucked into the woods and watchful as I approached the road. And there I saw a strange sight. It looked like a big cloud of snow was speeding down the road toward me, rolling along like a polar tumbleweed, you know, those big balls of dead plants you always see rolling across the desert in westerns? I quickly realized it was a big vehicle, driven very badly and way too fast.

Most people up here know how to handle a vehicle in winter conditions. Stefan started teaching me when he taught me how to drive when I was ten. Ever since then, he's let me practice on back roads that are never patrolled, and he's really challenged me to do stuff like brake too fast to cause a skid and then stay cool and steer out of it. He says I'm pretty good at it, and I agree. I think it's because it takes the same kind of ability to control your thoughts and stay calm that observing and hunting do. Anyway, I'm a hell of a lot better at it than whoever was driving down the road, that's for sure. As the vehicle got closer I saw it was the same kind of big, fancy car that Lori's big guy drove when he was up last year. And as the car got even closer and then turned onto the dirt road that serviced the Harwood cabin, I saw that the car was a Cadillac and it WAS Lori's Big Dude. And he was alone.

I was pretty curious about this, and also a little... worried. I didn't like the look on the guy's face or how tense he was. He didn't look like someone who was looking forward to a nice visit. He looked mad. But of course, it could have just been that the driving was scaring him because he was so bad at it. Whatever was going on, I decided to do some observing. Even though I figured the odds on the guy being aware of much going on around him were small, I kept to the woods, and because I'm so fast on my snowshoes and he had slowed wwwaaayyy down on the service road, I was pretty well able to keep up with him. He parked on the service road as most of the Harwood guests do, got out and walked around to open the passenger's front door. He bent to get a bottle that must have been lying on the floor on that side, opened it, threw his head back and took a long drink before putting the bottle back and closing the car door. Then he started walking. City guy – even though he was very tall, he really wasn't good at walking in deep snow. I was able to get ahead of him in the woods, and had already positioned myself at the watching station I'd used earlier, so I had a good view of the cabin. It was snowing, it was unlikely that I'd need to do much moving around, and it was likely that I'd be there for a while. So I took off my snowshoes, and made a kind of chair out of the snowshoes, sitting on one with the other one leaning against a tree as back support, and made myself comfortable. I took my binoculars and thermos of hot chocolate out of my pack and had actually managed to have a nice drink by the time Big Dude finally arrived.

He marched to the door and banged on it like he was a sheriff or something. I could hear Chuff and Zeke going nuts inside. The porch light was flipped on, but nothing happened for a minute or two. The dogs continued to howl. Then suddenly, they went quiet. The door opened, and Cass and Lori stepped out, dressed in parkas and boots. The dogs were with them, and Cass told them to sit and stay right away. They were good boys and did what they were told. Cass closed the door behind them, even though Big Dude kind of pointed toward it. I think he wanted to go in, but Cass and Lori weren't buying it. That was interesting, and I was glad. I'd never liked anything I saw when I was Just Watching that guy last year.

They talked for a while. I couldn't hear what they were saying, but after a few minutes, Cass seemed to signal that the guy should wait outside while she and Lori went back into the house. She had released the dogs from their stay and left them with the guy when she and Lori went back inside. Chuff's hackles were up, and he was sniffing around the guy like crazy, and then he lifted his leg and peed on his foot. I thought that was very funny, but Big Dude did not. I thought he was winding up to kick Chuffy when the door opened again, and the women came out. They all talked quietly for a minute, and then Cass opened the door, and they all went inside.

I settled in for a long watch. I felt very uneasy and figured I'd keep observing until I didn't feel that way any longer. I hoped this was just a short visit and that Cass and Lori wouldn't let the guy stay there that evening. I hadn't seen any sign of Noah, which made me feel that he wasn't there, that Cass and Lori were alone except for the dogs.

Things were quiet for quite a while, and I started to think I was being silly when the powerful floodlights were flipped on. Big Dude came out by himself. He headed through the lightly falling snow to the gazebo. Because of the floodlights, I could see him in the gazebo but with no detail, just the kind of black shape you get when you photograph someone with bright water in the background. He had reached into his parka and put some stuff on the table in the gazebo. The smaller item was a pack of cigarettes; I could tell when he lit one. And the larger shape was a bottle like the one he'd had in the car. He was drinking from it often. He stayed there for about half an hour and then headed back to the house.

He pushed open the door and stepped in. I couldn't see what was going on inside. But the door stayed open, which was weird, but which also allowed me to hear stuff. At first, there wasn't much to hear except the nice music kind of leaking out into the night. But after just a few seconds, there was a lot to hear. First, Chuff and Zeke went nuts. And then a few seconds later, I heard one of the women screaming. I was sure it was Lori, and she was screaming curses. I got up and started to run toward the cabin, leaving my stuff in the woods. I don't know what I was going to do. I didn't have a plan. I didn't even have a thought. I just found that I was on my feet and running automatically. But before I got out of the woods, all five of them exploded out of the cabin. I stopped, still in the woods, watching and ready to move again.

I couldn't believe what I was seeing. Cass had a huge sword, and Lori had a bat, and they and the dogs were backing Big Dude up into the yard until his back was against a big woodpile. And then Big Dude exploded. He charged at them the way a bear does. Zeke lunged for him and clamped onto the guy's leg. He was shaking his head and the guy along with it, as though he was going to tear chunks of his flesh off. Big Dude was screaming, and then Chuff, brave old Chuff, went for him. He went high; it was a damned good jump for an old dog. But the guy saw him coming and caught him, and twisted to throw him through the air back toward the woodpile. He was flying, still snarling as he flew, and I was frozen. I thought it was the end of Chuffy.

But Cass wasn't frozen. She grabbed the sword with both hands as if it was a bat. I couldn't figure out why she wasn't cutting her hands to the bone. And then she swung at the guy, the way you'd swing when playing baseball, at the same time hollering, "Motherfucker!" It was that amazing Cass holler I'd heard so many times before when she was calling Katrinka. That woman could yell! She connected with the sword someplace around his ribs with the sides of the sword rather than with the edge, which I figured might cut him in half. He fell, screaming, which kind of surprised me because he was wearing a heavy parka, and I didn't think she'd hit him all that hard. But then I realized she'd hit him on the side where he'd had the bottle stashed. I suspected he'd just been cut to shit.

So he was down and screaming, Lori was hugging Chuff, who was struggling by the woodpile, and Cass was doing this weird little sword dance. I finally realized the sword was inside a big silver holster, which was why she hadn't cut herself or sliced the guy in half. And now she was working like crazy to get the sword out of the holster, and it wasn't coming easily. The guy was trying to get up, so Lori went over and gave him a solid kick to the nuts. He went back down again, and by then, Cass had the sword out of its holster. It was a big, long, shiny, scary-looking weapon. Big Dude went still the second Cass placed the tip of the sword under his chin. I would have, too. Anyone would have; that was one hell of a weapon.

I realized I was almost standing on the road. No one had noticed, but I slipped back deeper into the woods, still close enough to the road to move quickly if I had to. But even though

I found it hard to believe, it looked like Cass and Lori had things under control. Cass kept the sword on the guy. Lori threw him a ski pole to help him walk, and then they made him walk in front of them and Zeke up the road. Chuff tried to follow but couldn't; he kept collapsing. It was obvious to me that the women were making the guy go back to his car. I watched them as I put on my backpack and snowshoes, and then, well-hidden in the woods, I stayed parallel to them on the road. Big Dude was in trouble. He'd kind of stagger a few steps and then fall, crawl his way back up, and do it again. I couldn't tell if it was because he was hurt or drunk or a wuss. I figured it was probably a combination of all three. One thing was for sure; despite his size, he was not a tough guy at all. Stefan would hardly have been slowed down by what this guy had experienced.

Once they got up the road, and the guy had been on his feet and moving for a while, Cass, Lori, and Zeke turned back. I didn't.

22

XAVIER – BIG DUDE'S DEPARTURE

I stayed in the woods overlooking the cabin service road and tracked Big Dude's progress toward where he'd parked his car. It was slow. A couple of times, he stumbled and fell to his knees. Each time, he stayed there slightly longer before he finally got to his feet again, using the ski pole to help. It reminded me of watching people on cross country skis for the first time, trying to get up after falling in deep snow. It was very hard work for them, very tiring, except that they aren't usually crying.

I think that's what the guy was doing. Burbly sounds were coming out of him that sounded like a combination of curse words, crying, and wheezing. I wondered if Cass had broken his ribs. One time when he fell to his knees, he just rolled over onto the side she hadn't hit, and kind of clutched his other side, and he wailed. Under my parka, I could feel my hair standing on end as I waited for him to get up again.

Except he didn't. He just lay there, like he'd given up. What a wuss! I did a pro-con analysis so fast that it was like lightning. I figured that if he lay there all night, it would be bad for Cass and Lori. Either he'd freeze or he wouldn't. Either way, it would be bad. So I came out of the woods onto the road behind him and then approached him as if it was totally normal for a kid on snowshoes to be trekking around in the dark. The guy was so messed up that he accepted my coming out of the snow and darkness as if it was expected. I squatted next to him and saw that there was blood on the snow where his head was; it looked like it was kind of leaking out of his mouth. I looked to see if the guy had a cut lip. He didn't, so I was hoping maybe he'd bitten his tongue. Before I could check or even say anything, he wheezed, "Where have you been? I've been waiting for you!"

I have no idea who he thought I was. I figured the guy's confusion worked to my advantage. I asked him, *"Je vous-aider?"* I'm not sure why I spoke to him in French. It might have been because I've done that before, successfully, so that the person I'm talking to will know less about me. Or it might have been that I was just being mean. I think it was probably that, and I decided that this guy was too sad for me to be mean to him. After that, I spoke to him in English.

The guy stank; I almost gagged when he breathed right into my face. I figured at least some of it was from the bottle that broke in his parka. But based on his breath, a fair bit of the stink was coming from him, a combination of alcohol and carrion. Each time I got a good whiff of his funk, I saw Chuffy flying through the air again and felt sad and mad at the same time. Despite that, I helped him get up. I put one of his arms around my shoulders and put the ski pole in the other one. I was still wearing my snowshoes, and I put one arm as far as I could around his back, trying to avoid where Cass whacked him and put both of my ski poles in my free hand. Good thing I'm strong; that guy was heavy. It took quite a while to get him to where the car was parked. He kept up that weird burbling talking, wheezing, crying thing he was doing almost the whole time. It was like a chant, "Fucking bitches tried to kill me! Fucking bitches tried to kill me!"

When we got to the car, he stopped and did that awful wailing thing again. "What?" I said to him. "What?"

"My keys! Where are my keys?" he wheeze-wailed at me as if he was a little kid, and I was his mother. My heart was thudding like crazy. It would be very bad if he didn't have his keys. But I stayed calm and told him to stand still while I went through the pockets of his parka. The keys were where I looked on my very first try, exactly where Stefan keeps his, in the inside zippered pocket of his parka. Another one of those meant to be kind of deals. I showed the guy the keys and then brushed enough snow off the car to unlock the doors.

He surprised me by going to the front passenger's door. The first thing he did was find the bottle I'd seen him drink from when he arrived. And then he just crawled into the passenger's seat. "Hey, are you coming?" he called to me, as though we had some kind of agreement. Well, maybe we did. I took my pack and snowshoes off, turned the car on, blasted the heat, found the scraper, and cleared the car off, happy that it was nice fluffy snow, not sticky or icy. Since he was in the passenger's seat, I slipped into the front seat.

The guy was still drinking and still repeating, "Fucking bitches tried to kill me." Every now and then, he gave a feeble little cough, and drool and blood spurted out of his mouth and onto his parka. The stink was bad, and the memory of Chuff flying through the air was worse. I took the bottle from him, and he moaned, put his head against his door, and just sort of slumped there, half-asleep. I decided I'd drive him to the village, where he could either get a room or sleep it off in the car. It was about fifteen kilometers away. That meant a good long trek back, but I'm a good long trekker. I got out and put my pack, snowshoes, and poles in the back seat. I pulled the driver's seat up to where I could reach the pedals, adjusted the mirrors, and put on my seatbelt. I did all the stuff Stefan taught me to do. Well, except for the guy's bottle, which I tucked away near me where he couldn't get it.

I started driving. It was a big heavy car, and it didn't have four-wheel drive, so I was glad the snow was light, even though it was already deep. But the heavy car tracked through it okay. I was very cautious and slow in making the turn onto the road to the village. No problem. After a few minutes, I figured I'd better start waking the guy up, so I opened the window he was slumping against. That worked. He woke up with a bang. "Fucking bitches tried to kill me!" he wheezed. *"Here we go again,"* I thought.

Except it turned out that he was not stuck on that one chant. The cold air blasting in from the window seemed to wake him up a bit. He looked at me and asked, "How long?"

I was amazed that he still didn't realize that I was a kid he didn't know, driving his car, but I just answered, "Not long."

He moaned and then asked, "Will there be someplace there where I can buy what I need?"

"What do you need?" I asked.

"A big fucking hunting knife," he said. He was slurring his words like a bad drunk, but I heard that clearly.

"What do you need a hunting knife for?" I asked him.

He looked at me, and it felt like he finally saw that I'm just a kid. "You ever had any pussy yet, kid?" he gasped. I didn't answer, but I guess he figured the answer was no because he acted as though I'd said that. So then he went into this wild all-over-the-place, crazy wheeze-talk about how many women he had fucked and how he's the greatest "cocksman" the world has ever seen. And he said that of all the women he'd had, Lori was the best, that no one could compare to her. He went on and on. When he said, "She has the sweetest pussy I ever ate. Just thinking about her pussy makes me hot," he tried to rub his crotch, which, if you remember, Lori had kicked not all that long ago.

When he reached for his crotch, he moaned and then started that crying, spurting blood thing again. And then he said something like this, though in-between the words and sentences, he continued to wheeze, moan, and cry, "Stick with me, kid. I'm going back there, and first, I'm going to fuck her cousin to death in front of her. Then I'm going to have her one more time. And

I'm going to let you go down on her. It will be something you'll never forget because it'll be the last time anyone ever does that to her. You'll be her last. Because I'm getting a big fucking knife, and after you and I both have at that cunt, I'm going to fuck her with the knife and cut her cunt right out of her body."

"Oh," I said. And then I handed him the bottle and suggested that he have a nice drink. The way he sucked at that thing was disgusting. If it had had a nipple on it, he would have looked like a greedy baby trying to suck. And if you're wondering, I have seen that. I remember going somewhere with my mother and seeing a lady nursing a young baby. So he was sucking away and doing his burbly chanting and wheezing shit, and I was driving very carefully. And when in a minute or two, I got to where the *chemin du Dépotoir* intersects the road to the village, I turned onto it. I was improvising.

The *chemin du Dépotoir* is the little road that goes to what used to be the official town dump. But most people at Lac Rouge just call it the Old Road because up until thirty years ago, that was the only road that connected to Lac Rouge. It is a very narrow, twisty road that snakes its way through rising woods on one side and a very long, steep ravine with no guardrails on the other. The ravine just drops into a bog when it's wet and into tangled underbrush when it's not. In the old days, in the winter and sometimes even at other seasons, people in cars sometimes plunged to their deaths if they made a mistake here. The road we use now and the new dump were built to stop this, so the only people who still use the old road are those who have stuff they want to get rid of quickly, easily, and illegally. Stefan hates that; he says that being an anarchist doesn't mean you can't also be a conservationist. He taught me winter-driving skills on that road, and when he did, he showed me a couple of places on the road where people just kind of backed up their trucks and shoved whatever was in there down the ravine. He was disgusted with this. When he showed me, I could see what looked like an old wood stove planted in the underbrush.

So I went to one of those unofficial drop-offs, but I didn't back up. I went in nose first and sat there for a minute to do what Stefan calls a reconnaissance. The snow was still falling, and it was still dark. I figured it was maybe nine or ten. Good. Most locals are in bed by then. I drove the car as close as I could get to the drop-off to the ravine. It was close. I put it in park, pulled the handbrake, turned the car off, and then looked over at Big Dude. He wasn't making any noise anymore, except the kind of hissing sound of his wheezing. I was pretty sure he was unconscious.

He was. That made my next task harder in some ways and easier in others, which didn't matter. Stefan always says, "You do what you gotta do," and I agree. I had to get the guy into the driver's seat. I pulled it way back to where it had been when I first got into the car. And then I had to pull the guy into the seat by leaning in from the driver's side. When I pulled at his parka, the top part of his body kind of collapsed toward the driver's side, lying over the big fancy console. I kneeled on the driver's seat and then lifted first his left and then his right leg into the driver's wheel. Then I pulled at his torso again. It was very hard work, but eventually, I succeeded. He was in the driver's seat, collapsed over the steering wheel. I figured that was okay.

I got my stuff out of the car and put it safely away from the action. Then I turned the car on. I had to put the guy's foot on the accelerator and push down on it hard to get it started. I put the car into gear and then tried to get it idling forward. Nope. So I had to do the stuff I've helped Stefan with so often with cars stuck in mud or snow; I found wood and underbrush to lie under the front wheels and then rocked the sucker. It took a while, and I was working so hard at pushing that I was almost dizzy, but eventually, the car came loose and started to move very slowly. It didn't have far to go, and, of course, I helped, pushing from the driver's door, which I had to keep open to make this happen. Big Dude was still completely out of it. The front wheels went over the edge, and the car kind of teetered for a second. I rocked it again, and then as it started to go, I slammed the driver's door. And just like that, very slowly, like in the movies, down it went.

In movies, they use slow motion throughout the whole fall. Not here. Once that heavy vehicle was truly over the edge, it gained speed, tearing through the trees and underbrush until it hit something that caused it to flip. I think it flipped three or four times before it got to the bottom. There was some pretty loud crashing until it stopped. And then, dead still, except for my tell-tale heart, which was booming so loud that I figured it could be heard back in Lac Rouge.

Once my heart and breathing calmed down, I did a thorough reconnaissance like Stefan taught me to do. I carefully inspected the site from several angles—from the top, mid-way down, and right from the bottom. It was yet another case of meant to be magic. The Caddy had landed top-side down, exactly in the middle of a huge patch of ice that I knew would become the bog once it thawed. When that happened in the spring, the car would sink, top-down, into the muck where it belonged. Right now, though, there was a ton of thick bushes you always see in marshland and bogs, growing out of the ice so thickly that even now, when I was looking for it, it was hard to make out the shape of the car. There was nothing glinty to catch whatever light there was or would be.

I stayed there for maybe an hour. It reminded me of what I did and how I felt after Jean-Luc went down—kind of shaky, but at the same time sort of flat, like whatever I should have been feeling was far away and unreachable. *Shit,* I thought. *I hope I don't get used to this.* I could almost hear Stefan's response to that in my head. "You do what you have to do. Doesn't mean you like it." Before I left, I used my binoculars while standing at the top. Between the snow, darkness, and distance, it was hard to see anything. I was looking for movement, but I didn't see any. In the time that I'd been waiting, the snow had already covered the car and tracks.

Before I put on my pack, I ate a couple of granola bars and drank some of my hot chocolate. It was only lukewarm but tasted very good. I figured I'd need energy for the trek back because my arms and legs felt very shaky.

But my body settled down once I got moving again. It was a challenging trek because, on both the old and new roads back to Lac Rouge, the woods on both sides of the road were steep. That meant I was always traveling on a side hill, which meant I had to use a fair bit of effort to avoid sliding. I did lots of switch-backs so that I wouldn't get sore from using only one side as my downhill side. The snow was soft and deep, and it was kind of fun, but it took a long time. Dawn was breaking by the time I got home.

The house was cold. I saw that Stefan was still sleeping in the chair where I'd left him. I didn't wake him up right away. I put my stuff away, put on the sweats I sleep in, and then I built a hot fire. I waited for the chill to come off the air, and then I put on water for coffee and hot chocolate, made a cup of each, and then took both to the living room. I gently shook Stefan and offered him the coffee. He smiled at me sleepily, and I felt a rush of some kind of sweet emotion for him. Stefan has a nice smile. "Thanks, son," he said. That was because he was still half-asleep. He rarely calls me son, just like I rarely call him Dad.

I told him I'd make breakfast, and he just kind of nodded while sipping his coffee. I like making breakfast for both of us, and I was hungry. I made pancakes, scrambled eggs, bacon, and lots of toast. I put it all on a platter that I put on the table and then went to get Stefan. He said it smelled great, and we sat down together and went at it. Anyone watching could have guessed that neither of us had dinner the night before, but neither of us mentioned that. We just ate and ate.

When I was so full I thought I'd burst, I made him another coffee and myself another hot chocolate and then sat down at the table with him again. "So, was this a celebration because you decided?" he asked me. I had no idea what he was talking about, but, of course, I didn't say that to him. Instead, I thought back to the conversation we had right before I left the house yesterday afternoon and realized he was talking about my birthday decision. That was the last thing he remembered, but to me, it felt like years had passed since then. I told him I had realized he was right. This was such an important decision that it made sense to take my time and review it many times and keep re-thinking it until I was completely certain. When I said that, he gave me that sleepy smile again and said, "I'm proud of you. It takes maturity to make a decision that way." Funny, I could sometimes tell that Stefan approved of stuff I did, but I think this was the first time he ever said he was proud of me.

23

CASS – AFTERSHOCKS

Cass and Noah missed most of the remainder of January at the cabin since they took a couple of weekends off because of Chuff. His movement had remained stiff and hobbled since his "fall" during Lori's visit. Back in Ottawa, Cass took him for a course of physiotherapy, religiously manipulated his limbs twice-daily at home, and took him to the closest aqua therapy facility twice a week. Chuff made good progress, but Cass didn't think he'd be ready to take on the rigors of deep snow for a few weeks. Plenty was going on in Ottawa during that period anyway.

Noah needed the time to tie up all the loose ends with his Calgary client, and by the end of the month, that relationship resumed its normal contours, with Noah happily ensconced in his home office once again and the revised software humming along nicely in Calgary. Meanwhile, Cass and her breeder had finally agreed on the best sire and dam for the upcoming litter, for which Cass would have the pick of the litter. The bitch went into heat in January, and the breeder felt that the mating had gone well and was likely to "take," meaning the mating would yield a pregnancy. It had taken place early in the month so that if all went well, puppies would be born around the end of February or the beginning of March, and the new Harwood puppy could be temperament-tested, chosen, and ready to go to the Harwood household in early May.

Cass followed her traditional Puppy Coming process by silently agonizing over her perceived upcoming infidelity to Chuff once the puppy arrived. She had gone through the same thing with each new puppy partner, feeling that she was betraying her established partner. She never resolved it, and she never let it stop her. She was a pro at handling self-imposed guilt and didn't let it intrude on her anticipation, which asserted itself most through the name game. Cass kept a list of dozens of options and combinations for the newcomer's registered and call names. Her practice over the years was to have this long list of options so that once the puppy arrived, they could quickly decide which name was most appropriate for that puppy. Since she and Noah liked to start teaching name recognition almost as soon as a puppy came home, she didn't like waiting more than a day or two before choosing the name.

She was also focused on further refining the program she'd developed for Chuff in the fall, before his big win. She had to be even more targeted and thoughtful with his training now because she didn't want to push Chuff to the point where he started to experience discomfort. She monitored carefully, hoping that the two of them could go into the ring together again. By mid-month, she felt that he'd be sufficiently recovered to return to both Lac Rouge and competition by the end of the month. And so she and Noah agreed they'd go back to the cabin at the end of January for a long weekend. It would be the first time Noah had been to Lac Rouge in the new year.

The dreams started as soon as they made that decision. Cass had been subject to sleep disturbances—nightmares, night terrors, and sleepwalking—throughout her childhood and early adult years. The older she got, the more infrequent they became. And when she met Noah, they just stopped. Secretly, Cass was embarrassed that it seemed that all she'd needed to get her psyche together was a good man. If that were true, it offended her feminist sensibilities. She never told anyone about these musings; this was another of those things too private to share.

When she was a kid and precociously reading Freudian dream theory, Cass was chagrinned by how transparent many of her nightmares were. There was one where a big boy in seventh grade bullied her. Her father appeared with a sword and cut the young man's legs off at the knees. Cass warily approached one of the severed legs and noticed something protruding from the severed limb. Reaching down, she extracted what appeared to be a blood-covered banana, which terminated in two small hanging plums. Upon awakening, the phallic imagery and vengeful emasculation were clear even to thirteen-year-old Cass, who subsequently never completely gave up her faith in Freudian interpretation even though she knew it had been largely discredited.

When she was a bit older, Cass discovered that she was a lucid dreamer, usually aware that she was dreaming and working to understand, interpret, and eventually alter her dreams even as they were unfolding. That was very much in play with the recurring nightmare that she experienced after the incident with Mike. In the dream, she was kayaking at Lac Rouge through the twisting stream where herons had flown above her and Lori during the preceding summer. She heard the lovely sound of the paddles churning through the water. As she approached the only deep spot in the black water, the water briefly churned, and then out of the water rose a man's bare hand and forearm—it was held aloft in a fist. No more water sounds. There was perfect stillness except for the steady drumbeat of a heart, at first slow and steady and then mounting in speed and volume until she was desperate to awaken herself, which she accomplished with a strangled scream.

Even as Noah shook her fully awake and soothed her, Cass was simultaneously shaken by the emotional impact of the dream, and acutely embarrassed by its lack of originality. Every fan of director John Boorman's movie version of the James Dickie classic *Deliverance* would recognize that arm rising out of the water as a cinematic icon of guilt. And then, just to whip it up, her subconscious had fed in an imagined soundtrack from *The Tell-Tale Heart.*

So to herself and herself only, Cass acknowledged that she felt guilty about the incident with Mike. It seemed to have worked out, thus validating the decisions taken. She was confident that if the story were ever to be told, it could be shaped to reveal sound reasoning. But even before the dreams started, she had felt a dark burden looming over her, like an invisible pendulum swinging ever-lower. Mike could have died, and out of a combination of loathing for him and unwillingness to deal with the consequences if the police became involved, she had initiated a course of action that now induced guilt—that exquisite emotion that she, a child of a Jewish upbringing she'd rejected, knew intimately.

Cass took action. First, she called Lori. Had she heard anything from or about Mike since her return? Lori reported that she had not but was not remotely surprised or upset about that. She had not expected to. They had no common social circle and no lingering ties or obligations. She was genuinely relieved that he was now out of her life, and she had started seeing someone new, about whom she was for the moment at least, enthused. If Lori was suffering any of the guilt-laden aftershocks that Cass was, she didn't allude to them.

So Cass, the accomplished lucid dreamer, took steps to alter the aftershocks. The second time she had the dream, as soon as the water started to churn, she followed the directions the lucid part of her gave: "Turn around! Now!" Dream Cass did. The next time the dream recurred, the voice intervened earlier, before the churn started, and the turnaround was successfully accomplished. And the time after that, no voice was required. As she paddled toward the twisting stream, Dream Cass decided to explore another part of the lake instead. Proud of her accomplishment, she told Noah about it without sharing her analysis of what the dream was about. As was typical under such circumstances, Noah looked at her blankly and said, "I don't get it." She hadn't expected him to; both had long accepted that some aspects of the other would never be understood but should be respected.

By the end of January, both Cass and Noah were feeling pleased with life and each other and were happy to return to the cabin. After their long absence, the snow was so deep that they decided to leave Chuff behind and snowshoe on the first day to set a foundation likely to be easier to ski and easier on Chuff on the second day. Though she kept looking for a flash of the orange backpack, Cass saw no sign of Xavier that day, though Zeke did an occasional alert-stop-and-scan. It could have been anything, though. Cass suspected there was carrion nearby. She had to relieve Zeke of a reasonably fresh deer hoof three times during that trek. He kept finding it again wherever she tried to stash it. He was very proud of himself. She eventually relegated it to the plastic bag in her pack reserved for such prizes.

Noah opted to stay at the cabin the next day while Cass skied, taking both Zeke and Chuff with her. It hadn't snowed the night before, and as she set out, she monitored Chuff carefully and felt he was doing well enough to withstand a foray to the back bush, following the route she and Noah had snowshoed flat the previous day. Shortly after she arrived at the trail that Noah, Yates, and Paul had created, which they had christened the Katrinka Bypass, the boys went on alert. Moments later, Zeke plunged into the woods, and watching the direction in which he was moving, Cass saw a flash of the orange backpack. Minutes later, Xavier and Zeke emerged back onto the trail together, and Cass had the now-familiar pleasure of watching Xavvy lope toward her on snowshoes.

He was coming fast, and Chuff surprised her by running out to greet him. At which point, Xavvy squatted on his snowshoes and threw his arms wide to receive him. When Cass caught up to them, Xavvy was still hugging Chuff, and Chuff was most uncharacteristically wriggling and tail wagging like a puppy as he sought to drive his face into the crook of the boy's shoulder. Cass didn't comment on it. She was getting used to the kid's mojo with dogs. It did not appear to have been limited to Katrinka. This canine mojo was part of Xavvy's appeal for Cass. She believed that it was an indicator of an innate relaxed authority that she found as attractive as dogs did.

Xavier, who was considerably faster on snowshoes than Cass was on skis, slowed down to accompany her on much of her trek. As in their previous encounter toward the end of Lori's visit, he invited and indeed initiated the kind of social small talk that had never been on the agenda before. Cass attributed it to what she perceived as his infatuation with Lori. He not only asked about Lori and if her trip back to Baltimore had been okay, but he also asked specifically, "Whatever happened to that big dude who was here with her last winter?"

"Oh, you saw him, did you? That was before we met, right?"

Xavier agreed and persisted, "So what happened to him? Is he still her boyfriend?" Cass responded that Lori had broken up with him and that she was glad—she hadn't liked him. "Neither did Chuffy," said Xavier. Cass, once again impressed with the astuteness of his observations, said, "Yeah, I can always trust Chuff's instincts." At that moment, Chuff was frisking next to Xavier like a puppy.

24

CASS – EARLY SPRING

It was a strange year at Lac Rouge. After what seemed like endless snow starting in early November, in early February, it just stopped, as though someone had pulled the plug—enough! There was already so much snow that, on cabin weekends, Cass could ski through early March. But because it was unseasonably warm, by then, the snow had turned soft and punky and unrewarding. By mid-month, it had receded into isolated patches only on hard-packed trails, and she was into the muddy hiking boots of Winter Receding. Uncharacteristically, it was a very short season, and for perhaps the second time in their long history at Lac Rouge, the Harwoods experienced a real spring, much more like those of Cass's childhood in Baltimore.

On a beautiful, warm spring day in early April, Noah accompanied Cass and the boys on what they had agreed would be a good long trek. Noah, who enjoyed trailblazing more than hiking, had mapped out a slightly different route originating from the Katrinka Bypass and took his compass and a small ax so that they could clear and mark it for the future if it proved pleasant. Cass enjoyed the rough stuff involved in setting a new trail and appreciated Noah taking the lead, given his considerably better navigation skills. So she followed him and kept an eye peeled for Xavvy, who she now encountered more often than not when she was by herself, and slightly less often when Noah accompanied her.

When they were well into their adventure, they both realized that Zeke had been out of sight for a while. Cass set to holler, and within a tolerable amount of time, they heard his bell coming toward them. When he emerged onto the trail in front of them, he was proudly displaying his new prize, which appeared to be a thoroughly yuck-encrusted snowmobile glove. Noah, who had been working on Zeke's retrieve, called, "Front!" and admonished him, saying, "Hold!" Then he said, "Give!" and Zeke—that very good boy—relinquished his prize as Noah reached for it, tentatively, given its rather sordid condition. "Good boy!" praised Noah, then looked down at what he held. "What the . . . ?" he remarked at first and then issued a garbled, "Aaargh!" of revulsion as he tossed the glove away. Before Zeke could go for it again, the usually quiet Noah roared, "Leave it! Stay!" and then turned to Cass, who was quickly approaching. "Cass," he said quietly, "I think there's a hand in that glove."

Cass Harwood's world twisted and whirled. "Are you sure?" she asked.

Noah, visibly pale, shrugged and suggested, "See what you think." With every fiber of her being resisting, Cass pulled on the plastic gloves she kept in her pack and picked up and inspected the tattered snowmobile glove. Inside lay a putrefied glop, but protruding from the top was the unmistakable remnant of a human wrist. She set it down very gently, as though it were fragile, and then turned away, gagging. The day had gone still except for the soundtrack from her recently vanquished nightmare: her own heart beating, progressively louder and faster. Could Noah not hear it?

Evidently, he could not. He came over to her, asking if she was okay. Even though she was visibly trembling and felt like all the blood in her body had whooshed into her feet so that if there were wind, she'd be doing the spastic dance of one of those inflatable advertising tube men, Cass nodded, then asked, "What now?"

The Harwoods quickly agreed that one of them needed to hoof it to Paul's place and enlist his aid in calling the *Sûreté du Québec*. The other needed to wait in situ, not touching that damned glove, to point investigators in the right direction when they showed up. Cass, who felt she'd shatter into atoms if she didn't get some movement to help ground her, volunteered to get Paul. She proposed taking the dogs with her so that they wouldn't intrude on things once the authorities arrived. But Noah suggested that Zeke, at least, might help lead searchers to where he'd made his find. And since Chuff had often displayed considerable brilliance in finding items as small as a favorite barrette of Cass's lost in the bush, they finally decided to leave both boys with Noah. Though they were seldom used in the bush, the Harwoods always carried leashes. To prevent the almost inevitable battles likely to ensue over the glove, both dogs were leashed and tethered to Noah before Cass left.

It took about an hour, walking at high speed, to make it to Paul's. During that time, still feeling light-headed and sick with dread, Cass reasoned with herself. Mike had left by car on the road. Even in the unlikely event that he exited his car and died, there was no way his body could have ended up where they found the hand in the back bush. She told herself that repeatedly. But lingering in her mind were echoes of the moose femur that kept reappearing randomly for years in a host of locations miles from where the moose died. Cass literally pinched herself and slapped her face to try to drive these thoughts away. All logic dictated that her terror was predicated far more on her nightmares than on any reasonable possibility that the orphaned hand was Mike's.

Once she got to Paul's, things unfolded quickly enough for a certain numbed calm to enfold her as Paul made the necessary calls and suggested that investigators might want to use ATVs to access the site where the hand had been found. Within an hour, an SQ truck, pulling a trailer with two ATVs, had arrived. The two officers followed Paul, with Cass behind him, to where Noah and the dogs waited. The Harwoods stood at a distance as the officers inspected the hand and then bagged it and placed it in what appeared to be an evidence box mounted on one of the ATVs.

One of the officers spoke good English and asked the Harwoods to show them where they thought Zeke had come from. Cass suggested that if she and Noah showed them where Zeke emerged from the woods, the officers might be able to follow his tracks. She knew damned well that Xavier would be able to, but even if she knew how to contact him, there was no way she wanted to get him involved in this mess. She suggested that if they took Zeke with them on leash and told him to find it, he might. To herself, she regretted that she'd never taken the time to register her boys in tracking classes, as so many of her friends had done. But despite that, she suspected that instinct might allow them to be helpful. Eventually, it was decided that Noah would accompany the officers on their search, with both Zeke and Chuff on leash.

Within forty-five minutes, Noah, the dogs, and one of the officers returned. Instructed to "Find It," at the bottom of a ravine, Chuff had located the remains of what appeared to be a hunter, clad in tattered camo, with a rifle next to him, and, of course, heavily scavenged by predators and thus totally unrecognizable. Noah told Cass one of the officers had asked him if he knew the man, and Noah had looked at him in disbelief. Whoever he was, the guy's own mother wouldn't have recognized him.

And Cass—happy, happy Cass! The dead guy was wearing camo! There was no way it was Mike! Now, she was light-headed with relief. She called upon her ability to calm herself and was confident that her glee was not evident when the SQ officer conferred with them after making several calls on his radio. He told them that a range of medical and investigative professionals would be showing up shortly and that they could leave if they wished to. After the Harwoods provided their contact information for both the cabin and Ottawa, Cass, Noah, and the dogs started for home. Curious to see the proceedings, Paul opted to stick around and watch from a distance, which the officer said he could do.

The Harwoods spent a schizophrenic evening, with Noah pale and quiet, and Cass doing everything she could to repress her relief-based glee. So both lay in bed that night, unable to sleep for very different reasons. Cass finally confided to Noah that as soon as the hand appeared, she'd been close to panic, thinking it might be Mike's. Having never realized the freight of guilt she'd been carrying, Noah was empathetic, with a slight undertone of derision. "When Mike left, he was well enough to drive his car. There is no way that he'd leave the car and then, for some unknown reason, crawl back to die in the bush." A covert part of Cass celebrated how closely his logic followed the lines she had tried to impose on herself with only partial success. She admitted to Noah that her dream of the hand rising, coupled with the recovery of a hand, had thoroughly spooked her. This evoked more soothing, laced with loving derision. Sleep crept into the Harwood household.

The next morning, they called Paul to see what intelligence he might have gathered at the discovery site. They were confident that there would be some. Paul, the gentle giant, had an unparalleled ability to schmooze in both official languages. He told them that while they were still in situ, the SQ officers had contacted their home base, to discover that there were no reports of missing white males—most probably hunters—in the area. The SQ would be working the case together with conservation officers, which evidently was a standard drill in investigating what might be a hunting fatality. But first and foremost, they needed to try to identify the guy, which could be a lengthy process unless there was enough left of him to get fingerprints and DNA, and even then, only if either his fingerprints or DNA were on file.

The morning after that, Paul called them as they were getting ready to return to Ottawa to tell them that he'd dropped into the auberge the night before to scope things out. He found that the discovery of the body was, of course, somehow known at the auberge. Everything found its way there, though no one professed to know how such "information" made its way into the rumor mill. Everyone was very eager to talk to Paul since he had been on the scene. No one had any idea who the hunter was. Most of the men at the auberge hunted in pairs or groups, and all their members were accounted for. But all the men with hunting licenses expected to be contacted. Evidently, that was standard procedure for any death that might be a hunting accident. Paul had mixed feelings about not having hunted this year. They all thought it would be interesting to be questioned.

And so, back to Ottawa, where Cass's interior glee was diminished by the reality of Chuff's aging. Given the rigors of the preceding weekend, she kept his training that week to a minimum, hopefully just enough to tweak his precision for the trials in which he was entered the upcoming weekend. And she and Chuff performed well there, but not as well as her friend Christianne, who won the High in Trial after taking first place in the Open class, competing against Cass and Chuff, and Noah and Zeke. Noah and Zeke nailed second place, leaving Cass and Chuff in third place. It was not the third-place finish, which she thought was entirely fair and correct, that drove Cass's decision-making. It was the fatigue she saw in Chuff on the Sunday evening after the two-day event was over. Though the idea of no longer competing with him saddened her terribly, it had been a long time coming. She would continue to train with Chuff for the pure joy of it for them both, but his competitive career was over.

Probably because of this decision, Cass found herself spending ever more time on the online puppy cam. The breeding for which she had the pick of the litter had indeed "taken," and the puppies had been born in March—five boys, three girls. Now four weeks old, the pups' eyes were open, and they were toddling about in the enhanced learning environment their breeder created for them. Each pup had a different colored collar, so Cass could identify them while watching them interact with each other and with the sensory and cognitive challenges like plastic bottles, mobiles, bird-wings, tiny ramps, and tunnels the breeder placed in their environment. There was one little boy Cass was mainly focused on, but she knew how much puppies change during the first eight weeks of life. At five weeks of age, Chuff hadn't been one of her top picks, and three weeks later, he was the standout. Nevertheless, as she played with her list of names, little Purple Collar was very much on her mind.

She was on the puppy cam when the phone rang on a Wednesday night. It was a representative of the *Sûreté du Québec*. She told Cass that officers investigating the death of the body found in the bush near Lac Rouge wanted to interview both Cass and Noah. Neither surprised nor worried about this, Cass immediately assented. Since she and Noah were headed to the cabin the next day and the investigators were doing other interviews in the area, it was agreed that an investigative team would come to the Harwood cabin on Friday morning.

Two officers showed up that morning—a female conservation officer and a male officer from the SQ. Both spoke fluent English and were extremely polite. After greeting the dogs and accepting a cup of coffee, they said they'd like to interview each of the Harwoods separately. Cass and Noah exchanged surprised looks but immediately agreed. Cass, eager to get on with it, suggested that she go first and that Noah take the dogs and retire to the gazebo until it was his turn. Suggestion accepted.

The first thing the officers told Cass was that the body had been identified a few days ago. "The body was that of Jean-Luc Tessier," the conservation officer said. It was clear that both officers were watching Cass's reaction very closely. She was so surprised that her response was totally unguarded. She kind of recoiled in her chair while exclaiming, "Jean-Luc? Really?" Yes, really, they assured her. Long a fan of crime documentaries, Cass immediately asked how he'd been identified and was told that Mr. Tessier had a criminal record, and thus his fingerprints were on file. Cass assumed that the hand that remained on the body was less putrefied than the foul mess she'd seen in the glove.

"You knew Mr. Tessier, didn't you?" Cass was asked. From this, Cass assumed that they were already acquainted with the Katrinka incident, either from previous interviews or conservation records. She saw no reason to dissemble and was completely honest with them about their minimal interactions with Jean-Luc before the incident and the total absence afterward. She told them about the message he'd sent them through Paul and the efforts they'd subsequently taken to avoid the Tessier property. She also told them about how she and Noah found the large field of marijuana not all that far from Jean-Luc's place. She stressed that they had no idea if it was in any way connected to Jean-Luc.

The officers asked Cass if either of the Harwoods had any firearms and if they hunted. They did not appear surprised to get a negative response to both of those questions. Cass figured it was obvious to them that the Harwoods had grown up urban and still retained much of that identity, despite the amount of time they spent at Lac Rouge.

There were only two questions that Cass found troubling. "*Madame* Harwood," said the SQ officer, "don't you think it is a pretty major coincidence that you had trouble with Mr. Tessier over the death of your dog and that it was also you who found his body?" Cass responded truthfully that if it was a coincidence, it was a very minor one. She probably spent more time in the bush in that area than anyone else in the Lac Rouge community, and she didn't find the body—her dogs did and brought it to her attention. The second question, the only one where she was not fulsome in her disclosure, was their query about whether she knew of anyone else that knew Mr. Tessier. She had already told them about Paul's interaction with him, and thus, of course, identified him in response to their question. For reasons she didn't quite understand, she did not mention Xavier. She figured if Noah did and they came back to her on that, she'd just say she'd forgotten. After all, he was just a kid. But she was surprised by how protective she felt about Xavier and how fiercely she hoped that Noah would also fail to mention Xavier if asked the same question.

There was no opportunity to consult with him. One of the officers escorted her to the gazebo and escorted Noah back to the cabin, preventing any conversation between them in the process. Cass, unaccountably nervous now, took the boys down to the beach. Even though the ice had just recently receded and still hovered in chunks and floes much further out on the lake, their bay was clear, and the boys were delighted to retrieve the bumpers—large plastic retrieving items—she threw for them. When Noah called her to rejoin them, she did so after confining the wet dogs to the sunny deck. She was still nervous but well-controlled. The officers had only one final question, which they asked them together. Could they account for their whereabouts during a specific one week period in November? Both Harwoods assumed this was the period during which it was likely that Jean-Luc had died. She asked the officers to wait while she retrieved her agenda. She was able to show the officers that they had been at dog events and coaching in Ottawa throughout the period. Yes, multiple people could confirm that. They provided names and phone numbers.

She was somewhat relieved when the officers left without any further questions. She was fully relieved when she and Noah compared notes and discovered that he also had failed to mention Xavier. In his case, he had forgotten or perhaps never even knew that the kid had done odd jobs for Jean-Luc. Cass couldn't remember if she'd told him or not. In any case, Noah agreed that mentioning Xavier was unnecessary. They did, however, give Paul a call to tell him to expect to be interviewed.

The next morning brought interesting revelations from Paul, who had spent the preceding evening at the auberge after moving again into information-gathering mode. The locals had figured out that the body found was Jean-Luc's or that he was somehow involved since investigative teams had been observed conducting what appeared to be extensive searches at the Tessier place. Officers were seen hauling large black plastic garbage bags from the utility building to waiting vans and then adding multiple computers from both the utility building and the house. This was even before Jean-Luc's brother showed up a few days ago, and the interviews of hunters had started.

Baptiste Tessier, Jean-Luc's younger brother, had still been there at the auberge. Paul was introduced to him and picked up his tab for the remainder of the evening. He learned from the dry-eyed Baptiste that he and the rest of the very small Tessier clan in Val d'Or had not been surprised to hear that Jean-Luc, who had been estranged from the family and who had been in and out of trouble since his teens, had met an untimely end. They had been considerably more surprised to learn that Jean-Luc owned property at Lac Rouge and that he'd had a will and left that property to Baptiste. He had traveled there to see what kind of property was now his and help in the investigation if he could.

He had been interviewed the preceding day but felt he'd been unable to provide any meaningful information since Jean-Luc was a good fifteen years older than he and had been estranged from the family and in and out of prison for most of Baptiste's life. But his knowledge of why Jean-Luc had been imprisoned in the past strengthened suspicions about the activity locals had observed at the Tessier place. Jean-Luc had been convicted in the past both of trafficking in marijuana and child porn. Well into the evening, when he had perhaps a bit too much to drink, Baptiste confided to Paul that as a child, he'd never been comfortable with the attention his older brother paid him on the rare occasions they had been together.

Having found the marijuana field with Noah and having seen disturbing pictures Jean-Luc took of Xavier, Cass was unsurprised by these revelations. No longer plagued by lingering guilt, she simply felt unclean after hearing what Paul told them. She needed to move. She abruptly announced that she was going for a hike, quickly called Zeke and Chuff, and took off, leaving the two Harwood men contentedly sipping coffee together. She hoped she'd encounter Xavvy.

25

XAVIER – JANUARY THROUGH APRIL

After a pretty busy and scary couple of months, starting with hunting season and going through until the time right after New Year's when Cass and Lori left, the next couple of months were quiet. I was glad. I felt like I had handled the scary stuff well and that my improvising skills were getting much better with practice, but I was happy to just kind of get back to normal. It happened gradually. There were still a couple of anxious times for me in January, but things calmed down after that.

Most of the anxious stuff in January was because of Chuff. Lori's guy was big, and he threw Chuff long and hard on that night. For days and even weeks after that, out of the blue, I'd suddenly see brave old Chuffy flying through the air and hitting that woodpile, and each time, I felt kind of sick and dizzy. But you know what? I realized after a while that it wasn't always "out of the blue." It was most likely to happen when Stefan got back from the auberge, where he'd had a few drinks. For some reason, that smell seemed to suddenly bring the picture of Chuff flying through the air into my mind. Or my eyes—I don't know which. What I was seeing felt very real, as though it was happening right then.

I think something Cass taught me when I helped her when she was training is probably what was going on. She told me that if a dog does a certain thing, say, like sitting when you tell him to, and that as soon as he does it, you give him a cookie, after a while when you tell him to sit, he's thinking "cookie coming" and is really glad to do it. Cass said that the dog "associates" the command with the cookie. I think maybe because it was such a scary night and scary sight to see Chuff in the air like that, that I started to "associate" the way the big guy smelled with what happened to Chuff. And not in a good "cookies coming" kind of way. If this doesn't stop, I figure I won't ever drink when I grow up. Stefan drinks every now and then, but he is not what they call a problem drinker on television. I guess I never will be either, which is good. But when I'm grown, I'd still like to be able to have a drink now and then like a regular guy.

Throughout this period, I felt kind of twitchy and uneasy. It was like constantly waking up and wanting to remember a dream that feels so close but then slips away. It was like a constant itch that I wanted to scratch but couldn't reach. I figured it was because I was so worried about Chuff. I could see, even the night that everything happened, that Cass, Lori, and Zeke were okay. But I didn't see Chuff again for a long time. I saw Cass and Lori skiing with Zeke before Lori left. But Chuff wasn't with them. They told me he was fine, but I wasn't sure I believed them. I don't remember much about my mother, but I remember that she tried to stop me from knowing about stuff she thought would make me sad. I think that's why she didn't tell me she was going to leave. Anyway, I figured maybe that's the way most women are and that Cass and Lori might not have been telling me the truth when they said Chuff was okay.

It was a couple of weeks before the Harwoods came back again, and once I realized they were back, I tracked them as they snowshoed through the back bush. Zeke was with them, but Chuff wasn't. I felt like crying. He wasn't like Katrinka, who had accepted me right away, kind of like a brother. Chuff wasn't like a brother. He was funny and brave and loved Cass like crazy, and he knew I'd try to take care of her, so we got along well, kind of like we were both soldiers. But in Chuff's mind, he was the captain. So when I didn't see him that day, I was afraid. I tracked Cass the next day when she was skiing without Noah, and I could see right away that both Zeke and Chuff were with her. Chuff was kind of dancing and grinning up at her like he always does.

I was so happy to see him that it felt like my heart was exploding out of my chest, but in a good way, not like the tell-tale heart. Or a different kind of tell-tale heart—one that beats loud because of happiness instead of guilt. I sort of ran up to them and hugged him, and he was just as happy to see me. I was happy not just about Chuff but also that Noah wasn't there because I figured I could ask Cass some stuff about Lori to kind of sniff around to see if she had anything to say about Lori's Big Dude having been there. All she said was that she didn't like that guy and was glad that Lori had broken up with him.

So that was all pretty good, except that after we had that little conversation, I realized I had not done a very good job of keeping my thoughts and feelings secret like Stefan taught me, and which I usually do really well. You know why I behaved that way that day. But I figured I kind of got away with it with Cass because I know she thought I was sort of in love with Lori. Stefan calls that "infatuation." He thinks I'm infatuated with Cass. I don't think I am; I think we are friends. That's why I did all the stuff I did. Stefan says you do everything for your family and friends. He is my family, and Cass is my friend. Lori might be a friend, but I admit that I am kind of infatuated with her, and I suspected Cass knew it and would think I was acting differently than I usually do because of that.

So those meetings in January were the last anxious moments for me for a while. Back at home, I finished reading all the short stories by Mr. Edgar Allen Poe. I liked them all but thought that it might be nice if at least a few of his storytellers were less . . . excitable. Stefan and I agreed that none of those guys would make much of a hunter. I knew that Mr. Poe had addiction problems and figured that was probably part of why everyone in his stories seemed so nervous. Meanwhile, the snow continued coming down forever and ever through early February, and the skiing and snowshoeing remained good all month. I "ran into" Cass and both dogs often on the weekends, and I'm sure she knew I wasn't trying to stay hidden the same way I used to. But that's the way it's supposed to be with friends, right?

In February, the big deal for me was that I finally finished the pros and cons list for my birthday present. A crossbow or a dog? I wanted both, so it was a tough decision, and I put a lot of thought into it. Stefan saw me working on my lists sometimes, but he didn't intrude; he just let me go about my "independent analysis" on my own. He'd been a lot more patient since he saw the new doctor. He was better about doing his exercises than ever before, and it seemed like that made a difference. He was hardly ever mean anymore. I'd always known that he was most likely to get that way when he was hurting. The only thing he said to me about my analysis was that I should try to come to a decision during February since it would take a while to get my present in time for my birthday in April.

So, in late-February, I told him I'd made my decision. He suggested we'd talk about it at our next lesson and use that to help us explore what he called "a logical argument." He explained that didn't mean we would fight about it, but that "argument" also implies a kind of logical case you build to support a decision. So that's what we did.

First, he asked me what my decision was, and I told him. Then he asked if he could see my pros and cons for each possibility. He called that an "option." After I gave him my lists, and he looked at them for a while, he said I had done a very good "options analysis." He asked me some questions about both pros and cons on each list and said I'd done a good job of thinking through all of them. He said he thought there was only one thing I should consider for both options that I hadn't listed. He called it the "learning curve," and explained that any time you start a new activity, you need to learn about it. For some things, that takes a lot of time and effort at the beginning. To help me understand, he drew it on a graph and showed me what's called a steep learning curve. Then he drew a couple of other graphs and explained that a learning curve can be steep and long, or steep and short, or gradual and long, or gradual and short, or any kind of shape in between those four patterns.

Stefan said that I would need to consider what I would do with my gift to figure out what kind of learning curve I would have. He asked if I thought that this gift would change the kind of hunting I do. I said I thought it would. So together, we worked out what the learning curve might be for each option. As it turned out, it was the same for both, so it didn't change my decision at all. Stefan told me that he didn't have any skills with either of my options but that he'd get us some books, and we'd figure it out together. I was fine with that.

As we finished our lesson, which I thought was a very fun one, Stefan reminded me that it would take a while to locate the right supplier for my gift. And he said that it was too personal for him to get for me because the "fit" had to be just right. So he said he'd get me some books and catalogs to look at and that we'd actually do some visits to maybe Gatineau, Montreal, or Ottawa to choose our supplier and make our purchase. This was unusual, and I admit, a bit exciting for me. I hardly ever went anywhere outside of Lac Rouge. I hoped wherever we went, we'd stop at a fast-food place. Once when I had a toothache, Stefan had taken me to a dentist in Gatineau, and on the way home, when the pain was gone, we stopped at a place called A&W and got hamburgers, fries, and milkshakes. It was delicious, even though I had to eat on only one side of my mouth.

So that was kind of a big deal for me during March. I looked over the books and catalogs and learned from them about the sort of stuff I should think about before we made our purchase. I wrote my questions down and gave them to Stefan, and he told me he'd phone different suppliers to ask my questions. I was okay with that because I don't know how to talk on the phone; I've never been allowed to. That's one of those things I know I'll have to learn if I'm ever going to be a real adult, and I hope it won't be a steep learning curve. But for this project, I was fine with Stefan making the phone calls. I don't know when he did it. I never heard it happening, so I guess he did it after I was asleep or when I was out observing. But we ended up making a couple of trips together, usually during the weekends. And we did stop at the A&W restaurant again, which was great. Because of the trips, I only saw Cass, or Cass and Noah, a couple of times during that period. I arranged things so that it still looked kind of like the old days when I was very cautious in meeting up with them because I wanted Cass to think the reason I'd been different in January was just because of Lori.

By the end of March, the snow was gone and anyone spending time in the bush was doing it on foot. Since it had snowed so much during hunting season, it was the first time that anyone, including me, the Harwoods, and their dogs, was back to walking through the back bush. I had a little background itching going on as I kept wondering if the spring would bring anyone an unpleasant surprise back there, so I wasn't all that surprised when I stepped into the kitchen one afternoon in April, and Stefan handed me a hot chocolate.

He asked me if I knew what *"déjà-vu"* meant. Of course, I speak French and understand what the words mean. But he explained that as a phrase, it described a new situation that feels like an old one—like you've been there before. He said, "Remember last year when I told you that Mrs. Harwood had some trouble way back in the bush and that her dog died?" I took a big sip of hot chocolate to cover the fact that I started holding my breath as soon as he said that. I knew he'd see that pretty quickly, so I let my breath out as if I was blowing on my chocolate to cool it. I told him that, of course, I remembered that. And then he told me that something sort of like that had happened again. He said that Cass's dogs had found a human hand and that the police had been out there and found the body. "Wow!" I said. "Who was it?"

I was sure that was a logical question and that I had asked it in a pretty casual way. But Stefan paused, and he looked at me in a different way than I ever remember him doing before. His eyes were kind of narrow, and you could see he was thinking stuff he wasn't saying. He looked the way he does when we're in the woods, and he hears something he's not sure about and is trying to figure out if we're safe to keep going.

Or maybe he didn't look that way. I used to trust my instincts and didn't have doubts about them. Stefan calls those kinds of doubts "second-guessing yourself," and I never did it until I started worrying about getting caught. Since then, though, I've been much less certain about trusting my instincts. I don't know if this is what guilt feels like. It, for sure, isn't as dramatic as the stuff Mr. Poe writes about. But for me, this new kind of uncertainty is not nice. It itches.

So, I think Stefan gave me a strange look, but I'm not sure. All he said afterward was that as far as he knew, no one yet knew who the dead guy was. He promised to let me know as soon as he heard more. And he did. It was maybe a week later, on a Saturday morning after he'd been to the auberge the night before that he told me the body had been identified, and that it was Jean-Luc.

I'd figured that this was coming and had been getting ready for it. It was time for some acting, and I'd kind of rehearsed in my mind how I thought I should play it. So I followed my script. We were both standing in the kitchen, finishing up the dishes, when he told me. I stopped drying and stood completely still. "Really?

Jean-Luc?" I asked, as I kind of dropped, heavy, as though my legs were weak with shock, onto a kitchen chair.

"Yes, really," Stefan said. He sat down with me and started with the questions. And the whole time, he was giving me the same sort of Alarm Show look I'd seen on his face earlier when he first told me about the discovery of the hand.

He asked when I last saw Jean-Luc, and I told him it was in early November. He asked why I hadn't seen him since then. I told him I didn't think he'd been around very much, and I'd kind of gone cold on him anyway. Which, of course, led him to ask about why that was. So I told him about the guy being lazy, which was okay for me because that's why there was work for me to do. But I said there was something creepy about the way he acted with me. I told him about the way he'd just take my picture without asking if he could use my camera. And about the way he'd traced my sweat and then sucked his finger. I made it sound like that happened on the last day I saw him in November.

That worked; I'd known it would. Even though Stefan is excellent at hiding his feelings, I watched his hands and saw them tighten into fists for a second so that his knuckles went white. I saw him take a deep breath and then release it while relaxing his hand and kind of loosening his whole body before he said anything else. Then he asked how I'd handled that, and I told him that I just kept my distance that day and decided to not work for him anymore. And that I hadn't seen him since then.

Stefan told me I'd done the right thing about trusting my instincts and not second-guessing myself. He said that the word at the auberge was that Jean-Luc had spent time in prison for drug trafficking and child porn. We both looked at each other for a minute, and then I shrugged and said, "Well, I guess I'm not too surprised to hear that."

Stefan told me that a team of police and conservation officers had started interviewing locals who either knew Tessier or who had hunting licenses. That was because Jean-Luc wasn't wearing a hunting vest, so it looked likely that he'd been killed accidentally by another hunter. But because of his record, they thought it might have been something else, like an intentional killing, not an accident. Like murder. "So," he said, "turns out to be a good thing that we didn't have hunting licenses this year, so we won't be interviewed. Unless anyone else knows that you knew the guy." He looked directly at me and asked, "Does anyone else know that you knew Tessier?" I looked directly back at him and told him that no one had ever seen us together, that I hadn't told anyone, and that I was sure Jean-Luc wouldn't have either because he was a very secretive guy.

And then Stefan told me that Paul Harwood, Cass's nephew, had also been at the auberge last night, and he'd said that Cass and Noah had been interviewed because they found the hand. And again, he looked directly into my eyes before he asked, "So you never told Mrs. Harwood that you knew Jean-Luc?"

I was kind of amazed because this was exactly what I had thought he'd say when I worked on my script in my head. But I was ready. I knew what to say and what to do. I was casual but put a tiny note of irritation into my voice, "Of course, not," I answered. "Why would I do that? She might be kind of emotional about it because of what happened to Katrinka. I didn't need that, so I just kept that to myself. Just like I keep everything else to myself like you've taught me to do." He gave me a long look, then he said that he was glad I still followed our family practice of saying little, which is part of the good anarchist tradition of avoiding any kind of government business or inquiries.

As you know, I have some secrets from Stefan, but I don't usually lie to him. But this time, I felt certain I had to—no second-guessing. I did not want Stefan to know that Cass knew that I'd spent time with Jean-Luc. I did not think about why I felt this way; I just respected it. At the same time, I was itching, itching, itching to find Cass and somehow, find out if she had said anything about me when she was interviewed. I was glad that it was a weekend and that I knew the Harwoods were around. Stefan went off to do some anarchist writing, and I told him I was going out to do some observations. Because I'd felt bad about scripting stuff and acting with Cass in the past, I decided to just improvise when I caught up with her.

26

CASS - APRIL MEETING IN THE BACK BUSH

Exercise always soothed Cass when she was unsettled, and that's how she was feeling after Paul's debriefing. As she eased into her usual ground-eating lope, she quickly decided that she and her boys were ready for a trek west into the back bush, where she was always more likely to encounter Xavier than on the east side. She still didn't know exactly how he tracked them, but she was confident he could find her any time he wanted to. Given Paul's report about how widespread was the knowledge that the remains found were those of Jean-Luc, she thought it likely that Xavier already knew about that. However, she didn't know whether that was likely to cause him to seek her out or avoid her.

But she put that aside. Xavvy would either find her or he wouldn't—it was up to him. Since there was nothing she could do about it one way or the other, it made sense to just give herself up to that rarest of experiences at Lac Rouge: warm sunshine and gentle breezes that usually didn't arrive until late May or early June when those charms were accompanied by heavy insect assaults and thickly-growing new underbrush. But this glorious day was too early in the year for that. She paused in a field to throw her head back, suck in the sun and the breeze, and for just a few minutes, immerse herself in the glory of a real spring, like a memory of childhood.

She took the Katrinka Bypass and was only a few minutes into one of her favorite trails when she saw Chuff and Zeke doing their curious routine: halt, heads up, ears swiveling, noses twitching. She scanned the bush in the direction that seemed to have their interest but failed to see the glimpse of orange she sought. She continued, and the next canine alert, about ten minutes later, seemed to be directed to the bush on the other side of the trail. And this time, Cass found the flash of the orange backpack that she'd hoped for. She waved and moved toward Xavier as he emerged from the woods, and both Zeke and Chuff frolicked forward to greet him. She and Xavier greeted one another casually, as was their habit.

Except when Lori was around, small talk was not a big part of Cass and Xavier's interactions. Both were comfortable without conversation unless there was something that needed to be said. Evidently, this time, there was, because—unprecedented—they both started to speak at the same time, with Cass saying, "Did you hear . . ." at the same time Xavvy said, "I heard that . . ." They both laughed, and Cass then took the lead.

"I guess you heard that Zeke found a human hand back there," she said, gesturing in the general direction, "a couple of weeks ago, and that the police found the dead guy it belonged to?" Xavier nodded. "Did you hear who it was?" she asked him.

He replied simply, "I heard it was Jean-Luc." Cass confirmed that and then told him that because she and Noah had found the hand, they had been interviewed by investigators yesterday.

"I've seen lots of those kinds of interviews on TV. Was it like that?" Xavier asked.

Cass responded that it was a lot more polite than most police interviews she'd seen on television.

Cass didn't want Xavier to recognize how focused she was on getting to the pivotal question about whether she knew anyone who knew Jean-Luc. She had already decided that the best way to impart that critical information was to bury it in a morass of detail, confident that if indeed that key piece of intelligence was important to clever Xavvy, he'd pick it out of the verbal slop around it. So she described the whole of the interview process for him—how she and Noah were separated, the questions she was asked, and how she answered them. Everything she recounted was factual, including that when she'd been asked about whether she knew anyone who knew Jean-Luc, she'd told them that her nephew Paul did. She didn't pause at that point in her account, but she made direct eye contact with the boy, who simply nodded. Without breaking conversational stride, Cass continued recounting the little that was left to tell about her interview.

Xavier asked only the kinds of questions a curious kid raised on television would. "Were they men or women? Did they speak good English? What were they wearing? Did they have guns? Were you nervous?" If he was dissembling, Cass couldn't see it. There was no hint of self-interest in his questions. She felt like an ass for having thought there might be an issue. But she was okay feeling like an ass and remained comfortable with and glad of her omission during the interview.

Xavier asked if she and Noah had compared notes on their interviews. She told him they had and discovered that they'd both responded in the same way. She thought it possible that there was a tiny millisecond "tell" at that point, that she saw a sigh that maybe looked like relief before Xavier converted it into a reasonably convincing response to the heat of the day, which caused him to grab a water bottle from his pack and take a long drink.

They continued together for quite a while. Cass told Xavier that she'd retired Chuff, and the kid was immediately concerned. "Won't that be hard for both of you?" he asked. Cass explained that she'd continue to train with Chuff, since training, far more than competition, was the foundation of their relationship. And since Noah and Zeke would keep competing, she and Chuff would be able to schmooze and have a different kind of fun at competitions, which she was looking forward to. And she told him that she and Noah would be bringing a new puppy into their household in a few weeks. "Really? Really?" Xavier exclaimed.

She suggested that Xavvy keep an eye on her training area in May, where he'd be most likely to meet the newcomer. "I will," Xavier promised as they parted paths as they usually did, at the start of the Katrinka Bypass.

27

CASS - EARLY MAY

Back in Ottawa, Cass became increasingly focused on the sweet anticipation and apprehension of Puppy Coming. Chuff was the source of her apprehension as she anticipated his reaction to a newcomer claiming much of her attention. Of course, he had been through this before with both Zeke and Katrinka, and he'd weathered those storms beautifully. But it wasn't Chuff's past or projected behavior that drove Cass's feelings; it was her discomfort with what she felt was her impending infidelity to him. Noah patiently and frequently pointed out that this was irrational. While Cass recognized the logic of his perspective, it was a relatively meager offset to her guilt-laden inner life.

But never mind. She'd been here before and did not allow apprehension to trump anticipation. When she and Noah arrived to observe the temperament testing of the litter, Cass was already sure, based on her puppy cam observations, that her choice would be Purple Collar. But once all the puppies had been tested, the breeder, the testers, and the Harwoods all agreed that both Purple Collar and Red Collar seemed equally well-suited to Cass's priorities. And so, the *pièce de résistance*. Everyone else retreated, and Cass was brought first one puppy, and then the other. She took as long as she felt she needed to play, cuddle, challenge, and observe each puppy. And in the end, Red Collar was her choice. The little dude projected an intense interest in her, coupled with a kind of stalwart cheerfulness, joyful confidence laced with assertion but devoid of aggression that simply made her happy and made her laugh. More than any other quality, Cass valued a dog that made her laugh.

So Red Collar went home with the Harwoods, tucked into Cass's sweatshirt, where he snoozed with his head nestled into her shoulder as Cass and Noah squabbled about names. All part of the Puppy Process. They knew it would somehow be amicably decided within a few days. And it was. As both watched the pup's introduction and speedy assimilation into their household, it was the little dude's sunny confidence, focus, curiosity, and cheerful acceptance of the mild admonishments his curiosity sometimes occasioned that impressed them most. Cass found herself singing bits and pieces of *Like A Rock*, a Bob Seeger classic, to the puppy, because she thought the brave resolve of the boy in the song so resembled what she saw in the puppy in front of her.

And so Red Collar was christened Trigold's Like a Rock. He spent his first two weeks with the Harwoods in Ottawa. The only uncomfortable aspect of those weeks was the process of the puppy and Chuff establishing a relationship. Chuff was cordial but completely devoid of interest in the avid advances of the pup, who had very quickly developed a giant case of hero worship for the household's senior dog. Each time he was approached by the newcomer, Chuff would turn his head away and adamantly refuse to acknowledge the approach. When the determined puppy would try to settle next to him, Chuff would simply walk away, leaving the little dude crestfallen, his chin on his front paws as he plotted his next attempt, which generally was exactly like his previous efforts. He was persistent but not creative.

Until the day that he realized a deep sleep might be his friend. He waited until Chuff was fast asleep and then silently crept toward him until he was furtively nestled between the older dog's chin and chest. At which point, Chuff awoke and absent-mindedly licked the puppy's face.

The puppy froze, as though he was momentarily incapable of responding to this piece of good fortune. And then he exploded, running madly throughout the house, literally bouncing off the walls in his glee. "He likes me! He really likes me!" From that point on, Chuff's tolerance quickly evolved into a far more intimate relationship than any he'd had with other dogs in the past. One of Cass's favorite photographs of that period showed Chuff sitting up proudly, with the pup in an identical posture between Chuff's front feet.

Shortly after this, the Harwoods decided it was time to introduce the newcomer to Lac Rouge. He handled the trip well, crying only briefly tucked into his crate in the back of the van. Once they arrived, he showed the cheerful resilience the Harwoods had already come to expect of him as he got his first introduction to the cabin, and in very small doses, the woods and lake. He thought that sitting on Cass's lap in the gazebo and watching hummingbirds bomb the feeders might just be the most fun ever. He emitted high-pitched yips of excitement, and his little body trembled with his desire to fly up and frolic with the peripatetic birds. Cass fell ever more deeply in love.

For a Golden puppy, the fun never ends. Guests! The pup had already met several of the Harwoods' friends, students, and neighbors and had shown the typical Golden affinity for humans. But when Yates arrived to spend a long weekend at the cabin, it was the pup's first prolonged exposure to another human. And Yates had always had very big canine mojo. He was probably Chuff and Zeke's favorite human, other than Cass, Noah, and Lori. As expected, the bond between Yates and the newcomer was already well-established by the time Paul dropped by for coffee that evening.

Paul had news. He'd been interviewed by the same officers who met with Cass and Noah and had little to add to their story. Before the Katrinka incident, he'd known who Jean-Luc was but hadn't met him. His description of his one interaction with the man when he visited him after Katrinka's death was in complete accord with what Cass and Noah had said. Paul described his interview as brief, cordial, and disappointing in that he'd been unable to extract any meaningful information about the progress of the investigation from the officers, despite his formidable best efforts.

However, that was not the case of his intelligence-gathering forays to the auberge while Cass and Noah had been away. The continuing speculation and surmise from the auberge regulars had been well-confirmed the previous evening when Baptiste Tessier reappeared and, once again, gladly accepted Paul's largesse. He said that investigators had told him that though they'd explored the small group of Jean-Luc's criminal cohort in Val-d'Or, they had found no one whom they considered to be a viable suspect in his death. So the conclusion they'd reached was that Tessier was the victim of a hunting accident. Though they had conducted an extensive investigation of local hunters, they could not identify any suspect in this accident. They told Baptiste that while the investigation was not yet considered closed, it had gone inactive and that he could proceed to make whatever arrangements he wanted with the property left to him by his brother.

So the mystery of who killed Jean-Luc Tessier remained, but it was of only incidental interest in the Harwood household. A bit ashamed at her insensitivity, Cass simply found herself relieved at no longer feeling compelled to conduct obsessive scans of the Tessier property as they made their way toward the Katrinka Bypass. She wanted to head there at some point during Yates' visit if Xavier didn't show up when she went to her training site on the east side. She'd told Yates about Xavier and was eager to have them meet and get Yates' take on the intriguing boy she'd befriended.

But her priority was to have Yates accompany her to the training site, where she'd work Chuff, and introduce the puppy to yet another new environment. That was her declared intent, but Cass, Noah, and Yates knew that it had been a long time since he last visited and that both he and Cass wanted and needed their regular walking visit. So Noah stayed back while Cass and Yates set off, accompanied by Chuff and the pup on a retractable leash. They carried his little crate with them. It was unwieldy, so they took turns and proceeded directly to the site, rather than taking a longer and more circuitous route.

Because Yates had been there for Paul's visit, he was already up to speed on all developments related to finding the macabre glove and the subsequent investigations. But in their occasional email exchanges and phone calls, Cass had given Yates only the most sanitized and abbreviated version of the incident with Mike: Cass and Lori at the cabin without Noah; Lori's bad boyfriend showed up and after promising to behave himself, didn't, which caused the women and the dogs to work together to oust him from the premises and leave him to drive himself to wherever he chose to go, in the dark and in the falling snow.

Now, with Yates, Cass felt she could finally unburden herself about the full extent of her terror from that episode and of the burden of guilt she'd subsequently experienced. So she did, and this unburdening resulted in her accessing the full array of emotions she'd experienced that night from which she'd been largely disassociated ever since except in her dreams. Yates questioned her gently, and Cass, who always prided herself on her ability to stay calm in any kind of stressful situation, shivered and wept at intervals during her recounting. By this time, they'd already reached the training site and deposited the now-exhausted puppy into his crate for a nap. They sat together on the stairs of the workshop, Chuff leaning against Cass, and Cass leaning against

Yates, who had both arms around her. No words were required—
the safe harbor of trust.

And then Chuff leaped to his feet: Wazzat? Head up, ears
swiveling, and nostrils probing the breeze.

28

XAVIER – EARLY MAY

As my fourteenth birthday approached, Stefan stayed in touch with the people we'd decided to get my gift from, and we put together a list of all the stuff we'd need so that I could work effectively with my present right from the start. It was on my birthday that we went and got both the present and all the other stuff we'd decided we'd need. It was expensive. I don't know how much money Stefan saved by not buying us hunting licenses in the fall, but I was grateful that he was willing to spend so much on my present. And on the way home, when we stopped at A&W, we even got these huge sundaes for dessert. Messy but good! When I was littlelittle, and my mom lived with us, I think maybe I remember that my birthday was a big deal. I'm not sure. But this was the first time that it seemed like a big deal for both Stefan and me. My present was what Stefan called an investment.

That seemed to mean that he wanted to talk to me about it—a lot. Mostly, he talked about how important it was for me to be responsible because with my present, any "lapse of attention" could be very dangerous. He said I'd have to be even more aware of where other people and animals are than I've ever been before to make sure I don't make a dangerous mistake. The first time he said this sort of thing, I paid careful attention. What he said made a lot of sense to me, and I told him that I agreed with him and that I would be very responsible. I reminded him that I'm always responsible, and he agreed and said it was why he allowed me to get my present. But I think he was a little nervous about it because he gave me the same talk a couple of times during the first couple of weeks after my birthday. After a while, I got a little tired of hearing it, but I tried hard to not let that show because I didn't want Stefan to get a backache. He always says that stress makes that happen, and I know that he gets stressed if I don't listen to him or I argue. So I didn't. I just agreed and agreed and agreed, and when I'd had too much agreement, I'd go outside and work on learning more about my present. I generally like learning stuff, and this was the best learning ever.

I kept an eye on the Harwood cabin, so I knew when they'd finally come back. I wondered if Cass got her puppy. When I observed their van in the driveway, I couldn't see anything that would tell me if she had or not. And then, another vehicle appeared. It was that guy who touches Cass too much. I didn't know if that meant anything about whether she had a puppy or not. I figured I'd check out the place where she trains in the morning to see what I could see. I wanted to be in place and track her on her way there, but I couldn't do that because Stefan decided we needed to fix our back stairs, which had gotten wobbly. So by the time we were done that, I figured she'd already be gone, and it would make sense to just make my way through the bush to get to the place on the east side where Cass does her dog training. I'd made a special kind of sling that I could put over my shoulder for carrying my present. I put the present into the sling, put the sling on my shoulder, and headed off.

I already had a few good places I'd used before to observe Cass when she trains. As I approached the one I'd decided on, I heard voices drifting through the woods and knew she was already there, and there was a man with her. Not Noah; I know his voice.

So I guessed it was the touchy guy, and when I got into position, I saw I was right. Whatever they were talking about, it looked like it was serious. Cass was doing most of the talking, and even though I couldn't hear what she was saying, I could get the music of her voice, and it wasn't happy. I could see Chuff felt that way too. Cass and the guy were standing up, and Chuff was pushing his way back and forth between Cass's legs. He does that when he's happy, when he wants her attention, and when he's stressed. I thought that this time, he was stressed. His ears were kind of down, and he wasn't holding his tail as high as usual. The guy asked questions every now and then, and I wondered whether his questions were what was upsetting Cass. At one point, after a question, Cass pushed Chuff aside and then stood like a baseball batter and pretended she was taking a swing. Then afterward, she put one hand on her ribs and pointed at them with her other hand. I think maybe she was telling the guy about how she hit Lori's Big Dude. I think maybe she was crying.

And then Mr. Touchy did what he always does, he kind of folded her up in a big hug. He sat down on the steps and pulled her down next to him, with her head on his shoulder. Chuffy settled next to Cass, with his head on her shoulder. I was fine with that. But I wasn't so fine with the way the guy had his arms around Cass. She didn't seem to mind; in fact, she seemed to like it in a quiet kind of way. But maybe she wasn't being responsible? I didn't want her to make some kind of mistake with this guy. I kept thinking about Noah. I knew he seemed okay with the way Cass and touchy guy were with each other, but . . .

But what? I didn't know. I just knew that I wanted, in fact, felt like I needed to do something. So I reached for my sling, put it over my shoulder, and headed out of the bush and into the open. Chuff knew I was there as soon as I moved. He jumped up from where he'd been leaning against Cass and did his Alarm Show. He knew exactly where to look, and as soon as I got out of the woods, he scampered to meet me, doing that good old Chuffy wag, where his big tail moves his whole body. I was reaching for my sling but decided to wait because Chuff might be in the way.

Cass saw me, waved, and stood up, pulling the touchy guy up with her. She came toward me, and he was right behind her. "Xavier," she said as she approached me, "I have someone I want you to meet. This is our friend Yates. He's been our best friend, mine and Noah's, forever." I thought Lori was her best friend and wanted to ask her about that, but I didn't get a chance.

"Great to finally meet you!" Yates said as he stuck his hand out for a handshake. When I took his hand to shake it, he kind of drew me forward with it and gave me a half-hug with his other arm. It surprised me, but you know what? It was okay because Yates had seriously good hands. He was like the opposite of Jean-Luc with his booger-slime hands. As soon as Yates touched me, I felt safe, which is kind of embarrassing to say, but it was true. So, I stopped worrying about what was going on with Cass and him. I had other stuff to think about right then, anyway, because my sling was starting to slip off my shoulder. "I've got something to show you," I told Cass. And then I reached into the sling and pulled out my puppy, who was just starting to wake up.

Cass did this unintentionally funny, exaggerated kind of surprise thing: her eyes went wide, her mouth opened in a great big O, and her hands went up as she exclaimed, "Oh my God, are you kidding me?" and then she scooched down to grab the puppy. She stood up, holding her to her chest and she looked so happy! "She's yours? You got a Golden puppy?" she asked. I told her that Stefan got me what I wanted for my birthday—a purebred Golden Retriever puppy.

"Have you named her yet?" Cass asked.

"Yes," I said. "Meet Vivamber's My Present." Cass kind of cocked her head at me, the way dogs do when they're curious.

"You know the word *present* means two different things in English, right?" she asked me, and I said I knew. So then she asked me which one I'd meant when I named my puppy. Was she my present, like my gift, or was she my present like *maintenant,* like right now? And I told her I meant it both ways. Which is true. "You are such a clever lad," she said. And then she asked me, "So what's her call name?"

"Katrinka. Her call name is Katrinka," I said.

There was a long pause while she just looked at me. Two tears just leaked out of her eyes. "That's a very good name," she told me. And she looked at me like she was asking permission as she held her arms out. I couldn't leave her standing there like that; it would have been mean. So I nodded and stepped in for the hug she was offering. Not too long or too tight. I'm not Yates. But it was nice, not creepy. We both stepped out of the hug at the same time. I thought that was interesting. Somehow, you both know when the hug is over, but I don't know how you know.

We all sat on the steps and watched Trinka trying to play with Chuff. She kept trying to bite the long flowy fur on his back legs. He was very patient with her. While we watched, Cass and Yates asked me all sorts of questions, like how we found the breeder and the kind of schedule I was following, and how I was teaching her not to poop and pee in the house. Cass congratulated me. She said I was doing a good job, and she asked how I knew to do all the stuff I was doing. I explained that Stefan brought me all kinds of books and magazines, and I'd studied them all hard.

And then, I heard a little whimper. I looked at Trinka, but it wasn't her. I looked at Cass. "You got your puppy too?" I asked.

"Yup," she said. "Come on." She took me over to a shaded spot near the workshop, where there was a little crate set up. Cass crouched down to open its door, and right away, a little black nose appeared. Then the front part of the puppy emerged. With his front feet out and the rest of his body still in the crate, he gave a great big yawn and stretch. Even though I couldn't see his rear-end, I could tell that it was up in the air while he stretched his front legs way out, like he was bowing. And while he was doing that, he looked up at Cass, and his whole face went brightbrightbright, and he kind of exploded out of the crate and into her arms. She held him to her chest the same way she'd held Katrinka and brought him over to me. He was a fat, solid-looking little guy. I didn't have to ask; you could just tell he was a boy, the same way most people who can see would be able to tell right off that Katrinka is a girl. She was scampering around, so Yates picked her up so that I could have a minute with Cass's little boy, who she'd handed to me. When I took him, he licked my nose right away and then started biting at my hair, which was kind of long. Like Katrinka, he was not afraid of meeting new people. It was just one more fun experience for them.

"Meet TriGold's Like a Rock," Cass said.

I kept cuddling him while I asked, "Why'd you name him that? What does Like a Rock mean?" She told me that it was the title of one of her favorite songs by a guy named Bob Seeger. Stefan likes him also, and so I'd heard some of his songs but not that one. I told her that. She told me that it's a song about how good, strong, and brave some boys are as they move from being boys to becoming men. And that she saw the same kind of qualities in her puppy. Then she sang the song for me. It was a nice song, and Cass has a pretty voice, not like a professional or anything, but pretty. And I could hear all the words well.

When she finished, I asked her, "So what's his call name? Rocky?" She paused, just for a second, and then looked right at me and said, "Good guess, but wrong. His call name is Xavvy."

I was . . . well, to tell the truth, I don't know what I was other than shocked. But not in a bad way. I didn't know you could go all still and blank with shock because of good stuff, but now I know you can. I must have looked weird because, after a second, Cass started to laugh. Not mean making-fun-of-you laughter, but the good we're-in-this-together-and-it's-funny laughter that Stefan and I have had together every now and then. And so I started to laugh too, and so did Yates. Then Chuff, who always loves it when people laugh, started to do the little laughing dance he does. And Katrinka and Xavvy, who we'd put down on the ground again, picked up the cues. I don't know if it was from Chuff or us, but I figured it was both. But they both started doing fat little puppy versions of Chuffy's laugh dance. So all of us were laughing together.

29

CASS – SUMMER

Just like the spring that preceded it, summer came early to Lac Rouge that year. The kayaking in mid-May, when Cass first got her boat into the water, offered deeper water because of the spring run-offs than she'd found before when "early in the season" usually meant later in May. So when Cass first headed down the twisting heron stream that she'd dreamt about during the preceding winter, she found a wider channel and deeper water than she usually experienced there. She almost didn't experience it because as she paddled toward the marshy north end of the lake, where she accessed the heron stream, she almost automatically passed it by. She shook herself; this had always been one of her favorite trips. Why had her body decided against it before her mind even got into the picture? She quickly realized that she was probably reacting to the subtle programming of her lucid dreaming when her dream voice instructed her to turn back.

A strong believer in confronting her fears, Cass immediately told her dream voice to fuck off and headed down the heron stream. She was well rewarded. The water was so deep that she sped over the remnants of an old beaver dam that usually had to be carefully navigated, and she experienced a tiny bit of white water as the stream twisted its way toward the marsh where it eventually terminated. No herons that day, but a trio of kingfishers squabbled as they hunted, flying low over the water and occasionally diving for a treat that, based on the vocalizations, was not to be shared.

On each subsequent trip Cass made, the water got lower, or the beaver dam got higher; it was hard to tell. But Cass was pretty sure that the dam was getting higher. It no longer had the look of decrepit abandonment, and it was no longer fully submerged. She was certain that there was an active work crew around. She hung around, hoping to spot some beavers in action. But she didn't have Xavier's patience and never spotted a crew member. By early June, it took considerable navigation skills to power her kayak over one of the few remaining spots in the dam that was still below the surface of the water. By the time Lori arrived for her annual summer visit, it was no longer possible to get over the dam, so the narrow, extremely twisty portions of the creek were no longer accessible. On the other hand, the dam was now so built-up that the sound of water constantly spilling over it sounded like the music of a waterfall—one of the loveliest summer songs Cass knew.

She wanted to share it with Lori, who had always loved the heron stream as much as Cass did. And Cass had done nothing to subvert that. Not wanting to besmirch Lori's pristine summer memories of Lac Rouge or awaken anxieties about the incident with Mike, Cass, who typically revealed all to Lori, had not told her about the series of nightmares she'd experienced in the aftermath of the incident with Mike. And she was confident that in her previous forays, she'd vanquished the initial nightmare hangover she'd experienced earlier.

So on one of the first days of Lori's summer visit, they left Noah and the dogs cheerfully ensconced in the gazebo and set off for a morning of kayaking. The trip to the north end and the heron stream was the last part of their adventure before heading home. As they navigated the sharp turn they had to make to enter the stream, the sound of the water spilling over the dam greeted them. Cass was leading, scanning for herons, hoping, hoping. She hadn't seen any in this part of the lake all season, so her eyes were primarily focused on the banks of the stream, where herons were most likely to perch, camouflaged in the graying driftwood and deadheads on the banks. Because of that, she was perhaps a bit late in seeing the little churn that appeared in the deepest part of the stream before the dam, exactly where the hand had emerged in her nightmare. Her visceral response was immediate. She stopped paddling as a trickle of adrenalin started what quickly turned into a powerful rush, as her focus on the churn in the water was replaced by the unmistakable sound of a sizable body plowing through the undergrowth immediately in front of the dam and diving into the stream. All she could see was a powerful, low-slung body, which could have been either a small bear or a large beaver. She quickly realized, given the proximity to the dam, that it must have been a beaver.

She was about to turn and tell Lori when she saw the stream of bubbles under the water, racing through it, directly toward her kayak. *Holy shit; it was going for them.* "Back up!" she yelled to Lori. "Back up!" She had not known that middle-aged women were capable of the kind of speed the cousins demonstrated as they raced backward toward the mouth of the stream. The pursuit ended before then, but they kept going until they were well back into the main body of the lake. The air was split by their exclamations, interspersed with mildly hysterical bursts of laughter, "Oh my God! Holy Shit! Jesus Christ!" Their kayaks drifted, each woman holding onto the other's paddle as they laughed, gasped, and slowly regained their equilibrium.

Eventually, enough calm was restored for Lori to turn to Cass and ask, "Was that real?"

"Was it real?" Cass exclaimed. "What do you mean? Of course, it was real. That was a real fucking beaver."

"No, no, that's not what I meant," said Lori. "I was terrified. Were you?" Cass confirmed that she had indeed been scared. "So what I meant was, was the danger real? Were we right to be afraid?" Cass told her that although it was relatively uncommon, there were well-documented reports and videos of beavers attacking humans, dogs, and kayaks, sometimes causing injury and damage and, occasionally, death. She suspected they'd encountered a protective mother, that the little churn she'd seen before the large animal hit the water was probably a kit that an angry mom was protecting.

So had they been in danger? Would the beaver have attacked if she'd caught up with the kayaks? Per usual, the bodily response had been way faster and more compelling than cognition. Cass didn't know if the danger had been real and never would. They headed for home.

30

XAVIER - SUMMER

Stefan had to make another trip to Ottawa in early July; it was time to check in with his doctor and his fellow-anarchists. As you know, he'd been leaving me alone during these trips for a long time, and before this, he had been very calm about it. This time, he remained calm. That is sort of who Stefan has become: a calm guy who is seldom mean, except when his back hurts. But being calm doesn't mean you can't give warnings. Stefan's started on my birthday and have continued since then, and they became frequent and long before he left for his trip. Be responsible! Be alert all the time! Look out for people and animals more than ever before! Recognize that things can escalate quickly! Be prepared to take action!

I've read youth novels where kids feel that their parents are nagging them. I think this might be nagging. But the funny thing is that when he started doing this in April, I was patient at first, and after that, I pretended to be patient. But as time has passed and I've started to understand more about why he acts this way, I don't have to act anymore because I now understand that Stefan is in love. He's infatuated with Katrinka, and he's afraid something bad will happen to her.

I've never seen him act like this before. He gets down on the floor to play with her. He laughs. He pulls her up onto this lap and uses his—very good, I suspect—hands to smooth her into sleep. Then he keeps stroking her, even after she's asleep. He is also inconsistent. That's something Cass has told me about. You can't keep changing the rules with dogs. You need to teach them what the rules are, help them to learn and understand the rules, and insist on the rules being followed. So if you're not going to let your puppy jump up on you and other people in greeting, you have to make that a rule and enforce it. Stefan is very bad both at making rules and enforcing them. So I make them, that's no problem. But then I have to figure out how to enforce Stefan to enforce my rules. He's a lot harder to train than Katrinka. But I'm okay with that. I like seeing how he is with her, and every now and then, I wonder what it would have been like if he'd been more like that with me when I was little.

Once Stefan left, I was grateful to have a couple of days for just me and Katrinka. But before I could start my Katrinka time, I needed to take a hike on my own. It was going to take a while, and I didn't like leaving her alone all that time, but I didn't have a choice. She was still too little to do that kind of hike with me and was now too big to carry in the sling for long periods. So I set up her x-pen, which Cass gave me as a welcome gift for Katrinka. It is like a big flexible metal cage that you can shape depending on where you are. I put the little bed that's usually in her crate in one corner and a bunch of her favorite toys nearby. I put a bucket of water she hasn't been able to spill in another corner, and then I put some newspaper in a far corner, in case she has to poop or pee. I didn't use that when I was house-training her. I just took her outside every hour so that she'd know that outside is where she needs to do her business. But I figured I'd be gone for about six hours and I didn't know if she could hold it that long. "I'm sorry, *chérie*," I said as I kissed her and put her in the x-pen. Then I put my lunch and my thermos of hot chocolate into my backpack, and off I went.

Even though I was walking and stayed mostly in the bush rather than on the road, I was surprised at how quickly I reached the *chemin du Dépotoir*. The trip had seemed endless in January. I guess that's no surprise. Within a couple of hours, I reached the place where I had dumped the Caddy. All I could see from the road was underbrush, no sign of anything that had been dumped. When I went further down, I saw that someone had been there since my last visit. There was an old, busted washing machine. Its glass door was open, as though the eye of that one-eyed myth guy, Cyclops, had popped out. All kinds of vines had invaded it and were flowing out of the open door. It was kind of pretty. And when I got out my binoculars, I could see what I'm sure was one of the tires of the Caddy, totally wrapped in vines, peeking out from under a corner of the one-eyed washing machine. It just looked like any old tire someone would toss out.

It was a beautiful sunny day, cooler than many July days, with a nice breeze. The birds were going nuts—lots of woodpeckers drumming away, songbirds going at it, blue-jays cursing each other out. There was no sign of hovering vultures or other carrion eaters and no bad smells. In fact, it was very peaceful. I found a nice big rock I could lean against about halfway up the ravine, one that allowed the sun to sneak in and bathe my raised face. I sat and had my lunch and drank some of my chocolate. I kept waiting for some tell-tale heart stuff to happen, but it never did. I guess I'm just not the kind of nervous, excitable guy Mr. Edgar Allen Poe must have been. I felt fine. I felt more than fine. I realized that for the first time in a long time, that low-key itch that seemed like it had become a part of who I'd become was gone. That made me think that someplace deep inside me, I must have been worried, and that now I wasn't anymore.

When I got home, I was relieved to not hear any noise as I approached our house. Because she'd never been left for a long time before, I was afraid that maybe Katrinka would cry or bark the whole time I was gone. Though she was quiet as I approached, the minute she heard me open the door, she started making little yelps and yips. I went to her x-pen even before I took my pack off and was amazed to see that she hadn't pooped or peed. She was so excited to see me that she didn't know what to do. So I picked her up and took her outside, and she peed and pooped right away. What a good girl! She got a lot of praise and cookies.

That night, I played with her. Sometimes play is just rolling around and petting and play-fighting or playing tug, which is one of her favorites. Sometimes it is the cookies game, where I tell her to do some of the commands Cass taught me to teach her, like "Sit" and "Down" and "Come." The rule is that I only tell her once, and if she does it right away, she gets a cookie. I'm careful to not do that for too long and to make it only one of the games we play. Cass said that makes them eager to do it, and so far, Cass has been right about all that kind of stuff. Katrinka loves to play, and she loves the lessons we take with Cass almost every week, and the games we learn there are some of her favorites.

The next morning, I decided to work on what Cass calls "With Me." It's like the heeling she does with her guys, which would be way too much to expect of a puppy. So it's much less demanding than that. Cass calls it part of the foundation for heeling. So far, Katrinka and I hadn't had too much success with it. Cass told me to be patient and just work on it for a few minutes at a time. I put Katrinka on her leash and try to get her to walk with me, and I turn around and go in the other direction whenever she gets distracted, which is all the time! I could get dizzy with all the turning around. I can't blame her. From her eye-level, there is so much stuff to grab her attention away from me: flowers, grasshoppers, butterflies, an itchy bum . . . the list goes on.

It was the same thing that morning. I was feeling kind of frustrated, so I stopped what I was doing. I agree with Cass that dogs know what you're feeling, and I didn't want her to think she was disappointing me. So I sat down and let her play while I tried to figure out how I could fix this. I knew that Cass would help me with it during our next lesson, but I agree with Stefan that you learn better when you figure it out yourself rather than having someone else teach you.

So I thought back to the first time I saw Cass and her dogs and how amazed I was at how they paid attention to her and how much they wanted to be with her and follow her. And I remembered that on that first day, I had figured out it was because of the way she moved—fast but relaxed—looking toward the horizon like she was speeding toward whatever she saw there, as though she was going somewhere good, and wanted to get there.

So I tried to do the same thing. I didn't think anything. I just closed my eyes and felt stuff. I felt the sun and the breeze. I felt how happy I was to finally have someone to love. I felt excited about the adventures we'd have together. And then, thinking nothing but feeling everything, I started to move. I moved with purpose. I didn't hesitate. And I trusted that Katrinka would be with me because she'd feel that wherever we were going was good and that she was safe because I would always take care of her. And I looked down at her while I walked and saw that it was working! I was moving fast; she was almost running next to me. She was looking up at me, and her little eyes were dancing, and she was laughing. It didn't last long; she's still a very young puppy, but it was a good start.

ACKNOWLEDGEMENTS

Many thanks to Anne and Jeff Bendig, who provided the background, context, and details needed for the hunting scenes and references. Hopefully, I have conveyed all of that faithfully. If there are errors or missteps, they are mine alone.

And many thanks also to these brave women, who dared to read my first draft and provide honest feedback: Kay LaBare, Jackie Pargament, Charlene Rothkopf, Paula Mancuso Rea, Judith Williams, Peggy Baxter, and Rejeanne Lalonde.

ABOUT THE AUTHOR

Ellie Beals grew up in Baltimore, Maryland, and moved to Canada when she was twenty years old. She spent most of her professional career as a management consultant in Ottawa, Ontario.

Dogs were a constant in Ellie's life from the time she was a child. In the mid-1990s, she started to train and compete in Obedience with Golden Retrievers with considerable success. In 2014, she had the highest-rated Canadian obedience dog (Fracas – upon whom Chuff is modeled), and her husband David Skinner had the second-rated dog. Over a ten-year period, both Ellie and David were regularly ranked among Canada's Top Ten Obedience competitors. They have an active coaching practice in Ottawa, having retired from their previous professional careers to spend more time playing with their dogs and students.

Like Cass and Noah Harwood, Ellie and David have a log cabin in Western Quebec, where Ellie is an avid wilderness recreationist, constantly accompanied by her dogs. As COVID-19 spread in March of 2020, she and David temporarily shut down their coaching practice and retreated to their cabin, where *Emergence* was written. Lac Rouge is not the real name of the lake on which they live. Everything else about the locale for *Emergence* is faithful to the character of the gentle Laurentian mountains of Western Quebec.

Made in the USA
Monee, IL
05 February 2021

59711662R00128